The Lighthouse

R. M. Ballantyne

(1865) .

Contents

Chapter One

The Rock

Early on a summer morning, about the beginning of the nineteenth century, two fishermen of Forfarshire wended their way to the shore, launched their boat, and put off to sea.

One of the men was tall and ill-favoured, the other, short and well-favoured. Both were square-built, powerful fellows, like most men of the class to which they belonged.

It was about that calm hour of the morning which precedes sunrise, when most living creatures are still asleep, and inanimate nature wears, more than at other times, the semblance of repose. The sea was like a sheet of undulating glass. A breeze had been expected, but, in defiance of expectation, it had not come, so the boatmen were obliged to use their oars. They used them well, however, insomuch that the land ere long appeared like a blue line on the horizon, then became tremulous and indistinct, and finally vanished in the mists of morning.

The men pulled "with a will,"—as seamen pithily express it,—and in silence. Only once during the first hour did the big, ill-favoured man venture a remark. Referring to the absence of wind, he said, that "it would be a' the better for landin' on the rock."

This was said in the broadest vernacular dialect, as, indeed, was everything that dropped from the fishermen's lips. We take the liberty of modifying it a little, believing that strict fidelity here would entail inevitable loss of sense to many of our readers.

The remark, such as it was, called forth a rejoinder from the short comrade, who stated his belief that "they would be likely to find somethin' there that day."

They then relapsed into silence.

Under the regular stroke of the oars the boat advanced steadily, straight out to sea. At first the mirror over which they skimmed was grey, and the foam at the cutwater leaden-coloured. By degrees they rowed, as it were, into a brighter region. The sea ahead lightened up, became pale yellow, then warmed into saffron, and, when the sun rose, blazed into liquid gold.

The words spoken by the boatmen, though few, were significant. The "rock" alluded to was the celebrated and much dreaded Inch Cape— more familiarly known as the Bell Rock—which being at that time unmarked by lighthouse or beacon of any kind, was the terror of mariners who were making for the firths of Forth and Tay. The "something" that was expected to be found there may be guessed at when we say that one of the fiercest storms that ever swept our eastern shores had just exhausted itself after strewing the coast with wrecks. The breast of ocean, though calm on the surface, as has been said, was still heaving with a mighty swell, from the effects of the recent elemental conflict.

"D'ye see the breakers noo, Davy?" enquired the ill-favoured man, who pulled the aft oar.

"Ay, and hear them, too," said Davy Spink, ceasing to row, and looking over his shoulder towards the seaward horizon.

"Yer een and lugs are better than mine, then," returned the ill-favoured comrade, who answered, when among his friends, to the name of Big Swankie, otherwise, and more correctly, Jock Swankie. "Od! I believe ye're right," he added, shading his heavy red brows with his heavier and redder hand, "that *is* the rock, but a man wad need the een o' an eagle to see onything in the face o' sik a bleezin' sun. Pull awa', Davy, we'll hae time to catch a bit cod or a haddy afore the rock's bare."

Influenced by these encouraging hopes, the stout pair urged their boat in the direction of a thin line of snow-white foam that lay apparently many miles away, but which was in reality not very far distant.

By degrees the white line expanded in size and became massive, as though a huge breaker were rolling towards them; ever and anon jets of foam flew high into the air from various parts of the mass, like smoke from a cannon's mouth. Presently, a low continuous roar became audible above the noise of the oars; as the boat advanced, the swells from the south-east could be seen towering upwards as they neared the foaming spot, gradually changing their broad-backed form, and coming on in majestic walls of green water, which fell with indescribable grandeur into the seething caldron. No rocks were visible, there was no apparent cause for this wild confusion in the midst of the otherwise calm sea. But the fishermen knew that the Bell Rock was underneath the foam, and that in less than an hour its jagged peaks would be left uncovered by the falling tide.

As the swell of the sea came in from the eastward, there was a belt of smooth water on the west side of the rock. Here the fishermen cast anchor, and, baiting their hand-lines, began to fish. At first they were unsuccessful, but before half an hour had elapsed, the cod began to nibble, and Big Swankie ere long hauled up a fish of goodly size. Davy Spink followed suit, and in a few minutes a dozen fish lay spluttering in the bottom of the boat.

"Time's up noo," said Swankie, coiling away his line.

"Stop, stop, here's a wallupper," cried Davy, who was an excitable man; "we better fish a while langer—bring the cleek, Swankie, he's ower big to—noo, lad, cleek him! that's it!—Oh–o–o–o!"

The prolonged groan with which Davy brought his speech to a sudden termination was in consequence of the line breaking and the fish escaping, just as Swankie was about to strike the iron hook into its side.

"Hech! lad, that was a guid ane," said the disappointed man with a sigh; "but he's awa'."

"Ay," observed Swankie, "and we must awa' too, so up anchor, lad. The rock's lookin' oot o' the sea, and time's precious."

The anchor was speedily pulled up, and they rowed towards the rock, the ragged edges of which were now visible at intervals in the midst of the foam which they created.

At low tide an irregular portion of the Bell Rock, less than a hundred yards in length, and fifty yards in breadth, is uncovered and left exposed for two or three hours. It does not appear in the form of a single mass or islet, but in a succession of serrated ledges of various heights, between and amongst which the sea flows until the tide has fallen pretty low. At full ebb the rock appears like a dark islet, covered with seaweed, and studded with deep pools of water, most of which are connected with the sea by narrow channels running between the ledges. The highest part of the rock does not rise more than seven feet above the level of the sea at the lowest tide.

To enter one of the pools by means of the channels above referred to is generally a matter of difficulty, and often of extreme danger, as the swell of the sea, even in calm weather, bursts over these ledges with such violence as to render the channels at times impassable. The utmost caution, therefore, is necessary.

Our fishermen, however, were accustomed to land there occasionally in search of the remains of wrecks, and knew their work well. They approached the rock on the lee-side, which was, as has been said, to the westward. To a spectator viewing them from any point but from the boat itself, it would have appeared that the reckless men were sailing into the jaws of certain death, for the breakers burst around them so confusedly in all directions that their instant destruction seemed inevitable. But Davy Spink, looking over his shoulder as he sat at the bow-oar, saw a narrow lead of comparatively still water in the midst of the foam, along which he guided the boat with consummate skill, giving only a word or two of direction to Swankie, who instantly acted in accordance therewith.

"Pull, pull, lad," said Davy.

Swankie pulled, and the boat swept round with its bow to the east just in time to meet a billow, which, towering high above its fellows, burst completely over the rocks, and appeared to be about to sweep away all before it. For a moment the boat was as if embedded in snow, then it sank once more into the lead among the floating tangle, and the men pulled with might and main in order to escape the next wave. They were just in time. It burst over the same rocks with greater violence than its predecessor, but the boat had gained the shelter of the next ledge, and lay floating securely in the deep, quiet pool within, while the men rested on their oars, and watched the chaos of the water rush harmlessly by.

In another moment they had landed and secured the boat to a projecting rock.

Few words of conversation passed between these practical men. They had gone there on particular business. Time and tide proverbially wait for no man, but at the Bell Rock they wait a much briefer period than elsewhere. Between low water and the time when it would be impossible to quit the rock without being capsized, there was only a space of two or three hours—sometimes more, frequently less—so it behoved the men to economise time.

Rocks covered with wet seaweed and rugged in form are not easy to walk over; a fact which was soon proved by Swankie staggering violently once or twice, and by Spink falling flat on his back. Neither paid attention to his comrade's misfortunes in this way. Each scrambled about actively, searching with care among the crevices of the rocks, and from time to time picking up articles which they thrust into their pockets or laid on their shoulders, according as weight and dimensions required.

In a short time they returned to their boat pretty well laden.

"Weel, lad, what luck?" enquired Spink, as Swankie and he met—the former with a grappling iron on his shoulder, the latter staggering under the weight of a mass of metal.

"Not much," replied Swankie; "nothin' but heavy metal this mornin', only a bit of a cookin' stove an' a cannon shot—that's all."

"Never mind, try again. There must ha' bin two or three wrecks on the rock this gale," said Davy, as he and his friend threw their burdens into the boat, and hastened to resume the search.

At first Spink was the more successful of the two. He returned to the boat with various articles more than once, while his comrade continued his rambles unsuccessfully. At last, however, Big Swankie came to a gully or inlet where a large mass of the _débris_ of a wreck was piled up in indescribable confusion, in the midst of which lay the dead body of an old man. Swankie's first impulse was to shout to his companion, but he checked himself, and proceeded to examine the pockets of the dead man.

Raising the corpse with some difficulty he placed it on the ledge of rock. Observing a ring on the little finger of the right hand, he removed it and put it hastily in his pocket. Then he drew a red morocco case from an inner breast pocket in the dead man's coat. To his surprise and delight he found that it contained a gold watch and several gold rings and brooches, in some of which were beautiful stones. Swankie was no judge of jewellery, but he could not avoid the conviction that these things must needs be valuable. He laid the case down on the rock beside him, and eagerly searched the other pockets. In one he found a large clasp-knife and a pencil-case; in another a leather purse, which felt heavy as he drew it out. His eyes sparkled at the first glance he got of the contents, for they were sovereigns! Just as he made this discovery, Davy Spink climbed over the ledge at his back, and Swankie hastily thrust the purse underneath the body of the dead man.

"Hallo! lad, what have ye there? Hey! watches and rings—come, we're in luck this mornin'."

"*We!*" exclaimed Swankie, somewhat sternly, "*you* didn't find that case."

"Na, lad, but we've aye divided, an' I dinna see what for we should change our plan noo."

"We've nae paction to that effec'—the case o' kickshaws is mine," retorted Swankie.

"Half o't," suggested Spink.

"Weel, weel," cried the other with affected carelessness, "I'd scorn to be sae graspin'. For the matter o' that ye may hae it all to yersel', but I'll hae the next thing we git that's worth muckle a' to *mysel'*."

So saying Swankie stooped to continue his search of the body, and in a moment or two drew out the purse with an exclamation of surprise.

"See, I'm in luck, Davy! Virtue's aye rewarded, they say. This is mine, and I doot not there'll be some siller intilt."

"Goold!" cried Davy, with dilated eyes, as his comrade emptied the contents into his large hand, and counted over thirty sovereigns.

"Ay, lad, ye can keep the what-d'ye-ca'-ums, and I'll keep the siller."

"I've seen that face before," observed Spink, looking intently at the body.

"Like enough," said Swankie, with an air of indifference, as he put the gold into his pocket. "I think I've seed it mysel'. It looks like auld Jamie Brand, but I didna ken him weel."

"It's just him," said Spink, with a touch of sadness. "Ay, ay, that'll fa' heavy on the auld woman. But, come, it'll no' do to stand haverin' this way. Let's see what else is on him."

They found nothing more of any value; but a piece of paper was discovered, wrapped up in oilskin, and carefully fastened with red tape, in the vest pocket of the dead man. It contained writing, and had been so securely wrapped up, that it was only a little damped. Davy Spink, who found it, tried in vain to read the writing; Davy's education had been neglected, so he was fain to confess that he could not make it out.

"Let *me* see't," said Swankie. "What hae we here? 'The sloop is hard an—an—'"

"'Fast,' maybe," suggested Spink.

"Ay, so 'tis. I canna make out the next word, but here's something about the jewel-case."

The man paused and gazed earnestly at the paper for a few minutes, with a look of perplexity on his rugged visage.

"Weel, man, what is't?" enquired Davy.

"Hoot! I canna mak' it oot," said the other, testily, as if annoyed at being unable to read it. He refolded the paper and thrust it into his bosom, saying, "Come, we're wastin' time. Let's get on wi' our wark."

"Toss for the jewels and the siller," said Spink, suggestively.

"Very weel," replied the other, producing a copper. "Heeds, you win the siller; tails, I win the box;—heeds it is, so the kickshaws is mine. Weel, I'm content," he added, as he handed the bag of gold to his comrade, and received the jewel-case in exchange.

In another hour the sea began to encroach on the rock, and the fishermen, having collected as much as time would permit of the wrecked materials, returned to their boat.

They had secured altogether above two hundredweight of old metal,—namely, a large piece of a ship's caboose, a hinge, a lock of a door, a ship's marking-iron, a soldier's bayonet, a cannon ball, a shoebuckle, and a small anchor, besides part of the cordage of the wreck, and the money and jewels before mentioned. Placing the heavier of these things in the bottom of the boat, they pushed off.

"We better take the corp ashore," said Spink, suddenly.

"What for? They may ask what was in the pockets," objected Swankie.

"Let them ask," rejoined the other, with a grin.

Swankie made no reply, but gave a stroke with his oar which sent the boat close up to the rocks. They both relanded in silence, and, lifting the dead body of the old man, laid it in the stern-sheets of the boat. Once more they pushed off.

Too much delay had been already made. The surf was breaking over the ledges in all directions, and it was with the utmost difficulty that they succeeded in getting clear out into deep water. A breeze which had sprung up from the east, tended to raise the sea a little, but when they finally got away from the dangerous reef, the breeze befriended them. Hoisting the foresail, they quickly left the Bell Rock far behind them, and, in the course of a couple of hours, sailed into the harbour of Arbroath.

Chapter Two

The Lovers and the Press-Gang

About a mile to the eastward of the ancient town of Arbroath the shore abruptly changes its character, from a flat beach to a range of, perhaps, the wildest and most picturesque cliffs on the east coast of Scotland. Inland the country is rather flat, but elevated several hundred feet above the level of the sea, towards which it slopes gently until it reaches the shore, where it terminates in abrupt, perpendicular precipices, varying from a hundred to two hundred feet in height. In many places the cliffs overhang the water, and all along the coast they have been perforated and torn up by the waves, so as to present singularly bold and picturesque outlines, with caverns, inlets, and sequestered "coves" of every form and size.

To the top of these cliffs, in the afternoon of the day on which our tale opens, a young girl wended her way,—slowly, as if she had no other object in view than a stroll, and sadly, as if her mind were more engaged with the thoughts within than with the magnificent prospect of land and sea without. The girl was:

"Fair, fair, with golden hair,"

And apparently about twenty years of age. She sought out a quiet nook among the rocks at the top of the cliffs; near to a circular chasm, with the name of which (at that time) we are not acquainted, but which was destined ere long to acquire a new name and celebrity from an incident which shall be related in another part of this story.

Curiously enough, just about the same hour, a young man was seen to wend his way to the same cliffs, and, from no reason whatever with which we happened to be acquainted, sought out the same nook! We say "he was seen," advisedly, for the maid with the golden hair saw him. Any ordinary observer would have said that she had scarcely raised her eyes from the ground since sitting down on a niece of flower-studded turf near the edge of the cliff, and that she certainly had not turned her head in the direction of the town. Yet she saw him,—however absurd the statement may appear, we affirm it confidently,—and knew that he was coming. Other eyes there were that also saw youth—eyes that would have caused him some degree of annoyance had he known they were upon him—eyes that he would have rejoiced to tinge with the colours black and blue! There were thirteen pair of them, belonging to twelve men and a lieutenant of the navy.

In those days the barbarous custom of impressment into the Royal Navy was in full operation. England was at war with France. Men were wanted to fight our battles, and when there was any difficulty in getting men, press-gangs were sent out to force them into the service. The youth whom we now introduce to the reader was a sailor, a strapping, handsome one, too; not, indeed, remarkable for height, being only a little above the average—five feet, ten inches or thereabouts—but noted for great depth of chest, breadth of shoulder, and development of muscle; conspicuous also for the quantity of close, clustering, light-brown curls down his head, and for the laughing glance of his dark-blue eye. Not a hero of romance, by any means. No, he was very matter of fact, and rather given to meditation than mischief.

The officer in charge of the press-gang had set his heart on this youth (so had another individual, of whom more anon!) but the youth, whose name was Ruby Brand, happened to have an old mother who was at that time in very bad health, and she had also set her heart, poor body, on the youth, and entreated him to stay at home just for one half-year. Ruby willingly consented, and from that time forward led the life of a dog in consequence of the press-gang.

Now, as we have said, he had been seen leaving the town by the lieutenant, who summoned his men and went after him—cautiously, however, in order to take him by surprise for Ruby, besides being strong and active as a lion, was slippery as an eel.

Going straight as an arrow to the spot where she of the golden hair was seated, the youth presented himself suddenly to her, sat down beside her, and exclaiming "Minnie", put his arm round her waist.

"Oh, Ruby, don't," said Minnie, blushing.

Now, reader, the "don't" and the blush had no reference to the arm round the waist, but to the relative position of their noses, mouths, and chins, a position which would have been highly improper and altogether unjustifiable but for the fact that Ruby was Minnie's accepted lover.

"Don't, darling, why not?" said Ruby in surprise.

"You're *so* rough," said Minnie, turning her head away.

"True, dear, I forgot to shave this morning."

"I don't mean that," interrupted the girl quickly, "I mean rude and—and—is that a sea-gull?"

"No, sweetest of your sex, it's a butterfly; but it's all the same, as my metaphysical Uncle

Ogilvy would undertake to prove to you, thus, a butterfly is white and a gull is white,—therefore, a gull is a butterfly."

"Don't talk nonsense, Ruby."

"No more I will, darling, if you will listen to me while I talk sense."

"What is it?" said the girl, looking earnestly and somewhat anxiously into her lover's face, for she knew at once by his expression that he had some unpleasant communication to make. "You're not going away?"

"Well, no—not exactly; you know I promised to stay with mother; but the fact is that I'm so pestered and hunted down by that rascally press-gang, that I don't know what to do. They're sure to nab me at last, too, and then I shall have to go away whether I will or no, so I've made up my mind as a last resource, to—" Ruby paused.

"Well?" said Minnie.

"Well, in fact to do what will take me away for a short time, but—" Ruby stopped short, and, turning his head on one side, while a look of fierce anger overspread his face, seemed to listen intently.

Minnie did not observe this action for a few seconds, but, wondering why he paused, she looked up, and in surprise exclaimed— "Ruby! what do you—"

"Hush! Minnie, and don't look round," said he in a low tone of intense anxiety, yet remaining immovably in the position which he had assumed on first sitting down by the girl's side, although the swelled veins of his neck and his flushed forehead told of a fierce conflict of feeling within. "It's the press-gang after me again. I got a glance of one o' them out of the tail of my eye, creeping round the rocks. They think I haven't seen them. Darling Minnie—one kiss. Take care of mother if I don't turn up soon."

"But how will you escape?"

"Hush, dearest girl! I want to have as much of you as I can before I go. Don't be afraid. They're honest British tars after all, and won't hurt *you*, Minnie."

Still seated at the girl's side, as if perfectly at his ease, yet speaking in quick earnest tones, and drawing her closely to him, Ruby waited until he heard a stealthy tread behind him. Then he sprang up with the speed of thought, uttered a laugh of defiance as the sailors rushed towards him, and leaping wildly off the cliff, fell a height of about fifty feet into the sea.

Minnie uttered a scream of horror, and fell fainting into the arms of the bewildered lieutenant.

"Down the cliffs—quick! he can't escape if you look alive. Stay, one of you, and look after this girl. She'll roll over the edge on recovering, perhaps."

It was easy to order the men down the cliffs, but not so easy for them to obey, for the rocks were almost perpendicular at the place, and descended sheer into the water.

"Surround the spot," shouted the lieutenant. "Scatter yourselves—away! there's no beach here."

The lieutenant was right. The men extended themselves along the top of the cliffs so as to prevent Ruby's escape, in the event of his trying to ascend them, and two sailors stationed themselves in ambush in the narrow pass at the spot where the cliffs terminate in the direction of the town.

The leap taken by Ruby was a bold one. Few men could have ventured it; indeed, the youth himself would have hesitated had he not been driven almost to desperation. But he was a practised swimmer and diver, and knew well the risk he ran. He struck the water with tremendous force and sent up a great mass of foam, but he had entered it perpendicularly, feet foremost, and in a few seconds returned to the surface so close to the cliffs that they overhung him, and thus effectually concealed him from his pursuers.

Swimming cautiously along for a short distance close to the rocks, he came to the entrance of a cavern which was filled by the sea. The inner end of this cave opened into a small hollow or hole among the cliffs, up the sides of which Ruby knew that he could climb, and thus reach the top unperceived, but, after gaining the summit, there still lay before him the difficulty of eluding those who watched there. He felt, however, that nothing could be gained by delay, so he struck at once into the cave, swam to the inner end, and landed. Wringing the water out of his clothes, he threw off his jacket and vest in order to be as unencumbered as possible, and then began to climb cautiously.

Just above the spot where Ruby ascended there chanced to be stationed a seaman named Dalls. This man had lain down flat on his breast, with his head close to the edge of the cliff, so as to observe narrowly all that went on below, but, being a stout, lethargic man, he soon fell fast asleep! It was just at the spot where this man lay that Ruby reached the summit. The ascent was very difficult. At each step the hunted youth had to reach his hand as high above his head as possible, and grasp the edge of a rock or a mass of turf with great care before venturing on another step. Had one of these points of rock, or one of these tufts of grass, given way, he would infallibly have fallen down the precipice and been killed. Accustomed to this style of climbing from infancy, however, he advanced without a sensation of fear.

On reaching the top he peeped over, and, seeing that no one was near, prepared for a rush. There was a mass of brown turf on the bank above him. He grasped it with all his force, and swung himself over the edge of the cliff. In doing so he nearly scalped poor Dalls, whose hair was the "turf" which he had seized, and who, uttering a hideous yell, leaped upon Ruby and tried to overthrow him. But Dalls had met his match. He received a blow on the nose that all but felled him, and instantly after a blow on each eye, that raised a very constellation of stars in his brain, and laid him prone upon the grass.

His yell, however, and the noise of the scuffle, were heard by those of the press-gang who were nearest to the scene of conflict. They rushed to the rescue, and reached the spot just as Ruby leaped over his prostrate foe and fled towards Arbroath. They followed with a cheer, which warned the two men in ambush to be ready. Ruby was lithe as a greyhound. He left his pursuers far behind him, and dashed down the gorge leading from the cliffs to the low ground beyond.

Here he was met by the two sailors, and by the lieutenant, who had joined them. Minnie was also there, having been conducted thither by the said lieutenant, who gallantly undertook to see her safe into the town, in order to prevent any risk of her being insulted by his men. On hearing the shout of those who pursued Ruby, Minnie hurried away, intending to get free from the gang, not feeling that the lieutenant's protection was either desirable or necessary.

When Ruby reached the middle of the gorge, which we have dignified with the name of "pass", and saw three men ready to dispute his passage, he increased his speed. When he was almost up to them he turned aside and sprang nimbly up the almost perpendicular wall of earth on his right. This act disconcerted the men, who had prepared to receive his charge and seize him, but Ruby jumped down on the shoulders of the one nearest, and crushed him to the ground with his weight. His clenched fist caught the lieutenant between the eyes and stretched him on his back—the third man wisely drew aside to let this human thunderbolt pass by!

He did pass, and, as the impetuous and quite irresistible locomotive is brought to a sudden pause when the appropriate brakes are applied, so was he brought to a sudden halt by Minnie a hundred yards or so farther on.

"Oh! don't stop," she cried eagerly, and hastily thrusting him away. "They'll catch you!"

Panting though he was, vehemently, Ruby could not restrain a laugh.

"Catch me! no, darling; but don't be afraid of them. They won't hurt you, Minnie, and they can't hurt me—except in the way of cutting short our interview. Ha! here they come. Goodbye, dearest; I'll see you soon again."

At that moment five or six of the men came rushing down the pass with a wild cheer. Ruby made no haste to run. He stood in an easy attitude beside Minnie; leisurely kissed her little hand, and gently smoothed down her golden hair. Just as the foremost pursuer came within fifteen yards or so of them, he said, "Farewell, my lassie, I leave you in good hands"; and then, waving his cap in the air, with a cheer of more than half-jocular defiance, he turned and fled towards Arbroath as if one of the nor'-east gales, in its wildest fury, were sweeping him over the land.

Chapter Three

Our Hero obliged to go to Sea

When Ruby Brand reached the outskirts of Arbroath, he checked his speed and walked into his native town whistling gently, and with his hands in his pockets, as though he had just returned from an evening walk. He directed his steps to one of the streets near the harbour, in which his mother's cottage was situated.

Mrs Brand was a delicate, little old woman—so little and so old that people sometimes wondered how it was possible that she could be the mother of such a stalwart son. She was one of those kind, gentle, uncomplaining, and unselfish beings, who do not secure much popularity or admiration in this world, but who secure obedient children, also steadfast and loving friends. Her favourite book was the Bible; her favourite hope in regard to earthly matters, that men should give up fighting and drinking, and live in peace; her favourite theory that the study of *truth* was the object for which man was created, and her favourite meal—tea.

Ruby was her only child. Minnie was the daughter of a distant relation, and, having been left an orphan, she was adopted by her. Mrs Brand's husband was a sailor. He commanded a small coasting sloop, of which Ruby had been the mate for several years. As we have said, Ruby had been prevailed on to remain at home for some months in order to please his mother, whose delicacy of health was such that his refusal would have injured her seriously; at least the doctor said so, therefore Ruby agreed to stay.

The sloop *Penguin*, commanded by Ruby's father, was on a voyage to Newcastle at that time, and was expected in Arbroath every day. But it was fated never more to cast anchor in that port. The great storm, to which reference has been made in a previous chapter, caused many wrecks on the shores of Britain. The *Penguin*, was one of the many.

In those days telegraphs, railroads, and penny papers did not exist. Murders were committed then, as now, but little was said, and less was known about them. Wrecks occurred then, as now, but few, except the persons immediately concerned, heard of them. "Destructive fires", "terrible accidents", and the familiar round of "appalling catastrophes" occurred then, as now, but their influence was limited, and their occurrence soon forgotten.

We would not be understood to mean that "now" (as compared with "then"), all is right and well; that telegraphs and railways and daily papers are all-potent and perfect. By no means. We have still much to learn and to do in these improved times; and, especially, there is wanting to a large extent among us a sympathetic telegraphy, so to speak, between the interior of our land and the sea-coast, which, if it existed in full and vigorous play, would go far to improve our condition, and raise us in the esteem of Christian nations. Nevertheless, as compared with now, the state of things then was lamentably imperfect.

The great storm came and went, having swept thousands of souls into eternity, and hundreds of thousands of pounds into nonentity. Lifeboats had not been invented. Harbours of refuge were almost unknown, and although our coasts bristled with dangerous reefs and headlands, lighthouses were few and far between. The consequence was, that wrecks were numerous; and so also were wreckers,—a class of men, who, in the absence of an efficient coastguard, subsisted to a large extent on what they picked up from the wrecks that were cast in their way, and who did not scruple, sometimes, to *cause* wrecks, by showing false lights in order to decoy vessels to destruction.

We do not say that all wreckers were guilty of such crimes, but many of them were so, and their style of life, at the best, had naturally a demoralising influence upon all of them.

The famous Bell Rock, lying twelve miles off the coast of Forfarshire, was a prolific source of destruction to shipping. Not only did numbers of vessels get upon it, but many others ran upon the neighbouring coasts in attempting to avoid it.

Ruby's father knew the navigation well, but, in the confusion and darkness of the furious storm, he miscalculated his position and ran upon the rock, where, as we have seen, his body was afterwards found by the two fishermen. It was conveyed by them to the cottage of Mrs Brand, and when Ruby entered he found his mother on her knees by the bedside, pressing the cold hand of his father to her breast, and gazing with wild, tearless eyes into the dead face.

We will not dwell upon the sad scenes that followed.

Ruby was now under the necessity of leaving home, because his mother being deprived of her husband's support naturally turned in distress to her son. But Ruby had no employment, and work could not be easily obtained at that time in the town, so there was no other resource left him but to go to sea. This he did in a small coasting sloop belonging to an old friend, who gave him part of his wages in advance to enable him to leave his mother a small provision, at least for a short time.

This, however, was not all that the widow had to depend on. Minnie Gray was expert with her needle, and for some years past had contributed not a little to the comforts of the household into which she had been adopted. She now set herself to work with redoubled zeal and energy. Besides this, Mrs Brand had a brother, a retired skipper, who obtained the complimentary title of Captain from his friends. He was a poor man, it is true, as regarded money, having barely sufficient for his own subsistence, but he was rich in kindliness and sympathy, so that he managed to make his small income perform wonders. On hearing of his brother-in-law's death, Captain Ogilvy hastened to afford all the consolation in his power to his sorrowing sister.

The captain was an eccentric old man, of rugged aspect. He thought that there was not a worse comforter on the face of the earth than himself, because, when he saw others in distress, his heart invariably got into his throat, and absolutely prevented him from saying a single word. He tried to speak to his sister, but all he could do was to take her hand and *weep*. This did the poor widow more good than any words could have done, no matter how eloquently or fitly spoken. It unlocked the fountain of her own heart, and the two wept together.

When Captain Ogilvy accompanied Ruby on board the sloop to see him off, and shook hands as he was about to return to the shore, he said— "Cheer up, Ruby; never say die so long as there's a shot in the looker. That's the advice of an old salt, an' you'll find it sound,

35

the more you ponder of it. W'en a young feller sails away on the sea of life, let him always go by chart and compass, not forgettin' to take soundin's w'en cruisin' off a bad coast. Keep a sharp lookout to wind'ard, an' mind yer helm—that's *my* advice to you lad, as ye go:—

"'A-sailin' down life's troubled stream,
 All as if it wor a dream.'"

The captain had a somewhat poetic fancy (at least he was impressed with the belief that he had), and was in the habit of enforcing his arguments by quotations from memory. When memory failed he supplemented with original composition.

"Goodbye, lad, an' Providence go wi' ye."

"Goodbye, uncle. I need not remind you to look after mother when I'm away."

"No, nephy, you needn't; I'll do it whether or not."

"And Minnie, poor thing, she'll need a word of advice and comfort now and then, uncle."

"And she shall have it, lad," replied the captain with a tremendous wink, which was unfortunately lost on the nephew, in consequence of its being night and unusually dark, "advice and comfort on demand, gratis; for:—

"'Woman, in her hours of ease,
  Is most uncommon hard to please;'

"But she *must* be looked arter, ye know, and made of, d'ye see? so Ruby, boy, farewell."

Half-an-hour before midnight was the time chosen for the sailing of the sloop *Termagant*, in order that she might get away quietly and escape the press-gang. Ruby and his uncle had taken the precaution to go down to the harbour just a few minutes before sailing, and they kept as closely as possible to the darkest and least-frequented streets while passing through the town.

Captain Ogilvy returned by much the same route to his sister's cottage, but did not attempt to conceal his movements. On the contrary, knowing that the sloop must have got clear of the harbour by that time, he went along the streets whistling cheerfully. He had been a noted, not to say noisy, whistler when a boy, and the habit had not forsaken him in his old age. On turning sharp round a corner, he ran against two men, one of whom swore at him, but the other cried—

"Hallo! messmate, yer musical the night. Hey, Captain Ogilvy, surely I seed you an' Ruby slinkin' down the dark side o' the market-gate half an 'oor ago?"

"Mayhap ye did, an' mayhap ye didn't," retorted the captain, as he walked on; "but as it's none o' your business to know, I'll not tell ye."

"Ay, ay? O but ye're a cross auld chap. Pleasant dreams t'ye."

This kindly remark, which was expressed by our friend Davy Spink, was lost on the captain, in consequence of his having resumed his musical recreation with redoubled energy, as he went rolling back to the cottage to console Mrs Brand, and to afford "advice and comfort gratis" to Minnie Gray.

Chapter Four

The Burglary

On the night in question, Big Swankie and a likeminded companion, who went among his comrades by the name of the Badger, had planned to commit a burglary in the town, and it chanced that the former was about that business when Captain Ogilvy unexpectedly ran against him and Davy Spink.

Spink, although a smuggler, and by no means a particularly respectable man, had not yet sunk so low in the scale of life as to be willing to commit burglary. Swankie and the Badger suspected this, and, although they required his assistance much, they were afraid to ask him to join, lest he should not only refuse, but turn against them. In order to get over the difficulty, Swankie had arranged to suggest to him the robbery of a store containing gin, which belonged to a smuggler, and, if he agreed to that, to proceed further and suggest the more important matter in hand. But he found Spink proof against the first attack.

"I tell 'ee, I'll hae naething to do wi't," said he, when the proposal was made.

"But," urged Swankie, "he's a smuggler, and a cross-grained hound besides. It's no' like robbin' an honest man."

"An' what are *we* but smugglers?" retorted Spink; "an' as to bein' cross-grained, you've naethin' to boast o' in that way. Na, na, Swankie, ye may do't yersel, I'll hae nae hand in't. I'll no objec' to tak a bit keg o' Auchmithie water (smuggled spirits) noo and then, or to pick up what comes to me by the wund and sea, but I'll steal frae nae man."

"Ay, man, but ye've turned awfu' honest all of a suddent," said the other with a sneer. "I wonder the thretty sovereigns I gied ye the other day, when we tossed for them and the case o' kickshaws, havena' brunt yer pooches."

Davy Spink looked a little confused.

"Aweel," said he, "it's o' nae use greetin' ower spilt milk, the thing's done and past noo, and I canna help it. Sae guidnight to 'ee."

Swankie, seeing that it was useless to attempt to gain over his comrade, and knowing that the Badger was waiting impatiently for him near the appointed house, hurried away without another word, and Davy Spink strolled towards his home, which was an extremely dirty little hut, near the harbour.

At the time of which we write, the town of Arbroath was neither so well lighted nor so well guarded as it now is. The two burglars found nothing to interfere with their deeds of darkness, except a few bolts and bars, which did not stand long before their expert hands.

Nevertheless, they met with a check from an unexpected quarter.

The house they had resolved to break into was inhabited by a widow lady, who was said to be wealthy, and who was known to possess a considerable quantity of plate and jewels. She lived alone, having only one old servant and a little girl to attend upon her. The house stood on a piece of ground not far from the ruins of the stately abbey which originated and gave celebrity to the ancient town of Aberbrothoc. Mrs Stewart's house was full of Eastern curiosities, some of them of great value, which had been sent to her by her son, then a major in the East India Company's service.

Now, it chanced that Major Stewart had arrived from India that very day, on leave of absence, all unknown to the burglars, who, had they been aware of the fact, would undoubtedly have postponed their visit to a more convenient season.

As it was, supposing they had to deal only with the old lady and her two servants, they began their work between twelve and one that night, with considerable confidence, and in great hopes of a rich booty.

A small garden surrounded the old house. It was guarded by a wall about eight feet high, the top of which bristled with bottle-glass. The old lady and her domestics regarded this terrible-looking defence with much satisfaction, believing in their innocence that no human creature could succeed in getting over it. Boys, however, were their only dread, and fruit their only care, when they looked complacently at the bottle-glass on the wall, and, so far, they were right in their feeling of security, for boys found the labour, risk, and danger to be greater than the worth of the apples and pears.

But it was otherwise with men. Swankie and the Badger threw a piece of thick matting on the wall; the former bent down, the latter stepped upon his back, and thence upon the mat; then he hauled his comrade up, and both leaped into the garden.

Advancing stealthily to the door, they tried it and found it locked. The windows were all carefully bolted, and the shutters barred. This they expected, but thought it as well to try each possible point of entrance, in the hope of finding an unguarded spot before having recourse to their tools. Such a point was soon found, in the shape of a small window, opening into a sort of scullery at the back of the house. It had been left open by accident. An entrance was easily effected by the Badger, who was a small man, and who went through the house with the silence of a cat, towards the front door. There were two lobbies, an inner and an outer, separated from each other by a glass door. Cautiously opening both doors, the

Badger admitted his comrade, and then they set to work.

A lantern, which could be uncovered or concealed in a moment, enabled them to see their way.

"That's the dinin'-room door," whispered the Badger.

"Hist! haud yer jaw," muttered Swankie; "I ken that as weel as you."

Opening the door, they entered and found the plate-chest under the sideboard.

It was open, and a grin of triumph crossed the sweet countenances of the friends as they exchanged glances, and began to put silver forks and spoons by the dozen into a bag which they had brought for the purpose.

When they had emptied the plate-chest, they carried the bag into the garden, and, climbing over the wall, deposited it outside. Then they returned for more.

Now, old Mrs Stewart was an invalid, and was in the habit of taking a little weak wine and water before retiring to rest at night. It chanced that the bottle containing the port wine had been left on the sideboard, a fact which was soon discovered by Swankie, who put the bottle to his mouth, and took a long pull.

"What is't?" enquired the Badger, in a low tone.

"Prime!" replied Swankie, handing over the bottle, and wiping his mouth with the cuff of his coat.

The Badger put the bottle to his mouth, but unfortunately for him, part of the liquid went down the "wrong throat". The result was that the poor man coughed, once, rather loudly. Swankie, frowning fiercely, and shaking his fist, looked at him in horror; and well he might, for the Badger became first red and then purple in the face, and seemed as if he were about to burst with his efforts to keep down the cough. It came, however, three times, in spite of him,—not violently, but with sufficient noise to alarm them, and cause them to listen for five minutes intently ere they ventured to go on with their work, in the belief that no one had been disturbed.

But Major Stewart had been awakened by the first cough. He was a soldier who had seen much service, and who slept lightly. He raised himself in his bed, and listened intently on hearing the first cough. The second cough caused him to spring up and pull on his trousers; the third cough found him halfway downstairs, with a boot-jack in his hand, and when the burglars resumed work he was peeping at them through the half-open door.

Both men were stooping over the plate-chest, the Badger with his back to the door, Swankie with his head towards it. The major raised the boot-jack and took aim. At the same moment the door squeaked, Big Swankie looked up hastily, and, in technical phraseology, "doused the glim." All was dark in an instant, but the boot-jack sped on its way notwithstanding. The burglars were accustomed to fighting, however, and dipped their heads. The boot-jack whizzed past, and smashed the pier-glass on the mantelpiece to a thousand atoms. Major Stewart being expert in all the devices of warfare, knew what to expect, and drew aside. He was not a moment too soon, for the dark lantern flew through the doorway, hit the opposite wall, and fell with a loud clatter on the stone floor of the lobby. The Badger followed at once, and received a random blow from the major that hurled him head over heels after the lantern.

There was no mistaking the heavy tread and rush of Big Swankie as he made for the door. Major Stewart put out his foot, and the burglar naturally tripped over it; before he could rise the major had him by the throat. There was a long, fierce struggle, both being powerful men; at last Swankie was hurled completely through the glass door. In the fall he disengaged himself from the major, and, leaping up, made for the garden wall, over which he succeeded in clambering before the latter could seize him. Thus both burglars escaped, and Major Stewart returned to the house half-naked,—his shirt having been torn off his back,—and bleeding freely from cuts caused by the glass door.

Just as he re-entered the house, the old cook, under the impression that the cat had got into the pantry, and was smashing the crockery, entered the lobby in her nightdress, shrieked "Mercy on us!" on beholding the major, and fainted dead away.

Major Stewart was too much annoyed at having failed to capture the burglars to take any notice of her. He relocked the door, and assuring his mother that it was only robbers, and that they had been beaten off, retired to his room, washed and dressed his wounds, and went to bed.

Meanwhile Big Swankie and the Badger, laden with silver, made for the shore, where they hid their treasure in a hole.

"I'll tell 'ee a dodge," said the Badger.

"What may that be?" enquired Swankie.

"You said ye saw Ruby Brand slinking down the market-gate, and that's he's off to sea?"

"Ay, and twa or three more folk saw him as weel as me."

"Weel, let's tak' up a siller spoon, or somethin', an' put it in the auld wife's garden, an' they'll think it was him that did it."

"No' that bad!" said Swankie, with a chuckle.

A silver fork and a pair of sugar-tongs bearing old Mrs Stewart's initials were accordingly selected for this purpose, and placed in the little garden in the front of Widow Brand's cottage.

Here they were found in the morning by Captain Ogilvy, who examined them for at least half-an-hour in a state of the utmost perplexity. While he was thus engaged one of the detectives of the town happened to pass, apparently in some haste.

"Hallo! Shipmate," shouted the captain.

"Well?" responded the detective.

"Did ye ever see silver forks an' sugar-tongs growin' in a garden before?"

"Eh?" exclaimed the other, entering the garden hastily; "let me see. Oho! this may throw some light on the matter. Did you find them here?"

"Ay, on this very spot."

"Hum. Ruby went away last night, I believe?"

"He did."

"Some time after midnight?" enquired the detective.

"Likely enough," said the captain, "but my chronometer ain't quite so reg'lar since we left the sea; it might ha' bin more,—mayhap less."

"Just so. You saw him off?"

"Ay; but you seem more than or'nar inquisitive to-day—"

"Did he carry a bundle?" interrupted the detective.

"Ay, no doubt."

"A large one?"

"Ay, a goodish big 'un."

"Do you know what was in it?" enquired the detective, with a knowing look.

"I do, for I packed it," replied the captain; "his kit was in it."

"Nothing more?"

"Nothin' as I knows of."

"Well, I'll take these with me just now," said the officer, placing the fork and sugar-tongs in his pocket. "I'm afraid, old man that your nephew has been up to mischief before he went away. A burglary was committed in the town last night, and this is some of the plate. You'll hear more about it before long, I dare say. Good day to you."

So saying, the detective walked quickly away, and left the captain in the centre of the garden staring vacantly before him in speechless amazement.

Chapter Five

The Bell Rock Invaded

A year passed away. Nothing more was heard of Ruby Brand, and the burglary was believed to be one of those mysteries which are destined never to be solved.

About this time great attention was being given by Government to the subject of lighthouses. The terrible number of wrecks that had taken place had made a deep impression on the public mind. The position and dangerous character of the Bell Rock, in particular, had been for a long time the subject of much discussion, and various unsuccessful attempts had been made to erect a beacon of some sort thereon.

There is a legend that in days of old one of the abbots of the neighbouring monastery of Aberbrothoc erected a bell on the Inchcape Rock, which was tolled in rough weather by the action of the waves on a float attached to the tongue, and thus mariners were warned at night and in foggy weather of their approach to the rock, the great danger of which consists in its being a sunken reef, lying twelve miles from the nearest land, and exactly in the course of vessels making for the firths of Forth and Tay. The legend further tells how that a Danish pirate, named Ralph the Rover, in a mischievous mood, cut the bell away, and that, years afterwards, he obtained his appropriate reward by being wrecked on the Bell Rock, when returning from a long cruise laden with booty.

Whether this be true or not is an open question, but certain it is that no beacon of any kind was erected on this rock until the beginning of the nineteenth century, after a great storm in 1799 had stirred the public mind, and set springs in motion, which from that time forward have never ceased to operate.

Many and disastrous were the shipwrecks that occurred during the storm referred to, which continued, with little intermission, for three days. Great numbers of ships were driven from their moorings in the Downs and Yarmouth Roads; and these, together with all vessels navigating the German Ocean at that time, were drifted upon the east coast of Scotland.

It may not, perhaps, be generally known that there are only three great inlets or estuaries to which the mariner steers when overtaken by easterly storms in the North Sea—namely, the Humber, and the firths of Forth and Moray. The mouth of the Thames is too much encumbered by sand-banks to be approached at night or during bad weather. The Humber is also considerably obstructed in this way, so that the Roads of Leith, in the Firth of Forth, and those of Cromarty, in the Moray Firth, are the chief places of resort in easterly gales. But both of these had their special risks.

On the one hand, there was the danger of mistaking the Dornoch Firth for the Moray, as it lies only a short way to the north of the latter; and, in the case of the Firth of Forth, there was the terrible Bell Rock.

Now, during the storm of which we write, the fear of those two dangers was so strong upon seamen that many vessels were lost in trying to avoid them, and much hardship was sustained by mariners who preferred to seek shelter in higher latitudes. It was estimated that no fewer than seventy vessels were either stranded or lost during that single gale, and many of the crews perished.

At one wild part of the coast, near Peterhead, called the Bullers of Buchan, after the first night of the storm, the wrecks of seven vessels were found in one cove, without a single survivor of the crews to give an account of the disaster.

The "dangers of the deep" are nothing compared with the *dangers of the shore*. If the hard rocks of our island could tell the tale of their experience, and if we landsmen could properly appreciate it, we should understand more clearly why it is that sailors love blue (in other words, deep) water during stormy weather.

In order to render the Forth more accessible by removing the danger of the Bell Rock, it was resolved by the Commissioners of Northern Lights to build a lighthouse upon it. This resolve was a much bolder one than most people suppose, for the rock on which the lighthouse was to be erected was a sunken reef, visible only at low tide during two or three hours, and quite inaccessible in bad weather. It was the nearest approach to building a house *in* the sea that had yet been attempted! The famous Eddystone stands on a rock which is *never quite* under water, although nearly so, for its crest rises a very little above the highest tides, while the Bell Rock is eight or ten feet under water at high tides.

It must be clear, therefore, to everyone, that difficulties, unusual in magnitude and peculiar in kind, must have stood in the way of the daring engineer who should undertake the erection of a tower on a rock twelve miles out on the stormy sea, and the foundation of which was covered with ten or twelve feet of water every tide; a tower which would have to be built *perfectly*, yet *hastily*; a tower which should form a comfortable home, fit for human beings to dwell in, and yet strong enough to withstand the utmost fury of the waves, not merely whirling round it, as might be the case on some exposed promontory, but rushing at it, straight and fierce from the wild ocean, in great blue solid billows that should burst in thunder on its sides, and rush up in scarcely less solid spray to its lantern, a hundred feet or more above its foundation.

An engineer able and willing to undertake this great work was found in the person of the late Robert Stevenson of Edinburgh, whose perseverance and talent shall be commemorated by the grandest and most useful monument ever raised by man, as long as the Bell Rock lighthouse shall tower above the sea.

It is not our purpose to go into the details of all that was done in the construction of this lighthouse. Our peculiar task shall be to relate those incidents connected with this work which have relation to the actors in our tale.

We will not, therefore, detain the reader by telling him of all the preliminary difficulties that were encountered and overcome in this "Robinson Crusoe" sort of work; how that a temporary floating lightship, named the *Pharos*, was prepared and anchored in the vicinity of the rock in order to be a sort of depot and rendezvous and guide to the three smaller vessels employed in the work, as well as a light to shipping generally, and a building-yard was established at Arbroath, where every single stone of the lighthouse was cut and nicely fitted before being conveyed to the rock. Neither shall we tell of the difficulties that arose in the matter of getting blocks of granite large enough for such masonry, and lime of a nature strong enough to withstand the action of the salt sea. All this, and a great deal more of a deeply interesting nature, must remain untold, and be left entirely to the reader's imagination. (See note 1.)

Suffice it to say that the work was fairly begun in the month of August, 1807; that a strong beacon of timber was built, which was so well constructed that it stood out all the storms that beat against it during the whole time of the building operations; that close to this beacon the pit or foundation of the lighthouse was cut down deep into the solid rock; that the men employed could work only between two and three hours at a time, and had to pump the water out of this pit each tide before they could resume operations; that the work could only be done in the summer months, and when engaged in it the men dwelt either in the *Pharos* floating light, or in one of the attending vessels, and were not allowed to go ashore— that is, to the mainland, about twelve miles distant; that the work was hard, but so novel and exciting that the artificers at last became quite enamoured of it, and that ere long operations were going busily forward, and the work was in a prosperous and satisfactory state of advancement.

Things were in this condition at the Bell Rock, when, one fine summer evening, our friend and hero, Ruby Brand, returned, after a long absence, to his native town.

Chapter Six

The Captain Changes His Quarters

It was fortunate for Ruby that the skipper of the vessel ordered him to remain in charge while he went ashore, because he would certainly have been recognised by numerous friends, and his arrival would speedily have reached the ears of the officers of justice, who seem to be a class of men specially gifted with the faculty of never forgetting. It was not until darkness had begun to settle down on the town that the skipper returned on board, and gave him leave to go ashore.

Ruby did not return in the little coaster in which he had left his native place. That vessel had been wrecked not long after he joined her, but the crew were saved, and Ruby succeeded in obtaining a berth as second mate of a large ship trading between Hull and the Baltic. Returning from one of his voyages with a pretty good sum of money in his pocket, he resolved to visit his mother and give it to her. He therefore went aboard an Arbroath schooner, and offered to work his passage as an extra hand. Remembering his former troubles in connexion with the press-gang, he resolved to conceal his name from the captain and crew, who chanced to be all strangers to him.

It must not be supposed that Mrs Brand had not heard of Ruby since he left her. On the contrary, both she and Minnie Gray got letters as frequently as the postal arrangements of those days would admit of; and from time to time they received remittances of money, which enabled them to live in comparative comfort. It happened, however, that the last of these remittances had been lost, so that Mrs Brand had to depend for subsistence on Minnie's exertions, and on her brother's liberality. The brother's power was limited, however, and Minnie had been ailing for some time past, in consequence of her close application to work, so that she could not earn as much as usual. Hence it fell out that at this particular time the widow found herself in greater pecuniary difficulties than she had ever been in before.

Ruby was somewhat of an original. It is probable that every hero is. He resolved to surprise his mother by pouring the money he had brought into her lap, and for this purpose had, while in Hull, converted all his savings into copper, silver, and gold. Those precious metals he stowed separately into the pockets of his huge pea-jacket, and, thus heavily laden, went ashore about dark, as soon as the skipper returned.

At this precise hour it happened that Mrs Brand, Minnie Gray, and Captain Ogilvy were seated at their supper in the kitchen of the cottage.

Two days previously the captain had called, and said to Mrs Brand—

"I tell 'ee what it is, sister, I'm tired of livin' a solitary bachelor life, all by myself, so I'm goin' to make a change, lass."

Mrs Brand was for some moments speechless, and Minnie, who was sewing near the window, dropped her hands and work on her lap, and looked up with inexpressible amazement in her sweet blue eyes.

"Brother," said Mrs Brand earnestly, "you don't mean to tell me that you're going to marry at *your* time of life?"

"Eh! what? Marry?"

The captain looked, if possible, more amazed than his sister for a second or two, then his red face relaxed into a broad grin, and he sat down on a chair and chuckled, wiping the perspiration (he seemed always more or less in a state of perspiration) from his bald head the while.

"Why, no, sister, I'm not going to marry; did I speak of marryin'?"

"No; but you spoke of being tired of a bachelor life, and wishing to change."

59

"Ah! you women," said the captain, shaking his head—"always suspecting that we poor men are wantin' to marry you. Well, pr'aps you ain't far wrong neither; but I'm not goin' to be spliced yet-a-while, lass. Marry, indeed!

"'Shall I, wastin' in despair,
  Die, 'cause why? a woman's rare?'"

"Oh! Captain Ogilvy, that's not rightly quoted," cried Minnie, with a merry laugh.

"Ain't it?" said the captain, somewhat put out; for he did not like to have his powers of memory doubted.

"No; surely women are not *rare*," said Minnie.

"Good ones are," said the captain stoutly.

"Well; but that's not the right word."

"What *is* the right word, then?" asked the captain with affected sternness, for, although by nature disinclined to admit that he could be wrong, he had no objection to be put right by Minnie.

"Die because a woman's f—," said Minnie, prompting him.

"F—, 'funny?'" guessed the captain.

"No; it's not 'funny,'" cried Minnie, laughing heartily.

"Of course not," assented the captain, "it could not be 'funny' nohow, because 'funny' don't rhyme with 'despair;' besides, lots o' women ain't funny a bit, an' if they was, that's no reason why a man should die for 'em; what *is* the word, lass?"

"What am *I*?" asked Minnie, with an arch smile, as she passed her fingers through the clustering masses of her beautiful hair.

"An angel, beyond all doubt," said the gallant captain, with a burst of sincerity which caused Minnie to blush and then to laugh.

"You're incorrigible, captain, and you are so stupid that it's of no use trying to teach you."

Mrs Brand—who listened to this conversation with an expression of deep anxiety on her meek face, for she could not get rid of her first idea that her brother was going to marry—here broke in with the question—

"When is it to be, brother?"

"When is what to be, sister?"

"The—the marriage."

"I tell you I *ain't* a-goin' to marry," repeated the captain; "though why a stout young feller like me, just turned sixty-four, *shouldn't* marry, is more than I can see. You know the old proverbs, lass—'It's never too late to marry;' 'Never ventur', never give in;' 'John Anderson my jo John, when we was first—first—'"

"Married," suggested Minnie.

"Just so," responded the captain, "and everybody knows that *he* was an old man. But no, I'm not goin' to marry; I'm only goin' to give up my house, sell off the furniture, and come and live with *you*."

"Live with me!" ejaculated Mrs Brand.

"Ay, an' why not? What's the use o' goin' to the expense of two houses when one'll do, an' when we're both raither scrimp o' the ready? You'll just let me have the parlour. It never was a comf'rable room to sit in, so it don't matter much your givin' it up; it's a good enough sleepin' and smokin' cabin, an' we'll all live together in the kitchen. I'll throw the whole of my treemendous income into the general purse, always exceptin' a few odd coppers, which I'll retain to keep me a-goin' in baccy. We'll sail under the same flag, an' sit round the same fire, an' sup at the same table, and sleep in the same—no, not exactly that, but under the same roof-tree, which'll be a more hoconomical way o' doin' business, you know; an' so, old girl, as the song says—

"'Come an' let us be happy together,
    For where there's a will there's a way,

An' we won't care a rap for the weather
  So long as there's nothin' to pay.'"

"Would it not be better to say, 'so long as there's *something* to pay?'" suggested Minnie.

"No, lass, it *wouldn't*," retorted the captain. "You're too fond of improvin' things. I'm a stanch old Tory, I am. I'll stick to the old flag till all's blue. None o' your changes or improvements for me."

This was a rather bold statement for a man to make who improved upon almost every line he ever quoted; but the reader is no doubt acquainted with parallel instances of inconsistency in good men even in the present day.

"Now, sister," continued Captain Ogilvy, "what d'ye think of my plan?"

"I like it well, brother," replied Mrs Brand with a gentle smile. "Will you come soon?"

"To-morrow, about eight bells," answered the captain promptly.

This was all that was said on the subject. The thing was, as the captain said, settled off-hand, and accordingly next morning he conveyed such of his worldly goods as he meant to retain possession of to his sister's cottage—"the new ship", as he styled it. He carried his traps on his own broad shoulders, and the conveyance of them cost him three distinct trips.

They consisted of a huge sea-chest, an old telescope more than a yard long, and cased in leather; a quadrant, a hammock, with the bedding rolled up in it, a tobacco-box, the enormous old Family Bible in which the names of his father, mother, brothers, and sisters were recorded; and a brown teapot with half a lid. This latter had belonged to the captain's mother, and, being fond of it, as it reminded him of the "old ooman", he was wont to mix his grog in it, and drink the same out of a teacup, the handle of which was gone, and the saucer of which was among the things of the past.

Notwithstanding his avowed adherence to Tory principles, Captain Ogilvy proceeded to make manifold radical changes and surprising improvements in the little parlour, insomuch that when he had completed the task, and led his sister carefully (for she was very feeble) to look at what he had done, she became quite incapable of expressing herself in ordinary language; positively refused to believe her eyes, and never again entered that room, but always spoke of what she had seen as a curious dream!

No one was ever able to discover whether there was not a slight tinge of underlying jocularity in this remark of Mrs Brand, for she was a strange and incomprehensible mixture of shrewdness and innocence; but no one took much trouble to find out, for she was so lovable that people accepted her just as she was, contented to let any small amount of mystery that seemed to be in her to remain unquestioned.

"The parlour" was one of those well-known rooms which are occasionally met with in country cottages, the inmates of which are not wealthy. It was reserved exclusively for the purpose of receiving visitors. The furniture, though old, threadbare, and dilapidated, was kept scrupulously clean, and arranged symmetrically. There were a few books on the table, which were always placed with mathematical exactitude, and a set of chairs, so placed as to give one mysteriously the impression that they were not meant to be sat upon. There was also a grate, which never had a fire in it, and was never without a paper ornament in it, the pink and white aspect of which caused one involuntarily to shudder.

But the great point, which was meant to afford the highest gratification to the beholder, was the chimney-piece. This spot was crowded to excess in every square inch of its area with ornaments, chiefly of earthenware, miscalled china, and shells. There were great white shells with pink interiors, and small brown shells with spotted backs. Then there were china cups and saucers, and china shepherds and shepherdesses, represented in the act of contemplating the heavens serenely, with their arms round each other's waists. There were also china dogs and cats, and a huge china cockatoo as a centre-piece; but there was not a single spot the size of a sixpence on which the captain could place his pipe or his tobacco-box!

"We'll get these things cleared away," said Minnie, with a laugh, on observing the perplexed look with which the captain surveyed the chimney-piece, while the changes above referred to were being made in the parlour; "we have no place ready to receive them just now, but I'll have them all put away to-morrow."

"Thank'ee, lass," said the captain, as he set down the sea-chest and seated himself thereon; "they're pretty enough to look at, d'ye see, but they're raither in the way just now, as my second mate once said of the rocks when we were cruising off the coast of Norway in search of a pilot."

The ornaments were, however, removed sooner than anyone had anticipated. The next trip that the captain made was for his hammock (he always slept in one), which was a long unwieldy bundle, like a gigantic bolster. He carried it into the parlour on his shoulder, and Minnie followed him.

"Where shall I sling it, lass?"

"Here, perhaps," said Minnie.

The captain wheeled round as she spoke, and the end of the hammock swept the mantelpiece of all its ornaments, as completely as if the besom of destruction had passed over it.

"Shiver my timbers!" gasped the captain, awestruck by the hideous crash that followed.

"You've shivered the ornaments at any rate," said Minnie, half-laughing and half-crying.

"So I have, but no matter. Never say die so long's there a shot in the locker. There's as good fish in the sea as ever come out of it; so bear a hand, my girl, and help me to sling up the hammock."

The hammock was slung, the pipe of peace was smoked, and thus Captain Ogilvy was fairly installed in his sister's cottage.

It may, perhaps, be necessary to remind the reader that all this is a long digression; that the events just narrated occurred a few days before the return of Ruby, and that they have been recorded here in order to explain clearly the reason of the captain's appearance at the supper table of his sister, and the position which he occupied in the family.

When Ruby reached the gate of the small garden, Minnie had gone to the captain's room to see that it was properly prepared for his reception, and the captain himself was smoking his pipe close to the chimney, so that the smoke should ascend it.

The first glance through the window assured the youth that his mother was, as letters had represented her, much better in health than she used to be. She looked so quiet and peaceful, and so fragile withal, that Ruby did not dare to "surprise her" by a sudden entrance, as he had originally intended, so he tapped gently at the window, and drew back.

The captain laid down his pipe and went to the door.

"What, Ruby!" he exclaimed, in a hoarse whisper.

"Hush, uncle! How is Minnie; where is she?"

"I think, lad," replied the captain in a tone of reproof, "that you might have enquired for your mother first."

"No need," said Ruby, pointing to the window; "I *see* that she is there and well, thanks be to God for that:— but Minnie?"

"She's well, too, boy, and in the house. But come, get inside. I'll explain, after."

This promise to "explain" was given in consequence of the great anxiety he, the captain, displayed to drag Ruby into the cottage.

The youth did not require much pressing, however. He no sooner heard that Minnie was well, than he sprang in, and was quickly at his mother's feet. Almost as quickly a fair vision appeared in the doorway of the inner room, and was clasped in the young sailor's arms with the most thorough disregard of appearances, not to mention propriety.

While this scene was enacting, the worthy captain was engaged in active proceedings, which at once amused and astonished his nephew, and the nature and cause of which shall be revealed in the next chapter.

Chapter Seven

Ruby in Difficulties

Having thrust his nephew into the cottage, Captain Ogilvy's first proceeding was to close the outer shutter of the window and fasten it securely on the inside. Then he locked, bolted, barred, and chained the outer door, after which he shut the kitchen door, and, in default of any other mode of securing it, placed against it a heavy table as a barricade.

Having thus secured the premises in front, he proceeded to fortify the rear, and, when this was accomplished to his satisfaction, he returned to the kitchen, sat down opposite the widow, and wiped his shining pate.

"Why, uncle, are we going to stand out a siege that you take so much pains to lock up?"

Ruby sat down on the floor at his mother's feet as he spoke, and Minnie sat down on a low stool beside him.

"Maybe we are, lad," replied the captain; "anyhow, it's always well to be ready—

"'Ready,   boys,   ready,
 We'll fight and we'll conquer again and again.'"

"Come uncle, explain yourself."

"Explain myself, nephy? I can neither explain myself nor anybody else. D'ye know, Ruby, that you're a burglar?"

"Am I, uncle? Well, I confess that that's news."

"Ay, but it's true though, at least the law in Arbroath says so, and if it catches you, it'll hang you as sure as a gun."

Here Captain Ogilvy explained to his nephew the nature of the crime that was committed on the night of his departure, the evidence of his guilt in the finding part of the plate in the garden, coupled with his sudden disappearance, and wound up by saying that he regarded him, Ruby, as being in a "reg'lar fix."

"But surely," said Ruby, whose face became gradually graver as the case was unfolded to him, "surely it must be easy to prove to the satisfaction of everyone that I had nothing whatever to do with this affair?"

"Easy to prove it!" said the captain in an excited tone; "wasn't you seen, just about the hour of the robbery, going stealthily down the street, by Big Swankie and Davy Spink, both of whom will swear to it."

"Yes, but *you* were with me, uncle."

"So I was, and hard enough work I had to convince them that I had nothin' to do with it myself, but they saw that I couldn't jump a stone wall eight foot high to save my life, much less break into a house, and they got no further evidence to convict me, so they let me off; but it'll go hard with you, nephy, for Major Stewart described the men, and one o' them was a big strong feller, the description bein' as like you as two peas, only their faces was blackened, and the lantern threw the light all one way, so he didn't see them well. Then, the things found in our garden,—and the villains will haul me up as a witness against you, for, didn't I find them myself?"

"Very perplexing; what shall I do?" said Ruby.

"Clear out," cried the captain emphatically.

"What! fly like a real criminal, just as I have returned home? Never. What say *you*, Minnie?"

"Stand your trial, Ruby. They cannot—they dare not—condemn the innocent."

"And you, mother?"

"I'm sure I don't know what to say," replied Mrs Brand, with a look of deep anxiety, as she passed her fingers through her son's hair, and kissed his brow. "I have seen the innocent condemned and the guilty go free more than once in my life."

"Nevertheless, mother, I will give myself up, and take my chance. To fly would be to give them reason to believe me guilty."

"Give yourself up!" exclaimed the captain, "you'll do nothing of the sort. Come, lad, remember I'm an old man, and an uncle. I've got a plan in my head, which I think will keep you out of harm's way for a time. You see my old chronometer is but a poor one,—the worse of the wear, like its master,—and I've never been able to make out the exact time that we went aboard the *Termagant* the night you went away. Now, can you tell me what o'clock it was?"

"I can."

"'Xactly?"

"Yes, exactly, for it happened that I was a little later than I promised, and the skipper pointed to his watch, as I came up the side, and jocularly shook his head at me. It was exactly eleven p.m."

"Sure and sartin o' that?" enquired the captain, earnestly.

"Quite, and his watch must have been right, for the town-clock rung the hour at the same time."

"Is that skipper alive?"

"Yes."

"Would he swear to that?"

"I think he would."

"D'ye know where he is?"

"I do. He's on a voyage to the West Indies, and won't be home for two months, I believe."

"Humph!" said the captain, with a disappointed look. "However, it can't be helped; but I see my way *now* to get you out o' this fix. You know, I suppose, that they're buildin' a lighthouse on the Bell Rock just now; well, the workmen go off to it for a month at a time, I believe, if not longer, and don't come ashore, and it's such a dangerous place, and troublesome to get to, that nobody almost ever goes out to it from this place, except those who have to do with it. Now, lad, you'll go down to the workyard the first thing in the mornin', before daylight, and engage to go off to work at the Bell Rock. You'll keep all snug and quiet, and nobody'll be a bit the wiser. You'll be earnin' good wages, and in the meantime I'll set about gettin' things in trim to put you all square."

"But I see many difficulties ahead," objected Ruby.

"Of course ye do," retorted the captain. "Did ye ever hear or see anything on this earth that hadn't rocks ahead o' some sort? It's our business to steer past 'em, lad, not to 'bout ship and steer away. But state yer difficulties."

"Well, in the first place, I'm not a stonemason or a carpenter, and I suppose masons and carpenters are the men most wanted there."

"Not at all, blacksmiths are wanted there," said the captain, "and I know that you were trained to that work as a boy."

"True, I can do somewhat with the hammer, but mayhap they won't engage me."

"But they *will* engage you, lad, for they are hard up for an assistant blacksmith just now, and I happen to be hand-and-glove with some o' the chief men of the yard, who'll be happy to take anyone recommended by me."

"Well, uncle, but suppose I do go off to the rock, what chance have you of making things appear better than they are at present?"

"I'll explain that, lad. In the first place, Major Stewart is a gentleman, out-and-out, and will listen to the truth. He swears that the robbery took place at one o'clock in the mornin', for he looked at his watch and at the clock of the house, and heard it ring in the town, just as the thieves cleared off over the wall. Now, if I can get your old skipper to take a run here on his return from the West Indies, he'll swear that you was sailin' out to the North Sea *before twelve*, and that'll prove that you *couldn't* have had nothin' to do with it, d'ye see?"

"It sounds well," said Ruby dubiously, "but do you think the lawyers will see things in the light you do?"

"Hang the lawyers! d'ye think they will shut their eyes to *the truth*?"

"Perhaps they may, in which case they will hang *me*, and so prevent my taking your advice to hang *them*," said Ruby.

"Well, well, but you agree to my plan?" asked the captain.

"Shall I agree, Minnie? it will separate me from you again for some time."

"Yet it is necessary," answered Minnie, sadly; "yes, I think you should agree to go."

"Very well, then, that's settled," said Ruby, "and now let us drop the subject, because I have other things to speak of; and if I must start before daylight my time with you will be short—"

"Come here a bit, nephy, I want to have a private word with 'ee in my cabin," said the captain, interrupting him, and going into his own room. Ruby rose and followed.

"You haven't any—"

The captain stopped, stroked his bald head, and looked perplexed.

"Well, uncle?"

"Well, nephy, you haven't—in short, have ye got any money about you, lad?"

"Money? yes, a *little*; but why do you ask?"

"Well, the fact is, that your poor mother is hard up just now," said the captain earnestly, "an' I've given her the last penny I have o' my own; but she's quite—"

Ruby interrupted his uncle at this point with a boisterous laugh. At the same time he flung open the door and dragged the old man with gentle violence back to the kitchen.

"Come here, uncle."

"But, avast! nephy, I haven't told ye all yet."

"Oh! don't bother me with such trifles just now," cried Ruby, thrusting his uncle into a chair and resuming his own seat at his mother's side; "we'll speak of that at some other time; meanwhile let me talk to mother."

"Minnie, dear," he continued, "who keeps the cash here; you or mother?"

"Well, we keep it between us," said Minnie, smiling; "your mother keeps it in her drawer and gives me the key when I want any, and I keep an account of it."

"Ah! well, mother, I have a favour to ask of you before I go."

"Well, *Ruby*?"

"It is that you will take care of my cash for me. I have got a goodish lot of it, and find it rather heavy to carry in my pockets—so, hold your apron steady and I'll give it to you."

Saying this he began to empty handful after handful of coppers into the old woman's apron; then, remarking that "that was all the browns", he began to place handful after handful of shillings and sixpences on the top of the pile until the copper was hid by silver.

The old lady, as usual when surprised, became speechless; the captain smiled and Minnie laughed, but when Ruby put his hand into another pocket and began to draw forth golden sovereigns, and pour them into his mother's lap, the captain became supremely amazed, the old woman laughed, and,—so strangely contradictory and unaccountable is human nature,—Minnie began to cry.

Poor girl! the tax upon her strength had been heavier than anyone knew, heavier than she could bear, and the sorrow of knowing, as she had come to know, that it was all in vain, and that her utmost efforts had failed to "keep the wolf from the door", had almost broken her down. Little wonder, then, that the sight of sudden and ample relief upset her altogether.

But her tears, being tears of joy, were soon and easily dried—all the more easily that it was Ruby who undertook to dry them.

Mrs Brand sat up late that night, for there was much to tell and much to hear. After she had retired to rest the other three continued to hold converse together until grey dawn began to appear through the chinks in the window-shutters. Then the two men rose and went out, while Minnie laid her pretty little head on the pillow beside Mrs Brand, and sought, and found, repose.

Chapter Eight

The Scene Changes—Ruby is Vulcanised

As Captain Ogilvy had predicted, Ruby was at once engaged as an assistant blacksmith on the Bell Rock. In fact, they were only too glad to get such a powerful, active young fellow into their service; and he was shipped off with all speed in the sloop *Smeaton*, with a few others who were going to replace some men who had become ill and were obliged to leave.

A light westerly breeze was blowing when they cast off the moorings of the sloop.

"Goodbye, Ruby," said the captain, as he was about to step on the pier. "Remember your promise, lad, to keep quiet, and don't try to get ashore, or to hold communication with anyone till you hear from me."

"All right, uncle, I won't forget, and I'll make my mind easy, for I know that my case is left in good hands."

Three hours elapsed ere the *Smeaton* drew near to the Bell Rock. During this time, Ruby kept aloof from his fellow-workmen, feeling disposed to indulge the sad thoughts which filled his mind. He sat down on the bulwarks, close to the main shrouds, and gazed back at the town as it became gradually less and less visible in the faint light of morning. Then he began to ponder his unfortunate circumstances, and tried to imagine how his uncle would set about clearing up his character and establishing his innocence; but, do what he would, Ruby could not keep his mind fixed for any length of time on any subject or line of thought, because of a vision of sweetness which it is useless to attempt to describe, and which was always accompanied by, and surrounded with, a golden halo.

At last the youth gave up the attempt to fix his thoughts, and allowed them to wander as they chose, seeing that they were resolved to do so whether he would or no. The moment these thoughts had the reins flung on their necks, and were allowed to go where they pleased, they refused, owing to some unaccountable species of perversity, to wander at all, but at once settled themselves comfortably down beside the vision with golden hair, and remained there.

This agreeable state of things was rudely broken in upon by the hoarse voice of the mate shouting—

"Stand by to let go the anchor."

Then Ruby sprang on the deck and shook himself like a great mastiff, and resolved to devote himself, heart and soul, from that moment, to the work in which he was about to engage.

The scene that presented itself to our hero when he woke up from his dreams would have interested and excited a much less enthusiastic temperament than his.

The breeze had died away altogether, just as if, having wafted the *Smeaton* to her anchorage, there were no further occasion for its services. The sea was therefore quite calm, and as there had only been light westerly winds for some time past, there was little or none of the swell that usually undulates the sea. One result of this was, that, being high water when the *Smeaton* arrived, there was no sign whatever of the presence of the famous Bell Rock. It lay sleeping nearly two fathoms below the sea, like a grim giant in repose, and not a ripple was there to tell of the presence of the mariner's enemy.

The sun was rising, and its slanting beams fell on the hulls of the vessels engaged in the service, which lay at anchor at a short distance from each other. These vessels, as we have said, were four in number, including the *Smeaton*. The others were the *Sir Joseph Banks*, a small schooner-rigged vessel; the *Patriot*, a little sloop; and the *Pharos* lightship, a large clumsy-looking Dutch-built ship, fitted with three masts, at the top of which were the lanterns. It was intended that this vessel should do duty as a lightship until the lighthouse should be completed.

Besides these there were two large boats, used for landing stones and building materials on the rock.

These vessels lay floating almost motionless on the calm sea, and at first there was scarcely any noise aboard of them to indicate that they were tenanted by human beings, but when the sound of the *Smeaton's* cable was heard there was a bustle aboard of each, and soon faces were seen looking inquisitively over the sides of the ships.

The *Smeaton's* boat was lowered after the anchor was let go, and the new hands were transferred to the *Pharos*, which was destined to be their home for some time to come.

Just as they reached her the bell rang for breakfast, and when Ruby stepped upon the deck he found himself involved in all the bustle that ensues when men break off from work and make preparation for the morning meal.

There were upwards of thirty artificers on board the lightship at this time. Some of these, as they hurried to and fro, gave the new arrivals a hearty greeting, and asked, "What news from the shore?" Others were apparently too much taken up with their own affairs to take notice of them.

While Ruby was observing the busy scene with absorbing interest, and utterly forgetful of the fact that he was in any way connected with it, an elderly gentleman, whose kind countenance and hearty manner gave indication of a genial spirit within, came up and accosted him:

"You are our assistant blacksmith, I believe?"

"Yes, sir, I am," replied Ruby, doffing his cap, as if he felt instinctively that he was in the presence of someone of note.

"You have had considerable practice, I suppose, in your trade?"

"A good deal, sir, but not much latterly, for I have been at sea for some time."

"At sea? Well, that won't be against you here," returned the gentleman, with a meaning smile. "It would be well if some of my men were a little more accustomed to the sea, for they suffer much from sea-sickness. You can go below, my man, and get breakfast. You'll find your future messmate busy at his, I doubt not. Here, steward," (turning to one of the men who chanced to pass at the moment,) "take Ruby Brand—that is your name, I think?"

"It is, sir."

"Take Brand below, and introduce him to James Dove as his assistant."

The steward escorted Ruby down the ladder that conducted to those dark and littered depths of the ship's hull that were assigned to the artificers as their place of abode. But amidst a good deal of unavoidable confusion, Ruby's practised eye discerned order and arrangement everywhere.

"This is your messmate, Jamie Dove," said the steward, pointing to a massive dark man, whose outward appearance was in keeping with his position as the Vulcan of such an undertaking as he was then engaged in. "You'll find him not a bad feller if you only don't cross him." He added, with a wink, "His only fault is that he's given to spoilin' good victuals, being raither floored by sea-sickness if it comes on to blow ever so little."

"Hold your clapper, lad," said the smith, who was at the moment busily engaged with a mess of salt pork, and potatoes to match. "Who's your friend?"

"No friend of mine, though I hope he'll be one soon," answered the steward. "Mr Stevenson told me to introduce him to you as your assistant."

The smith looked up quickly, and scanned our hero with some interest; then, extending his great hard hand across the table, he said, "Welcome, messmate; sit down, I've only just begun."

Ruby grasped the hand with his own, which, if not so large, was quite as powerful, and shook the smith's right arm in a way that called forth from that rough-looking individual a smile of approbation.

"You've not had breakfast, lad?"

"No, not yet," said Ruby, sitting down opposite his comrade.

"An' the smell here don't upset your stummick, I hope?"

The smith said this rather anxiously.

"Not in the least," said Ruby with a laugh, and beginning to eat in a way that proved the truth of his words; "for the matter o' that, there's little smell and no motion just now."

"Well, there isn't much," replied the smith, "but, woe's me! you'll get enough of it before long. All the new landsmen like you suffer horribly from sea-sickness when they first come off."

"But I'm not a landsman," said Ruby.

"Not a landsman!" echoed the other. "You're a blacksmith, aren't you?"

"Ay, but not a landsman. I learned the trade as a boy and lad; but I've been at sea for some time past."

"Then you won't get sick when it blows?"

"Certainly not; will *you*?"

The smith groaned and shook his head, by which answer he evidently meant to assure his friend that he would, most emphatically.

"But come, it's of no use groanin' over what can't be helped. I get as sick as a dog every time the wind rises, and the worst of it is I don't never seem to improve. Howsever, I'm all right when I get on the rock, and that's the main thing."

Ruby and his friend now entered upon a long and earnest conversation as to their peculiar duties at the Bell Rock, with which we will not trouble the reader.

After breakfast they went on deck, and here Ruby had sufficient to occupy his attention and to amuse him for some hours.

As the tide that day did not fall low enough to admit of landing on the rock till noon, the men were allowed to spend the time as they pleased. Some therefore took to fishing, others to reading, while a few employed themselves in drying their clothes, which had got wet the previous day, and one or two entertained themselves and their comrades with the music of the violin and flute. All were busy with one thing or another, until the rock began to show its black crest above the smooth sea. Then a bell was rung to summon the artificers to land.

This being the signal for Ruby to commence work, he joined his friend Dove, and assisted him to lower the bellows of the forge into the boat. The men were soon in their places, with their various tools, and the boats pushed off— Mr Stevenson, the engineer of the building, steering one boat, and the master of the *Pharos*, who was also appointed to the post of landing-master, steering the other.

They landed with ease on this occasion on the western side of the rock, and then each man addressed himself to his special duty with energy. The time during which they could work being short, they had to make the most of it.

"Now, lad," said the smith, "bring along the bellows and follow me. Mind yer footin', for it's slippery walkin' on them tangle-covered rocks. I've seen some ugly falls here already."

"Have any bones been broken yet?" enquired Ruby, as he shouldered the large pair of bellows, and followed the smith cautiously over the rocks.

"Not yet; but there's been an awful lot o' pipes smashed. If it goes on as it has been, we'll have to take to metal ones. Here we are, Ruby, this is the forge, and I'll be bound you never worked at such a queer one before. Hallo! Bremner!" he shouted to one of the men.

"That's me," answered Bremner.

"Bring your irons as soon as you like! I'm about ready for you."

"Ay, ay, here they are," said the man, advancing with an armful of picks, chisels, and other tools, which required sharpening.

He slipped and fell as he spoke, sending all the tools into the bottom of a pool of water; but, being used to such mishaps, he arose, joined in the laugh raised against him, and soon fished up the tools.

"What's wrong!" asked Ruby, pausing in the work of fixing the bellows, on observing that the smith's face grew pale, and his general expression became one of horror. "Not sea-sick, I hope?"

"Sea-sick," gasped the smith, slapping all his pockets hurriedly, "it's worse than that; I've forgot the matches!"

Ruby looked perplexed, but had no consolation to offer.

"That's like you," cried Bremner, who, being one of the principal masons, had to attend chiefly to the digging out of the foundation-pit of the building, and knew that his tools could not be sharpened unless the forge fire could be lighted.

"Suppose you hammer a nail red-hot," suggested one of the men, who was disposed to make game of the smith.

"I'll hammer your nose red-hot," replied Dove, with a most undovelike scowl, "I could swear that I put them matches in my pocket before I started."

"No, you didn't," said George Forsyth, one of the carpenters—a tall loose-jointed man, who was chiefly noted for his dislike to getting into and out of boats, and climbing up the sides of ships, because of his lengthy and unwieldy figure—"No, you didn't, you turtle-dove, you forgot to take them; but I remembered to do it for you; so there, get up your fire, and confess yourself indebted to me for life."

"I'm indebted to 'ee for fire," said the smith, grasping the matches eagerly. "Thank'ee, lad, you're a true Briton."

"A tall 'un, rather," suggested Bremner.

"Wot never, never, never will be a slave," sang another of the men.

"Come, laddies, git up the fire. Time an' tide waits for naebody," said John Watt, one of the quarriers. "We'll want thae tools before lang."

The men were proceeding with their work actively while those remarks were passing, and ere long the smoke of the forge fire arose in the still air, and the clang of the anvil was added to the other noises with which the busy spot resounded.

The foundation of the Bell Rock Lighthouse had been carefully selected by Mr Stevenson; the exact spot being chosen not only with a view to elevation, but to the serrated ridges of rock, that might afford some protection to the building, by breaking the force of the easterly seas before they should reach it; but as the space available for the purpose of building was scarcely fifty yards in diameter, there was not much choice in the matter.

The foundation-pit was forty-two feet in diameter, and sunk five feet into the solid rock. At the time when Ruby landed, it was being hewn out by a large party of the men. Others were boring holes in the rock near to it, for the purpose of fixing the great beams of a beacon, while others were cutting away the seaweed from the rock, and making preparations for the laying down of temporary rails to facilitate the conveying of the heavy stones from the boats to their ultimate destination. All were busy as bees. Each man appeared to work as if for a wager, or to find out how much he could do within a given space of time.

To the men on the rock itself the aspect of the spot was sufficiently striking and peculiar, but to those who viewed it from a boat at a short distance off it was singularly interesting, for the whole scene of operations appeared like a small black spot, scarcely above the level of the waves, on which a crowd of living creatures were moving about with great and incessant activity, while all around and beyond lay the mighty sea, sleeping in the grand tranquillity of a calm summer day, with nothing to bound it but the blue sky, save to the northward, where the distant cliffs of Forfar rested like a faint cloud on the horizon.

The sounds, too, which on the rock itself were harsh and loud and varied, came over the water to the distant observer in a united tone, which sounded almost as sweet as soft music.

The smith's forge stood on a ledge of rock close to the foundation-pit, a little to the north of it. Here Vulcan Dove had fixed a strong iron framework, which formed the hearth. The four legs which supported it were let into holes bored from six to twelve inches into the rock, according to the inequalities of the site. These were wedged first with wood and then with iron, for as this part of the forge and the anvil was doomed to be drowned every tide, or twice every day, besides being exposed to the fury of all the storms that might chance to blow, it behoved them to fix things down with unusual firmness.

The block of timber for supporting the anvil was fixed in the same manner, but the anvil itself was left to depend on its own weight and the small stud fitted into the bottom of it.

The bellows, however, were too delicate to be left exposed to such forces as the stormy winds and waves, they were therefore shipped and unshipped every tide, and conveyed to and from the rock in the boats with the men.

Dove and Ruby wrought together like heroes. They were both so powerful that the heavy implements they wielded seemed to possess no weight when in their strong hands, and their bodies were so lithe and active as to give the impression of men rejoicing, revelling, in the enjoyment of their work.

"That's your sort; hit him hard, he's got no friends," said Dove, turning a mass of red-hot metal from side to side, while Ruby pounded it with a mighty hammer, as if it were a piece of putty.

"Fire and steel for ever," observed Ruby, as he made the sparks fly right and left. "Hallo! the tide's rising."

"Ho! so it is," cried the smith, finishing off the piece of work with a small hammer, while Ruby rested on the one he had used and wiped the perspiration from his brow. "It always serves me in this way, lad," continued the smith, without pausing for a moment in his work. "Blow away, Ruby, the sea is my greatest enemy. Every day, a'most, it washes me away from my work. In calm weather, it creeps up my legs, and the legs o' the forge too, till it gradually puts out the fire, and in rough weather it sends up a wave sometimes that sweeps the whole concern black out at one shot."

"It will *creep* you out to-day, evidently," said Ruby, as the water began to come about his toes.

"Never mind, lad, we'll have time to finish them picks this tide, if we work fast."

Thus they toiled and moiled, with their heads and shoulders in smoke and fire, and their feet in water.

Gradually the tide rose.

"Pump away, Ruby! Keep the pot bilin', my boy," said the smith.

"The wind blowin', you mean. I say, Dove, do the other men like the work here?"

"Like it, ay, they like it well. At fist we were somewhat afraid o' the landin' in rough weather, but we've got used to that now. The only bad thing about it is in the rolling o' that horrible *Pharos*. She's so bad in a gale that I sometimes think she'll roll right over like a cask. Most of us get sick then, but I don't think any of 'em are as bad as me. They seem to be gettin' used to that too. I wish I could. Another blow, Ruby."

"Time's up," shouted one of the men.

"Hold on just for a minute or two," pleaded the smith, who, with his assistant, was by this time standing nearly knee-deep in water.

The sea had filled the pit some time before, and driven the men out of it. These busied themselves in collecting the tools and seeing that nothing was left lying about, while the men who were engaged on those parts of the rocks that were a few inches higher, continued their labours until the water crept up to them. Then they collected their tools, and went to the boats, which lay awaiting them at the western landing-place.

"Now, Dove," cried the landing-master, "come along; the crabs will be attacking your toes if you don't."

"It's a shame to gi'e Ruby the chance o' a sair throat the very first day," cried John Watt.

"Just half a minute more," said the smith, examining a pickaxe, which he was getting up to that delicate point of heat which is requisite to give it proper temper.

While he gazed earnestly into the glowing coals a gentle hissing sound was heard below the frame of the forge, then a gurgle, and the fire became suddenly dark and went out!

"I knowed it! always the way!" cried Dove, with a look of disappointment. "Come, lad, up with the bellows now, and don't forget the tongs."

In a few minutes more the boats pushed off and returned to the *Pharos*, three and a half hours of good work having been accomplished before the tide drove them away.

Soon afterwards the sea overflowed the whole of the rock, and obliterated the scene of those busy operations as completely as though it had never been!

Chapter Nine

Storms and Troubles

A week of fine weather caused Ruby Brand to fall as deeply in love with the work at the Bell Rock as his comrades had done.

There was an amount of vigor and excitement about it, with a dash of romance, which quite harmonized with his character. At first he had imagined it would be monotonous and dull, but in experience he found it to be quite the reverse.

Although there was uniformity in the general character of the work, there was constant variety in many of the details; and the spot on which it was carried on was so circumscribed, and so utterly cut off from all the world, that the minds of those employed became concentrated on it in a way that aroused strong interest in every trifling object.

There was not a ledge or a point of rock that rose ever so little above the general level that was not named after, and intimately associated with, some event or individual. Every mass of seaweed became a familiar object. The various little pools and inlets, many of them not larger than a dining-room table, received high-sounding and dignified names—such as *Port Stevenson, Port Erskine, Taylor's Track, Neill's Pool*, and etcetera. Of course the fish that frequented the pools, and the shell-fish that covered the rock, became subjects of much attention, and, in some cases, of earnest study.

Robinson Crusoe himself did not pry into the secrets of his island-home with half the amount of assiduity that was displayed at this time by many of the men who built the Bell Rock Lighthouse. The very fact that their time was limited acted as a spur, so that on landing each tide they rushed hastily to the work, and the amateur studies in natural history to which we have referred were prosecuted hurriedly during brief intervals of rest. Afterwards, when the beacon house was erected, and the men dwelt upon the rock, these studies (if we may not call them amusements) were continued more leisurely, but with unabated ardour, and furnished no small amount of comparatively thrilling incident at times.

One fine morning, just after the men had landed, and before they had commenced work, "Long Forsyth", as his comrades styled him, went to a pool to gather a little dulse, of which there was a great deal on the rock, and which was found to be exceedingly grateful to the palates of those who were afflicted with sea-sickness.

He stooped over the pool to pluck a morsel, but paused on observing a beautiful fish, about a foot long, swimming in the clear water, as quietly as if it knew the man to be a friend, and were not in the least degree afraid of him.

Forsyth was an excitable man, and also studious in his character. He at once became agitated and desirous of possessing that fish, for it was extremely brilliant and variegated in colour. He looked round for something to throw at it, but there was nothing within reach. He sighed for a hook and line, but as sighs never yet produced hooks or lines he did not get one.

Just then the fish swam slowly to the side of the pool on which the man kneeled, as if it actually desired more intimate acquaintance. Forsyth lay flat down and reached out his hand toward it; but it appeared to think this rather too familiar, for it swam slowly beyond his reach, and the man drew back. Again it came to the side, much nearer. Once more Forsyth lay down, reaching over the pool as far as he could, and insinuating his hand into the water. But the fish moved off a little.

Thus they coquetted with each other for some time, until the man's comrades began to observe that he was "after something."

"Wot's he a-doin' of?" said one.

"Reachin' over the pool, I think," replied another.

"Ye don't mean he's sick?" cried a third.

The smile with which this was received was changed into a roar of laughter as poor Forsyth's long legs were seen to tip up into the air, and the whole man to disappear beneath the water. He had overbalanced himself in his frantic efforts to reach the fish, and was now making its acquaintance in its native element!

The pool, although small in extent, was so deep that Forsyth, long though he was, did not find bottom. Moreover, he could not swim, so that when he reached the surface he came up with his hands first and his ten fingers spread out helplessly; next appeared his shaggy head, with the eyes wide open, and the mouth tight shut. The moment the latter was uncovered, however, he uttered a tremendous yell, which was choked in the bud with a gurgle as he sank again.

The men rushed to the rescue at once, and the next time Forsyth rose he was seized by the hair of the head and dragged out of the pool.

It has not been recorded what became of the fish that caused such an alarming accident, but we may reasonably conclude that it sought refuge in the ocean cavelets at the bottom of that miniature sea, for Long Forsyth was so very large, and created such a terrible disturbance therein, that no fish exposed to the full violence of the storm could have survived it!

"Wot a hobject!" exclaimed Joe Dumsby, a short, thickset, little Englishman, who, having been born and partly bred in London, was rather addicted to what is styled chaffing. "Was you arter a mermaid, shipmate?"

"Av coorse he was," observed Ned O'Connor, an Irishman, who was afflicted with the belief that he was rather a witty fellow, "av coorse he was, an' a merry-maid she must have bin to see a human spider like him kickin' up such a dust in the say."

"He's like a drooned rotten," observed John Watt; "tak' aff yer claes, man, an' wring them dry."

"Let the poor fellow be, and get along with you," cried Peter Logan, the foreman of the works, who came up at that moment.

With a few parting remarks and cautions, such as,—"You'd better bring a dry suit to the rock next time, lad," "Take care the crabs don't make off with you, boy," "and don't be gettin' too fond o' the girls in the sea," etcetera, the men scattered themselves over the rock and began their work in earnest, while Forsyth, who took the chaffing in good part, stripped himself and wrung the water out of his garments.

Episodes of this kind were not unfrequent, and they usually furnished food for conversation at the time, and for frequent allusion afterwards.

But it was not all sunshine and play, by any means.

Not long after Ruby joined, the fine weather broke up, and a succession of stiff breezes, with occasional storms, more or lees violent, set in. Landing on the rock became a matter of extreme difficulty, and the short period of work was often curtailed to little more than an hour each tide.

The rolling of the *Pharos* lightship, too, became so great that sea-sickness prevailed to a large extent among the landsmen. One good arose out of this evil, however. Landing on the Bell Rock invariably cured the sickness for a time, and the sea-sick men had such an intense longing to eat of the dulse that grew there, that they were always ready and anxious to get into the boats when there was the slightest possibility of landing.

Getting into the boats, by the way, in a heavy sea, when the lightship was rolling violently, was no easy matter. When the fine weather first broke up, it happened about midnight, and the change commenced with a stiff breeze from the eastward. The sea rose at once, and, long before daybreak, the *Pharos* was rolling heavily in the swell, and straining violently at the strong cable which held her to her moorings.

About dawn Mr Stevenson came on deck. He could not sleep, because he felt that on his shoulders rested not only the responsibility of carrying this gigantic work to a satisfactory conclusion, but also, to a large extent, the responsibility of watching over and guarding the lives of the people employed in the service.

"Shall we be able to land to-day, Mr Wilson?" he said, accosting the master of the *Pharos*, who has been already introduced as the landing-master.

"I think so; the barometer has not fallen much; and even although the wind should increase a little, we can effect a landing by the Fair Way, at Hope's Wharf."

"Very well, I leave it entirely in your hands; you understand the weather better than I do, but remember that I do not wish my men to run unnecessary or foolish risk."

It may be as well to mention here that a small but exceedingly strong tramway of iron-grating had been fixed to the Bell Rock at an elevation varying from two to four feet above it, and encircling the site of the building. This tramway or railroad was narrow, not quite three feet in width; and small trucks were fitted to it, so that the heavy stones of the building might be easily run to the exact spot they were to occupy. From this circular rail several branch lines extended to the different creeks where the boats deposited the stones. These lines, although only a few yards in length, were dignified with names—as, *Kennedy's Reach,*

Logan's Reach, Watt's Reach, and *Slight's Reach*. The ends of them, where they dipped into the sea, were named *Hope's Wharf, Duff's Wharf, Rae's Wharf*, etcetera; and these wharves had been fixed on different sides of the rock, so that, whatever wind should blow, there would always be one of them on the lee-side available for the carrying on of the work.

Hope's Wharf was connected with *Port Erskine*, a pool about twenty yards long by three or four wide, and communicated with the side of the lighthouse by *Watt's Reach*, a distance of about thirty yards.

About eight o'clock that morning the bell rang for breakfast. Such of the men as were not already up began to get out of their berths and hammocks.

To Ruby the scene that followed was very amusing. Hitherto all had been calm and sunshine. The work, although severe while they were engaged, had been of short duration, and the greater part of each day had been afterwards spent in light work, or in amusement. The summons to meals had always been a joyful one, and the appetites of the men were keenly set.

Now, all this was changed. The ruddy faces of the men were become green, blue, yellow, and purple, according to temperament, but few were flesh-coloured or red. When the bell rang there was a universal groan below, and half a dozen ghostlike individuals raised themselves on their elbows and looked up with expressions of the deepest woe at the dim skylight. Most of them speedily fell back again, however, partly owing to a heavy lurch of the vessel, and partly owing to indescribable sensations within.

"Blowin'!" groaned one, as if that single word comprehended the essence of all the miseries that seafaring man is heir to.

"O dear!" sighed another, "why did I ever come here?"

"Och! murder, I'm dyin', send for the praist an' me mother!" cried O'Connor, as he fell flat down on his back and pressed both hands tightly over his mouth.

The poor blacksmith lost control over himself at this point and—found partial relief!

The act tended to relieve others. Most of the men were much too miserable to make any remark at all, a few of them had not heart even to groan; but five or six sat up on the edge of their beds, with a weak intention of turning out. They sat there swaying about with the motions of the ship in helpless indecision, until a tremendous roll sent them flying, with unexpected violence, against the starboard bulkheads.

"Come, lads," cried Ruby, leaping out of his hammock, "there's nothing like a vigorous jump to put sea-sickness to flight."

"Humbug!" ejaculated Bremner, who owned a little black dog, which lay at that time on the pillow gazing into his master's green face, with wondering sympathy.

"Ah, Ruby," groaned the smith, "it's all very well for a sea-dog like you that's used to it, but—"

James Dove stopped short abruptly. It is not necessary to explain the cause of his abrupt silence. Suffice it to say that he did not thereafter attempt to finish that sentence.

"Steward!" roared Joe Dumsby.

"Ay, ay, shipmate, what's up?" cried the steward, who chanced to pass the door of the men's sleeping-place, with a large dish of boiled salt pork, at the moment.

"Wot's up?" echoed Dumsby. "Everythink that ever went into me since I was a hinfant must be 'up' by this time. I say, is there any chance of gettin' on the rock to-day?"

"O yes. I heard the cap'n say it would be quite easy, and they seem to be makin' ready now, so if any of 'ee want breakfast you'd better turn out."

This speech acted like a shock of electricity on the wretched men. In a moment every bed was empty, and the place was in a bustle of confusion as they hurriedly threw on their clothes.

Some of them even began to think of the possibility of venturing on a hard biscuit and a cup of tea, but a gust of wind sent the fumes of the salt pork into the cabin at the moment, and the mere idea of food filled them with unutterable loathing.

Presently the bell rang again. This was the signal for the men to muster, the boats being ready alongside. The whole crew at once rushed on deck, some of them thrusting biscuits into their pockets as they passed the steward's quarters. Not a man was absent on the roll being called. Even the smith crawled on deck, and had spirit enough left to advise Ruby not to forget the bellows; to which Ruby replied by recommending his comrade not to forget the matches.

Then the operation of embarking began.

The sea at the time was running pretty high, with little white flecks of foam tipping the crests of the deep blue waves. The eastern sky was dark and threatening. The black ridges of the Bell Rock were visible only at times in the midst of the sea of foam that surrounded them. Anyone ignorant of their nature would have deemed a landing absolutely impossible.

The *Pharos*, as we have said, was rolling violently from side to side, insomuch that those who were in the boats had the greatest difficulty in preventing them from being stove in; and getting into these boats had much the appearance of an exceedingly difficult and dangerous feat, which active and reckless men might undertake for a wager.

But custom reconciles one to almost anything. Most of the men had had sufficient experience by that time to embark with comparative ease. Nevertheless, there were a few whose physical conformation was such that they could do nothing neatly.

Poor Forsyth was one of these. Each man had to stand on the edge of the lightship, outside the bulwarks, holding on to a rope, ready to let go and drop into the boat when it rose up and met the vessel's roll. In order to facilitate the operation a boat went to either side of the ship, so that two men were always in the act of watching for an opportunity to spring. The active men usually got in at the first or second attempt, but others missed frequently, and were of course "chaffed" by their more fortunate comrades.

The embarking of "Long Forsyth" was always a scene in rough weather, and many a narrow escape had he of a ducking. On the present occasion, being very sick, he was more awkward than usual.

"Now, Longlegs," cried the men who held the boat on the starboard side, as Forsyth got over the side and stood ready to spring, "let's see how good you'll be to-day."

He was observed by Joe Dumsby, who had just succeeded in getting into the boat on the port side of the ship, and who always took a lively interest in his tall comrade's proceedings.

"Hallo! is that the spider?" he cried, as the ship rolled towards him, and the said spider appeared towering high on the opposite bulwark, sharply depicted against the grey sky.

It was unfortunate for Joe that he chanced to be on the opposite side from his friend, for at each roll the vessel necessarily intervened and hid him for a few seconds from view.

Next roll, Forsyth did not dare to leap, although the gunwale of the boat came within a foot of him. He hesitated, the moment was lost, the boat sank into the hollow of the sea, and the man was swung high into the air, where he was again caught sight of by Dumsby.

"What! are you there yet?" he cried. "You must be fond of a swing—"

Before he could say more the ship rolled over to the other side, and Forsyth was hid from view.

"Now, lad, now! now!" shouted the boat's crew, as the unhappy man once more neared the gunwale.

Forsyth hesitated. Suddenly he became desperate and sprang, but the hesitation gave him a much higher fall than he would otherwise have had; it caused him also to leap wildly in a sprawling manner, so that he came down on the shoulders of his comrades "all of a lump". Fortunately they were prepared for something of the sort, so that no damage was done.

When the boats were at last filled they pushed off and rowed towards the rock. On approaching it the men were cautioned to pull steadily by Mr Stevenson, who steered the leading boat.

It was a standing order in the landing department that every man should use his greatest exertions in giving to the boats sufficient velocity to preserve their steerage way in entering the respective creeks at the rock, that the contending seas might not overpower them at places where the free use of the oars could not be had on account of the surrounding rocks or the masses of seaweed with which the water was everywhere encumbered at low tide. This order had been thoroughly impressed upon the men, as carelessness or inattention to it might have proved fatal to all on board.

As the leading boat entered the fairway, its steersman saw that more than ordinary caution would be necessary; for the great green billows that thundered to windward of the rock came sweeping down on either side of it, and met on the lee-side, where they swept onward with considerable, though much abated force.

"Mind your oars, lads; pull steady," said Mr Stevenson, as they began to get amongst the seaweed.

The caution was unnecessary as far as the old hands were concerned; but two of the men happened to be new hands, who had come off with Ruby, and did not fully appreciate the necessity of strict obedience. One of these, sitting at the bow-oar, looked over his shoulder, and saw a heavy sea rolling towards the boat, and inadvertently expressed some fear. The other man, on hearing this, glanced round, and in doing so missed a stroke of his oar. Such a preponderance was thus given to the rowers on the opposite side, that when the wave struck the boat, it caught her on the side instead of the bow, and hurled her upon a ledge of shelving rocks, where the water left her. Having been *canted* to seaward, the next billow completely filled her, and, of course, drenched the crew.

Instantly Ruby Brand and one or two of the most active men leaped out, and, putting forth all their strength, turned the boat round so as to meet the succeeding sea with its bow first. Then, after making considerable efforts, they pushed her off into deep water, and finally made the landing-place. The other boat could render no assistance; but, indeed, the whole thing was the work of a few minutes.

As the boats could not conveniently leave the rock till flood-tide, all hands set to work with unwonted energy in order to keep themselves warm, not, however, before they ate heartily of their favourite dulse—the blacksmith being conspicuous for the voracious manner in which he devoured it.

Soon the bellows were set up; the fire was kindled, and the ring of the anvil heard; but poor Dove and Ruby had little pleasure in their work that day; for the wind blew the smoke and sparks about their faces, and occasionally a higher wave than ordinary sent the spray flying round them, to the detriment of their fire. Nevertheless they plied the hammer and bellows unceasingly.

The other men went about their work with similar disregard of the fury of the elements and the wet condition of their garments.

Chapter Ten

The Rising of the Tide—A Narrow Escape

The portion of the work that Mr Stevenson was now most anxious to get advanced was the beacon.

The necessity of having an erection of this kind was very obvious, for, in the event of anything happening to the boats, there would be no refuge for the men to fly to; and the tide would probably sweep them all away before their danger could be known, or assistance sent from the attendant vessels. Every man felt that his personal safety might depend on the beacon during some period of the work. The energies of all, therefore, were turned to the preliminary arrangements for its erection.

As the beacon would require to withstand the utmost fury of the elements during all seasons of the year, it was necessary that it should be possessed of immense strength.

In order to do this, six cuttings were made in the rock for the reception of the ends of the six great beams of the beacon. Each beam was to be fixed to the solid rock by two strong and massive bats, or stanchions, of iron. These bats, for the fixing of the principal and diagonal beams and bracing-chains, required fifty-four holes, each measuring a foot and a half deep, and two inches wide. The operation of boring such holes into the solid rock, was not an easy or a quick one, but by admirable arrangements on the part of the engineer, and steady perseverance on the part of the men, they progressed faster than had been anticipated.

Three men were attached to each jumper, or boring chisel; one placed himself in a sitting posture, to guide the instrument, and give it a turn at each blow of the hammer; he also sponged and cleaned out the hole, and supplied it occasionally with a little water, while the other two, with hammers of sixteen pounds weight, struck the jumper alternately, generally bringing the hammer with a swing round the shoulder, after the manner of blacksmith work.

Ruby, we may remark in passing, occupied himself at this work as often as he could get away from his duties at the forge, being particularly fond of it, as it enabled him to get rid of some of his superabundant energy, and afforded him a suitable exercise for his gigantic strength. It also tended to relieve his feelings when he happened to think of Minnie being so near, and he so utterly and hopelessly cut off from all communication with her.

But to return to the bat-holes. The three men relieved each other in the operations of wielding the hammers and guiding the jumpers, so that the work never flagged for a moment, and it was found that when the tools were of a very good temper, these holes could be sunk at the rate of one inch per minute, including stoppages. But the tools were not always of good temper; and severely was poor Dove's temper tried by the frequency of the scolds which he received from the men, some of whom were clumsy enough, Dove said, to spoil the best tempered tool in the world.

But the most tedious part of the operation did not lie in the boring of these holes. In order that they should be of the required shape, two holes had to be bored a few inches apart from each other, and the rock cut away from between them. It was this latter part of the work that took up most time.

Those of the men who were not employed about the beacon were working at the foundation-pit.

While the party were thus busily occupied on the Bell Rock, an event occurred which rendered the importance of the beacon, if possible, more obvious than ever, and which well-nigh put an end to the career of all those who were engaged on the rock at that time.

The *Pharos* floating light lay at a distance of above two miles from the Bell Rock; but one of the smaller vessels, the sloop *Smeaton*, lay much closer to it, and some of the artificers were berthed aboard of her, instead of the floating light.

Some time after the landing of the two boats from the *Pharos*, the *Smeaton's* boat put off and landed eight men on the rock; soon after which the crew of the boat pushed off and returned to the *Smeaton* to examine her riding-ropes, and see that they were in good order, for the wind was beginning to increase, and the sea to rise.

The boat had no sooner reached the vessel than the latter began to drift, carrying the boat along with her. Instantly those on board endeavoured to hoist the mainsail of the *Smeaton*, with the view of working her up to the buoy from which she had parted; but it blew so hard, that by the time she was got round to make a tack towards the rock, she had drifted at least three miles to leeward.

The circumstance of the *Smeaton* and her boat having drifted was observed first by Mr Stevenson, who prudently refrained from drawing attention to the fact, and walked slowly to the farther point of the rock to watch her. He was quickly followed by the landing-master, who touched him on the shoulder, and in perfect silence, but with a look of intense anxiety, pointed to the vessel.

"I see it, Wilson. God help us if she fails to make the rock within a very short time," said Mr Stevenson.

"She will *never* reach us in time," said Wilson, in a tone that convinced his companion he entertained no hope.

"Perhaps she may," he said hurriedly; "she is a good sailer."

"Good sailing," replied the other, "cannot avail against wind and tide together. No human power can bring that vessel to our aid until long after the tide has covered the Bell Rock."

Both remained silent for some time, watching with intense anxiety the ineffectual efforts of the little vessel to beat up to windward.

In a few minutes the engineer turned to his companion and said, "They cannot save us, Wilson. The two boats that are left—can they hold us all?"

The landing-master shook his head. "The two boats," said he, "will be completely filled by their own crews. For ordinary rough weather they would be quite full enough. In a sea like that," he said, pointing to the angry waves that were being gradually lashed into foam by the increasing wind, "they will be overloaded."

"Come, I don't know that, Wilson; we may devise something," said Mr Stevenson, with a forced air of confidence, as he moved slowly towards the place where the men were still working, busy as bees and all unconscious of the perilous circumstances in which they were placed.

As the engineer pondered the prospect of deliverance, his thoughts led him rather to despair than to hope. There were thirty-two persons in all upon the rock that day, with only two boats, which, even in good weather, could not unitedly accommodate more than twenty-four sitters. But to row to the floating light with so much wind and in so heavy a sea, a complement of eight men for each boat was as much as could with propriety be attempted, so that about half of their number was thus unprovided for. Under these circumstances he felt that to despatch one of the boats in expectation of either working the *Smeaton* sooner up to the rock, or in hopes of getting her boat brought to their assistance would, besides being useless, at once alarm the workmen, each of whom would probably insist upon taking to his own boat, and leaving the eight men of the *Smeaton* to their chance. A scuffle might ensue, and he knew well that when men are contending for life the results may be very disastrous.

For a considerable time the men remained in ignorance of the terrible conflict that was going on in their commander's breast. As they wrought chiefly in sitting or kneeling postures, excavating the rock or boring with jumpers, their attention was naturally diverted from everything else around them. The dense volumes of smoke, too, that rose from the forge fire, so enveloped them as to render distant objects dim or altogether invisible.

While this lasted,—while the numerous hammers were going and the anvil continued to sound, the situation of things did not appear so awful to the only two who were aware of what had occurred. But ere long the tide began to rise upon those who were at work on the lower parts of the beacon and lighthouse. From the run of the sea upon the rock, the forge fire was extinguished sooner than usual; the volumes of smoke cleared away, and objects became visible in every direction.

After having had about three hours' work, the men began pretty generally to make towards their respective boats for their jackets and socks.

Then it was that they made the discovery that one boat was absent.

Only a few exclamations were uttered. A glance at the two boats and a hurried gaze to seaward were sufficient to acquaint them with their awful position. Not a word was spoken by anyone. All appeared to be silently calculating their numbers, and looking at each other with evident marks of perplexity depicted in their countenances. The landing-master, conceiving that blame might attach to him for having allowed the boat to leave the rock, kept a little apart from the men.

All eyes were turned, as if by instinct, to Mr Stevenson. The men seemed to feel that the issue lay with him.

The engineer was standing on an elevated part of the rock named Smith's Ledge, gazing in deep anxiety at the distant *Smeaton*, in the hope that he might observe some effort being made, at least, to pull the boat to their rescue.

Slowly but surely the tide rose, overwhelming the lower parts of the rock; sending each successive wave nearer and nearer to the feet of those who were now crowded on the last ledge that could afford them standing-room.

The deep silence that prevailed was awful! It proved that each mind saw clearly the impossibility of anything being devised, and that a deadly struggle for precedence was inevitable.

Mr Stevenson had all along been rapidly turning over in his mind various schemes which might be put in practice for the general safety, provided the men could be kept under command. He accordingly turned to address them on the perilous nature of their circumstances; intending to propose that all hands should strip off their upper clothing when the higher parts of the rock should be laid under water; that the seamen should remove every unnecessary weight and encumbrance from the boats; that a specified number of men should go into each boat; and that the remainder should hang by the gunwales, while the boats were to be rowed gently towards the *Smeaton*, as the course to the floating light lay rather to windward of the rock.

But when he attempted to give utterance to his thoughts the words refused to come. So powerful an effect had the awful nature of their position upon him, that his parched tongue could not articulate. He learned, from terrible experience, that saliva is as necessary to speech as the tongue itself.

Stooping hastily, he dipped his hand into a pool of salt water and moistened his mouth. This produced immediate relief and he was about to speak, when Ruby Brand, who had stood at his elbow all the time with compressed lips and a stern frown on his brow, suddenly took off his cap, and waving it above his head, shouted "A boat! a boat!" with all the power of his lungs.

All eyes were at once turned in the direction to which he pointed, and there, sure enough, a large boat was seen through the haze, making towards the rock.

Doubtless many a heart there swelled with gratitude to God, who had thus opportunely and most unexpectedly sent them relief at the eleventh hour; but the only sound that escaped them was a cheer, such as men seldom give or hear save in cases of deliverance in times of dire extremity.

The boat belonged to James Spink, the Bell Rock pilot, who chanced to have come off express from Arbroath that day with letters.

We have said that Spink came off *by chance*; but, when we consider all the circumstances of the case, and the fact that boats seldom visited the Bell Rock at any time, and *never* during bad weather, we are constrained to feel that God does in His mercy interfere sometimes in a peculiar and special manner in human affairs, and that there was something more and higher than mere chance in the deliverance of Stevenson and his men upon this occasion.

The pilot-boat, having taken on board as many as it could hold, set sail for the floating light; the other boats then put off from the rock with the rest of the men, but they did not reach the *Pharos* until after a long and weary pull of three hours, during which the waves broke over the boats so frequently as to necessitate constant baling.

When the floating light was at last reached, a new difficulty met them, for the vessel rolled so much, and the men were so exhausted, that it proved to be a work of no little toil and danger to get them all on board.

Long Forsyth, in particular, cost them all an infinite amount of labour, for he was so sick, poor fellow, that he could scarcely move. Indeed, he did at one time beg them earnestly to drop him into the sea and be done with him altogether, a request with which they of course refused to comply. However, he was got up somehow, and the whole of them were comforted by a glass of rum and thereafter a cup of hot coffee.

Ruby had the good fortune to obtain the additional comfort of a letter from Minnie, which, although it did not throw much light on the proceedings of Captain Ogilvy (for that sapient seaman's proceedings were usually involved in a species of obscurity which light could not penetrate), nevertheless assured him that something was being done in his behalf, and that, if he only kept quiet for a time, all would be well.

The letter also assured him of the unalterable affection of the writer, an assurance which caused him to rejoice to such an extent that he became for a time perfectly regardless of all other sublunary things, and even came to look upon the Bell Rock as a species of paradise, watched over by the eye of an angel with golden hair, in which he could indulge his pleasant dreams to the utmost.

That he had to indulge those dreams in the midst of storm and rain and smoke, surrounded by sea and seaweed, workmen and hammers, and forges and picks, and jumpers and seals, while his strong muscles and endurance were frequently tried to the uttermost, was a matter of no moment to Ruby Brand.

All experience goes to prove that great joy will utterly overbear the adverse influence of physical troubles, especially if those troubles are without, and do not touch the seats of life within. Minnie's love, expressed as it was in her own innocent, truthful, and straightforward way, rendered his body, big though it was, almost incapable of containing his soul. He pulled the oar, hammered the jumper, battered the anvil, tore at the bellows, and hewed the solid Bell Rock with a vehemence that aroused the admiration of his comrades, and induced Jamie Dove to pronounce him to be the best fellow the world ever produced.

Chapter Eleven

A Storm and a Dismal State of Things on Board the Pharos

From what has been said at the close of the last chapter, it will not surprise the reader to be told that the storm which blew during that night had no further effect on Ruby Brand than to toss his hair about, and cause a ruddier glow than usual to deepen the tone of his bronzed countenance.

It was otherwise with many of his hapless comrades, a few of whom had also received letters that day, but whose pleasure was marred to some extent by the qualms within.

Being Saturday, a glass of rum was served out in the evening, according to custom, and the men proceeded to hold what is known by the name of "Saturday night at sea."

This being a night that was usually much enjoyed on board, owing to the home memories that were recalled, and the familiar songs that were sung; owing, also, to the limited supply of grog, which might indeed cheer, but could not by any possibility inebriate, the men endeavoured to shake off their fatigue, and to forget, if possible, the rolling of the vessel.

The first effort was not difficult, but the second was not easy. At first, however, the gale was not severe, so they fought against circumstances bravely for a time.

"Come, lads," cried the smith, in a species of serio-comic desperation, when they had all assembled below, "let's drink to sweethearts and wives."

"Hear, hear! Bless their hearts! Sweethearts and wives!" responded the men. "Hip, hip!"

The cheer that followed was a genuine one.

"Now for a song, boys," cried one of the men, "and I think the last arrivals are bound to sing first."

"Hear, hear! Ruby, lad, you're in for it," said the smith, who sat near his assistant.

"What shall I sing?" enquired Ruby.

"Oh! let me see," said Joe Dumsby, assuming the air of one who endeavoured to recall something. "Could you come Beet'oven's symphony on B flat?"

"Ah! howld yer tongue, Joe," cried O'Connor, "sure the young man can only sing on the sharp kays; ain't he always sharpin' the tools, not to speak of his appetite?"

"You've a blunt way of speaking yourself, friend," said Dumsby, in a tone of reproof.

"Hallo! stop your jokes," cried the smith; "if you treat us to any more o' that sort o' thing we'll have ye dipped over the side, and hung up to dry at the end o' the mainyard. Fire away, Ruby, my tulip!"

"Ay, that's hit," said John Watt. "Gie us the girl ye left behind ye."

Ruby flushed suddenly, and turned towards the speaker with a look of surprise.

"What's wrang, freend? Hae ye never heard o' that sang?" enquired Watt.

"O yes, I forgot," said Ruby, recovering himself in some confusion. "I know the song—I—I was thinking of something—of—"

"The girl ye left behind ye, av coorse," put in O'Connor, with a wink.

"Come, strike up!" cried the men.

Ruby at once obeyed, and sang the desired song with a sweet, full voice, that had the effect of moistening some of the eyes present.

The song was received enthusiastically.

"Your health and song, lads" said Robert Selkirk, the principal builder, who came down the ladder and joined them at that moment.

"Thank you, now it's my call," said Ruby. "I call upon Ned O'Connor for a song."

"Or a speech," cried Forsyth.

"A spaitch is it?" said O'Connor, with a look of deep modesty. "Sure, I never made a spaitch in me life, except when I axed Mrs O'Connor to marry me, an' I never finished that spaitch, for I only got the length of 'Och! darlint,' when she cut me short in the middle with 'Sure, you may have me, Ned, and welcome!'"

"Shame, shame!" said Dove, "to say that of your wife."

"Shame to yersilf," cried O'Connor indignantly. "Ain't I payin' the good woman a compliment, when I say that she had pity on me bashfulness, and came to me help when I was in difficulty?"

"Quite right, O'Connor; but let's have a song if you won't speak."

"Would ye thank a cracked tay-kittle for a song?" said Ned. "Certainly not," replied Peter Logan, who was apt to take things too literally.

"Then don't ax *me* for wan," said the Irishman, "but I'll do this for ye, messmates: I'll read ye the last letter I got from the mistress, just to show ye that her price is beyond all calkerlation."

A round of applause followed this offer, as Ned drew forth a much-soiled letter from the breast pocket of his coat, and carefully unfolding it, spread it on his knee.

"It begins," said O'Connor, in a slightly hesitating tone, "with some expressions of a—a—raither endearin' charackter, that perhaps I may as well pass."

"No, no," shouted the men, "let's have them all. Out with them, Paddy!"

"Well, well, av ye *will* have them, here they be.

"'**Galway**.

"'My own purty darlin' as has bin my most luved sin' the day we wos marrit, you'll be grieved to larn that the pig's gone to its long home.'"

Here O'Connor paused to make some parenthetical remarks with which, indeed, he interlarded the whole letter.

"The pig, you must know, lads, was an old sow as belonged to me wife's gran'-mother, an' besides bein' a sort o' pet o' the family, was an uncommon profitable crature. But to purceed. She goes on to say,— 'We waked her' (that's the pig, boys) 'yisterday, and buried her this mornin'. Big Rory, the baist, was for aitin' her, but I wouldn't hear of it; so she's at rest, an' so is old Molly Mallone. She wint away just two minutes be the clock before the pig, and wos buried the day afther. There's no more news as I knows of in the parish, except that your old flame Mary got married to Teddy O'Rook, an' they've been fightin' tooth an' nail ever since, as I towld ye they would long ago. No man could live wid that woman. But the schoolmaster, good man, has let me off the cow. Ye see, darlin', I towld him ye wos buildin' a palace in the say, to put ships in afther they wos wrecked on the coast of Ameriky, so ye couldn't be expected to send home much money at prisint. An' he just said, "Well, well, Kathleen, you may just kaip the cow, and pay me whin ye can." So put that off yer mind, my swait Ned.

"'I'm sorry to hear the Faries rowls so bad, though what the Faries mains is more nor I can tell.' (I spelled the word quite krect, lads, but my poor mistress hain't got the best of eyesight.) 'Let me know in yer nixt, an' be sure to tell me if Long Forsyth has got the bitter o' say-sickness. I'm koorius about this, bekaise I've got a receipt for that same that's infallerable, as his Riverence says. Tell him, with my luv, to mix a spoonful o' pepper, an' two o' salt, an' wan o' mustard, an' a glass o' whisky in a taycup, with a sprinklin' o' ginger; fill it up with goat's milk, or ass's, av ye can't git goat's; bait it in a pan, an' drink it as hot as he can—hotter, if possible. I niver tried it meself, but they say it's a suverin' remidy; and if it don't do no good, it's not likely to do much harm, bein' but a waik mixture. Me own belaif is, that the milk's a mistake, but I suppose the doctors know best.

"'Now, swaitest of men, I must stop, for Neddy's just come in howlin' like a born Turk for his tay; so no more at present from, yours till deth, Kathleen O'Connor.'"

"Has she any sisters?" enquired Joe Dumsby eagerly, as Ned folded the letter and replaced it in his pocket.

"Six of 'em," replied Ned; "every one purtier and better nor another."

"Is it a long way to Galway?" continued Joe.

"Not long; but it's a coorious thing that Englishmen never come back from them parts whin they wance ventur' into them."

Joe was about to retort when the men called for another song.

"Come, Jamie Dove, let's have 'Rule, Britannia.'"

Dove was by this time quite yellow in the face, and felt more inclined to go to bed than to sing; but he braced himself up, resolved to struggle manfully against the demon that oppressed him.

It was in vain! Poor Dove had just reached that point in the chorus where Britons stoutly affirm that they "never, never, never shall be slaves," when a tremendous roll of the vessel caused him to spring from the locker, on which he sat, and rush to his berth.

There were several of the others whose self-restraint was demolished by this example; these likewise fled, amid the laughter of their companions, who broke up the meeting and went on deck.

The prospect of things there proved, beyond all doubt, that Britons never did, and never will, rule the waves.

The storm, which had been brewing for some time past, was gathering fresh strength every moment, and it became abundantly evident that the floating light would have her anchors and cables tested pretty severely before the gale was over.

About eight o'clock in the evening the wind shifted to east-south-east; and at ten it became what seamen term a *hard gale*, rendering it necessary to veer out about fifty additional fathoms of the hempen cable. The gale still increasing, the ship rolled and laboured excessively, and at midnight eighty fathoms more were veered out, while the sea continued to strike the vessel with a degree of force that no one had before experienced.

That night there was little rest on board the *Pharos*. Everyone who has been "at sea" knows what it is to lie in one's berth on a stormy night, with the planks of the deck only a few inches from one's nose, and the water swashing past the little port that *always* leaks; the seas striking against the ship; the heavy sprays falling on the decks; and the constant rattle and row of blocks, spars, and cordage overhead. But all this was as nothing compared with the state of things on board the floating light, for that vessel could not rise to the seas with the comparatively free motions of a ship, sailing either with or against the gale. She tugged and strained at her cable, as if with the fixed determination of breaking it, and she offered all the opposition of a fixed body to the seas.

Daylight, though ardently longed for, brought no relief. The gale continued with unabated violence. The sea struck so hard upon the vessel's bows that it rose in great quantities, or, as Ruby expressed it, in "green seas", which completely swept the deck as far aft as the quarterdeck, and not unfrequently went completely over the stern of the ship.

Those "green seas" fell at last so heavily on the skylights that all the glass was driven in, and the water poured down into the cabins, producing dire consternation in the minds of those below, who thought that the vessel was sinking.

"I'm drowned intirely," roared poor Ned O'Connor, as the first of those seas burst in and poured straight down on his hammock, which happened to be just beneath the skylight.

Ned sprang out on the deck, missed his footing, and was hurled with the next roll of the ship into the arms of the steward, who was passing through the place at the time.

Before any comments could be made the dead-lights were put on, and the cabins were involved in almost absolute darkness.

"Och! let me in beside ye," pleaded Ned with the occupant of the nearest berth.

"Awa' wi' ye! Na, na," cried John Watt, pushing the unfortunate man away. "Cheinge yer wat claes first, an' I'll maybe let ye in, if ye can find me again i' the dark."

While the Irishman was groping about in search of his chest, one of the officers of the ship passed him on his way to the companion ladder, intending to go on deck. Ruby Brand, feeling uncomfortable below, leaped out of his hammock and followed him. They had both got about halfway up the ladder when a tremendous sea struck the ship, causing it to tremble from stem to stern. At the same moment someone above opened the hatch, and putting his head down, shouted for the officer, who happened to be just ascending.

"Ay, ay," replied the individual in question.

Just as he spoke, another heavy sea fell on the deck, and, rushing aft like a river that has burst its banks, hurled the seaman into the arms of the officer, who fell back upon Ruby, and all three came down with tons of water into the cabin.

The scene that followed would have been ludicrous, had it not been serious. The still rising sea caused the vessel to roll with excessive violence, and the large quantity of water that had burst in swept the men, who had jumped out of their beds, and all movable things, from side to side in indescribable confusion. As the water dashed up into the lower tier of beds, it was found necessary to lift one of the scuttles in the floor, and let it flow into the limbers of the ship.

Fortunately no one was hurt, and Ruby succeeded in gaining the deck before the hatch was reclosed and fastened down upon the scene of discomfort and misery below.

This state of things continued the whole day. The seas followed in rapid succession, and each, as it struck the vessel, caused her to shake all over. At each blow from a wave the rolling and pitching ceased for a few seconds, giving the impression that the ship had broken adrift, and was running with the wind; or in the act of sinking; but when another sea came, she ranged up against it with great force. This latter effect at last became the regular intimation to the anxious men below that they were still riding safely at anchor.

No fires could be lighted, therefore nothing could be cooked, so that the men were fain to eat hard biscuits—those of them at least who were able to eat at all—and lie in their wet blankets all day.

At ten in the morning the wind had shifted to north-east, and blew, if possible, harder than before, accompanied by a much heavier swell of the sea; it was therefore judged advisable to pay out more cable, in order to lessen the danger of its giving way.

During the course of the gale nearly the whole length of the hempen cable, of 120 fathoms, was veered out, besides the chain-moorings, and, for its preservation, the cable was carefully "served", or wattled, with pieces of canvas round the windlass, and with leather well greased in the hawse-hole, where the chafing was most violent.

As may readily be imagined, the gentleman on whom rested nearly all the responsibility connected with the work at the Bell Rock, passed an anxious and sleepless time in his darkened berth. During the morning he had made an attempt to reach the deck, but had been checked by the same sea that produced the disasters above described.

About two o'clock in the afternoon great alarm was felt in consequence of a heavy sea that struck the ship, almost filling the waist, and pouring down into the berths below, through every chink and crevice of the hatches and skylights. From the motion being suddenly checked or deadened, and from the flowing in of the water above, every individual on board thought that the ship was foundering—at least all the landsmen were fully impressed with that idea.

Mr Stevenson could not remain below any longer. As soon as the ship again began to range up to the sea, he made another effort to get on deck. Before going, however, he went through the various apartments, in order to ascertain the state of things below.

Groping his way in darkness from his own cabin he came to that of the officers of the ship. Here all was quiet, as well as dark. He next entered the galley and other compartments occupied by the artificers; here also all was dark, but not quiet, for several of the men were engaged in prayer, or repeating psalms in a full tone of voice, while others were protesting that if they should be fortunate enough to get once more ashore, no one should ever see them afloat again; but so loud was the creaking of the bulkheads, the dashing of water, and the whistling noise of the wind, that it was hardly possible to distinguish words or voices.

The master of the vessel accompanied Mr Stevenson, and, in one or two instances, anxious and repeated enquiries were made by the workmen as to the state of things on deck, to all of which he returned one characteristic answer— "It can't blow long in this way, lads; we *must* have better weather soon."

The next compartment in succession, moving forward, was that allotted to the seamen of the ship. Here there was a characteristic difference in the scene. Having reached the middle of the darksome berth without the inmates being aware of the intrusion, the anxious engineer was somewhat reassured and comforted to find that, although they talked of bad weather and cross accidents of the sea, yet the conversation was carried on in that tone and manner which bespoke ease and composure of mind.

"Well, lads," said Mr Stevenson, accosting the men, "what think you of this state of things? Will the good ship weather it?"

"Nae fear o' her, sir," replied one confidently, "she's light and new; it'll tak' a heavy sea to sink her."

"Ay," observed another, "and she's got little hold o' the water, good ground-tackle, and no top-hamper; she'll weather anything, sir."

Having satisfied himself that all was right below, Mr Stevenson returned aft and went on deck, where a sublime and awful sight awaited him. The waves appeared to be what we hear sometimes termed "mountains high." In reality they were perhaps about thirty feet of unbroken water in height, their foaming crests being swept and torn by the furious gale. All beyond the immediate neighbourhood of the ship was black and chaotic.

Upon deck everything movable was out of sight, having either been stowed away below previous to the gale, or washed overboard. Some parts of the quarter bulwarks were damaged by the breach of the sea, and one of the boats was broken, and half-full of water.

There was only one solitary individual on deck, placed there to watch and give the alarm if the cable should give way, and this man was Ruby Brand, who, having become tired of having nothing to do, had gone on deck, as we have seen, and volunteered his services as watchman.

Ruby had no greatcoat on, no overall of any kind, but was simply dressed in his ordinary jacket and trousers. He had thrust his cap into his pocket in order to prevent it being blown away, and his brown locks were streaming in the wind. He stood just aft the foremast, to which he had lashed himself with a gasket or small rope round his waist, to prevent his falling on the deck or being washed overboard. He was as thoroughly wet as if he had been drawn through the sea, and this was one reason why he was so lightly clad, that he might wet as few clothes as possible, and have a dry change when he went below.

There appeared to be a smile on his lips as he faced the angry gale and gazed steadily out upon the wild ocean. He seemed to be enjoying the sight of the grand elemental strife that was going on around him. Perchance he was thinking of someone not very far away— with golden hair!

Mr Stevenson, coupling this smile on Ruby's face with the remarks of the other seamen, felt that things were not so bad as they appeared to unaccustomed eyes, nevertheless he deemed it right to advise with the master and officers as to the probable result, in the event of the ship drifting from her moorings.

"It is my opinion," said the master, on his being questioned as to this, "that we have every chance of riding out the gale, which cannot continue many hours longer with the same fury; and even if she should part from her anchor, the storm-sails have been laid ready to hand, and can be bent in a very short time. The direction of the wind being nor'-east, we could sail up the Forth to Leith Roads; but if this should appear doubtful, after passing the May we can steer for Tyningham Sands, on the western side of Dunbar, and there run the ship ashore. From the flatness of her bottom and the strength of her build, I should think there would be no danger in beaching her even in a very heavy sea."

This was so far satisfactory, and for some time things continued in pretty much the state we have just described, but soon after there was a sudden cessation of the straining motion of the ship which surprised everyone. In another moment Ruby shouted "All hands a-hoy! ship's adrift!"

The consternation that followed may be conceived but not described. The windlass was instantly manned, and the men soon gave out that there was no strain on the cable. The mizzen-sail, which was occasionally bent for the purpose of making the ship ride easily, was at once set; the other sails were hoisted as quickly as possible, and they bore away about a mile to the south-westward, where, at a spot that was deemed suitable, the best-bower anchor was let go in twenty fathoms water.

Happily the storm had begun to abate before this accident happened. Had it occurred during the height of the gale, the result might have been most disastrous to the undertaking at the Bell Rock.

Having made all fast, an attempt was made to kindle the galley fire and cook some food.

"Wot are we to 'ave, steward?" enquired Joe Dumsby, in a feeble voice.

"Plumduff, my boy, so cheer up," replied the steward, who was busy with the charming ingredients of a suet pudding, which was the only dish to be attempted, owing to the ease with which it could be both cooked and served up.

Accordingly, the suet pudding was made; the men began to eat; the gale began to "take off", as seaman express it; and, although things were still very far removed from a state of comfort, they began to be more endurable; health began to return to the sick, and hope to those who had previously given way to despair.

Chapter Twelve

Bell Rock Billows—An Unexpected Visit—A Disaster and a Rescue

It is pleasant, it is profoundly enjoyable, to sit on the margin of the sea during the dead calm that not unfrequently succeeds a wild storm, and watch the gentle undulations of the glass-like surface, which the very gulls seem to be disinclined to ruffle with their wings as they descend to hover above their own reflected images.

It is pleasant to watch this from the shore, where the waves fall in low murmuring ripples, or from the ship's deck, far out upon the sea, where there is no sound of water save the laving of the vessel's bow as she rises and sinks in the broad-backed swell; but there is something more than pleasant, there is, something deeply and peculiarly interesting, in the same scene when viewed from such a position as the Bell Rock; for there, owing to the position of the rock and the depth of water around it, the observer beholds, at the same moment, the presence, as it were, of storm and calm.

The largest waves there are seen immediately after a storm has passed away, not during its continuance, no matter how furious the gale may have been, for the rushing wind has a tendency to blow down the waves, so to speak, and prevent their rising to their utmost height. It is when the storm is over that the swell rises; but as this swell appears only like large undulations, it does not impress the beholder with its magnitude until it draws near to the rock and begins to feel the checking influence of the bottom of the sea. The upper part of the swell, having then greater velocity than the lower parts assumes more and more the form of a billow. As it comes on it towers up like a great green wall of glittering glass, moving with a grand, solemn motion, which does not at first give the idea of much force or impetus. As it nears the rock, however, its height (probably fifteen or twenty feet) becomes apparent; its velocity increases; the top, with what may be termed gentle rapidity, rushes in advance of the base; its dark green side becomes concave; the upper edge lips over, then curls majestically downwards, as if bowing to a superior power, and a gleam of light flashes for a moment on the curling top. As yet there is no sound; all has occurred in the profound silence of the calm, but another instant and there is a mighty crash—a deafening roar; the great wall of water has fallen, and a very sea of churning foam comes leaping, bursting, spouting over rocks and ledges, carrying all before it with a tremendous sweep that seems to be absolutely irresistible until it meets the higher ledges of rock, when it is hurled back, and retires with a watery hiss that suggests the idea of baffled rage.

But it is not conquered. With the calm majesty of unalterable determination, wave after wave comes on, in slow, regular succession, like the inexhaustible battalions of an unconquerable foe, to meet with a similar repulse again and again.

There is, however, this peculiar difference between the waves on the ordinary seashore and the billows on the Bell Rock, that the latter, unlike the former, are not always defeated. The spectator on shore plants his foot confidently at the very edge of the mighty sea, knowing that "thus far it may come, but no farther." On the Bell Rock the rising tide makes the conflict, for a time, more equal. Now, the rock stands proudly above the sea: anon the sea sweeps furiously over the rock with a roar of "Victory!"

Thus the war goes on, and thus the tide of battle daily and nightly ebbs and flows all the year round.

But when the cunning hand of man began to interfere, the aspect of things was changed, the sea was forced to succumb, and the rock, once a dreaded enemy, became a servant of the human race. True, the former rages in rebellion still, and the latter, although compelled to uphold the light that warns against itself, continues its perpetual warfare with the sea; but both are effectually conquered by means of the wonderful intelligence that God has given to man, and the sea for more than half a century has vainly beat against the massive tower whose foundation is on the Bell Rock.

But all this savours somewhat of anticipation. Let us return to Ruby Brand, in whose interest we have gone into this long digression; for he it was who gazed intently at the mingled scene of storm and calm which we have attempted to describe, and it was he who thought out most of the ideas which we have endeavoured to convey.

Ruby had lent a hand to work the pump at the foundation-pit that morning. After a good spell at it he took his turn of rest, and, in order to enjoy it fully, went as far out as he could upon the seaward ledges, and sat down on a piece of rock to watch the waves.

While seated there, Robert Selkirk came and sat down beside him. Selkirk was the principal builder, and ultimately laid every stone of the lighthouse with his own hand. He was a sedate, quiet man, but full of energy and perseverance. When the stones were landed faster than they could be built into their places, he and Bremner, as well as some of the other builders, used to work on until the rising tide reached their waists.

"It's a grand sight, Ruby," said Selkirk, as a larger wave than usual fell, and came rushing in torrents of foam up to their feet, sending a little of the spray over their heads.

"It is indeed a glorious sight," said Ruby. "If I had nothing to do, I believe I could sit here all day just looking at the waves and thinking."

"Thinkin'?" repeated Selkirk, in a musing tone of voice. "Can ye tell, lad, what ye think about when you're lookin' at the waves?"

Ruby smiled at the oddness of the question.

"Well," said he, "I don't think I ever thought of that before."

"Ah, but *I* have!" said the other, "an' I've come to the conclusion that for the most part we don't think, properly speakin', at all; that our thoughts, so to speak, think for us; that they just take the bit in their teeth and go rumblin' and tumblin' about anyhow or nohow!"

Ruby knitted his brows and pondered. He was one of those men who, when they don't understand a thing, hold their tongues and think.

"And," continued Selkirk, "it's curious to observe what a lot o' nonsense one thinks too when one is lookin' at the waves. Many a time I have pulled myself up, thinkin' the most astonishin' stuff ye could imagine."

"I would hardly have expected this of such a grave kind o' man as you," said Ruby.

"Mayhap not. It is not always the gravest looking that have the gravest thoughts."

"But you don't mean to say that you never think sense," continued Ruby, "when you sit looking at the waves?"

"By no means," returned his companion; "I'm only talking of the way in which one's thoughts will wander. Sometimes I think seriously enough. Sometimes I think it strange that men can look at such a scene as that, and scarcely bestow a thought upon Him who made it."

"Speak for yourself, friend," said Ruby, somewhat quickly; "how know you that other men don't think about their Creator when they look at His works?"

"Because," returned Selkirk, "I find that I so seldom do so myself, even although I wish to and often try to; and I hold that every man, no matter what he is or feels, is one of a class who think and feel as he does; also, because many people, especially Christians, have told me that they have had the same experience to a large extent; also, and chiefly, because, as far as unbelieving man is concerned, the Bible tells me that 'God is not in all his thoughts.' But, Ruby, I did not make the remark as a slur upon men in general, I merely spoke of a fact,—an unfortunate fact,—that it is not natural to us, and not easy, to rise from nature to nature's God, and I thought you would agree with me."

"I believe you are right," said Ruby, half-ashamed of the petulance of his reply; "at any rate, I confess you are right as far as I am concerned."

As Selkirk and Ruby were both fond of discussion, they continued this subject some time longer, and there is no saying how far they would have gone down into the abstruse depths of theology, had not their converse been interrupted by the appearance of a boat rowing towards the rock.

"Is yonder craft a fishing boat, think you?" said Ruby, rising and pointing to it.

"Like enough, lad. Mayhap it's the pilot's, only it's too soon for him to be off again with letters. Maybe it's visitors to the rock, for I see something like a woman's bonnet."

As there was only one woman in the world at that time as far as Ruby was concerned (of course putting his mother out of the question!), it will not surprise the reader to be told that the youth started, that his cheek reddened a little, and his heart beat somewhat faster than usual. He immediately smiled, however, at the absurdity of supposing it possible that the woman in the boat could be Minnie, and as the blacksmith shouted to him at that moment, he turned on his heel and leaped from ledge to ledge of rock until he gained his wonted place at the forge.

Soon he was busy wielding the fore-hammer, causing the sparks to fly about himself and his comrade in showers, while the anvil rang out its merry peal.

Meanwhile the boat drew near. It turned out to be a party of visitors, who had come off from Arbroath to see the operations at the Bell Rock. They had been brought off by Spink, the pilot, and numbered only three—namely, a tall soldier-like man, a stout sailor-like man, and a young woman with—yes,—with golden hair.

Poor Ruby almost leaped over the forge when he raised his eyes from his work and caught sight of Minnie's sweet face. Minnie had recognised her lover before the boat reached the rock, for he stood on an elevated ledge, and the work in which he was engaged, swinging the large hammer round his shoulder, rendered him very conspicuous. She had studiously concealed her face from him until quite close, when, looking him straight in the eyes without the least sign of recognition, she turned away.

We have said that the first glance Ruby obtained caused him to leap nearly over the forge; the second created such a revulsion of feeling that he let the fore-hammer fall.

"Hallo! Got a spark in yer eye?" enquired Dove, looking up anxiously.

It flashed across Ruby at that instant that the look given him by Minnie was meant to warn him not to take any notice of her, so he answered the smith's query with "No, no; I've only let the hammer fall, don't you see? Get on, old boy, an don't let the metal cool."

The smith continued his work without further remark, and Ruby assisted, resolving in his own mind to be a little more guarded as to the expression of his feelings.

Meanwhile Mr Stevenson received the visitors, and showed them over the works, pointing out the peculiarities thereof, and the difficulties that stood in the way.

Presently he came towards the forge, and said, "Brand, the stout gentleman there wishes to speak to you. He says he knew you in Arbroath. You can spare him for a few minutes, I suppose, Mr Dove?"

"Well, yes, but not for long," replied the smith. "The tide will soon be up, and I've enough to do to get through with all these."

Ruby flung down his hammer at the first word, and hastened to the ledge of rock where the visitors were standing, as far apart from the workmen as the space of the rock would admit of.

The stout gentleman was no other than his uncle, Captain Ogilvy, who put his finger to his lips as his nephew approached, and gave him a look of mystery that was quite sufficient to put the latter on his guard. He therefore went forward, pulled off his cap, and bowed respectfully to Minnie, who replied with a stiff curtsy, a slight smile, and a decided blush.

Although Ruby now felt convinced that they were all acting a part, he could scarcely bear this cold reception. His impulse was to seize Minnie in his arms; but he did not even get the comfort of a cold shake of the hand.

"Nephy," said the captain in a hoarse whisper, putting his face close to that of Ruby, "mum's the word! Silence, mystery, an' all that sort o' thing. Don't appear to be an old friend, lad; and as to Minnie here—

"'O no, we never mention her, Her name it's never heard.'

"Allow me to introduce you to Major Stewart, whose house you broke into, you know, Ruby, when:—

"'All in the Downs the fleet was moored,'

"At least when the *Termagant* was waitin' for you to go aboard."

Here the captain winked and gave Ruby a facetious poke in the ribs, which was not quite in harmony with the ignorance of each other he was endeavouring to inculcate.

"Young man," said the major quietly, "we have come off to tell you that everything is in a prosperous state as regards the investigation into your innocence—the private investigation I mean, for the authorities happily know nothing of your being here. Captain Ogilvy has made me his confidant in this matter, and from what he tells me I am convinced that you had nothing to do with this robbery. Excuse me if I now add that the sight of your face deepens this conviction."

Ruby bowed to the compliment.

"We were anxious to write at once to the captain of the vessel in which you sailed," continued the major, "but you omitted to leave his full name and address when you left. We were afraid to write to you, lest your name on the letter might attract attention, and induce a premature arrest. Hence our visit to the rock to-day. Please to write the address in this pocket-book."

The major handed Ruby a small green pocket-book as he spoke, in which the latter wrote the full name and address of his late skipper.

"Now, nephy," said the captain, "we must, I'm sorry to say, bid ye good day, and ask you to return to your work, for it won't do to rouse suspicion, lad. Only keep quiet here, and do yer dooty—'England expects *every* man to do his dooty'—and as sure as your name's Ruby all will be shipshape in a few weeks."

"I thank you sincerely," said Ruby, addressing the major, but looking at Minnie.

Captain Ogilvy, observing this, and fearing some display of feeling that would be recognised by the workmen, who were becoming surprised at the length of the interview, placed himself between Minnie and her lover.

"No, no, Ruby," said he, solemnly. "I'm sorry for ye, lad, but it won't do. Patience is a virtue, which, taken at the flood, leads on to fortune."

"My mother?" said Ruby, wishing to prolong the interview.

"Is well," said the captain. "Now, goodbye, lad, and be off."

"Goodbye, Minnie," cried Ruby, stepping forward suddenly and seizing the girl's hand; then, wheeling quickly round, he sprang over the rocks, and returned to his post.

"Ha! it's time," cried the smith. "I thought you would never be done makin' love to that there girl. Come, blaze away!"

Ruby felt so nettled by the necessity that was laid upon him of taking no notice of Minnie, that he seized the handle of the bellows passionately, and at the first puff blew nearly all the fire away.

"Hallo! messmate," cried the smith, clearing the dust from his eyes; "what on airth ails ye? You've blowed the whole consarn out!"

Ruby made no reply, but, scraping together the embers, heaped them up and blew more gently.

In a short time the visitors re-entered their boat, and rowed out of the creek in which it had been lying.

Ruby became so exasperated at not being able even to watch the boat going away, that he showered terrific blows on the mass of metal the smith was turning rapidly on the anvil.

"Not so fast, lad; not so fast," cried Dove hurriedly.

Ruby's chafing spirit blew up just at that point; he hit the iron a crack that knocked it as flat as a pancake, and then threw down the hammer and deliberately gazed in the direction of the boat.

The sight that met his eyes appalled him. The boat had been lying in the inlet named Port Stevenson. It had to pass out to the open sea through *Wilson's Track*, and past a small outlying rock named *Gray's Rock*—known more familiarly among the men as *Johnny Gray*. The boat was nearing this point, when the sea, which had been rising for some time, burst completely over the seaward ledges, and swept the boat high against the rocks on the left. The men had scarcely got her again into the track when another tremendous billow, such as we have already described, swept over the rocks again and swamped the boat, which, being heavily ballasted, sank at once to the bottom of the pool.

It was this sight that met the horrified eyes of Ruby when he looked up.

He vaulted over the bellows like an antelope, and, rushing over *Smith's Ledge* and *Trinity Ledge*, sprang across *Port Boyle*, and dived head foremost into *Neill's Pool* before any of the other men, who made a general rush, could reach the spot.

A few powerful strokes brought Ruby to the place where the major and the captain, neither of whom could swim, were struggling in the water. He dived at once below these unfortunates, and almost in a second, reappeared with Minnie in his arms.

A few seconds sufficed to bring him to *Smith's Ledge*, where several of his comrades hauled him and his burden beyond the reach of the next wave, and where, a moment or two later, the major and captain with the crew of the boat were landed in safety.

To bear the light form of Minnie in his strong arms to the highest and driest part of the rock were the work of a few moments to Ruby. Brief though those moments were, however, they were precious to the youth beyond all human powers of calculation, for Minnie recovered partial consciousness, and fancying, doubtless, that she was still in danger, flung her arms round his neck, and grasped him convulsively. Reader, we tell you in confidence that if Ruby had at that moment been laid on the rack and torn limb from limb, he would have cheered out his life triumphantly. It was not only that he knew she loved him—*that* he knew before,—but he had saved the life of the girl he loved, and a higher terrestrial happiness can scarcely be attained by man.

Laying her down as gently as a mother would her first-born, Ruby placed a coat under her head, and bade his comrades stand back and give her air. It was fortunate for him that one of the foremen, who understood what to do, came up at this moment, and ordered him to leave off chafing the girl's hand with his wet fists, and go get some water boiled at the forge if he wanted to do her good.

Second words were not needed. The bellows were soon blowing, and the fire glowed in a way that it had not done since the works at the Bell Rock began. Before the water quite boiled some tea was put in, and, with a degree of speed that would have roused the jealousy of any living waiter, a cup of tea was presented to Minnie, who had recovered almost at the moment Ruby left her.

She drank a little, and then closing her eyes, moved her lips silently for a few seconds.

Captain Ogilvy, who had attended her with the utmost assiduity and tenderness as soon as he had wrung the water out of his own garments, here took an opportunity of hastily pouring something into the cup out of a small flask. When Minnie looked up again and smiled, he presented her with the cup. She thanked him, and drank a mouthful or two before perceiving that it had been tampered with.

"There's something in it," she said hurriedly.

"So there is, my pet," said the captain, with a benignant smile, "a little nectar, that will do you more good than all the tea. Come now, don't shake your head, but down with it all, like a good child."

But Minnie was proof against persuasion, and refused to taste any more.

"Who was it that saved me, uncle?" (She had got into the way of calling the captain "uncle.")

"Ruby Brand did it, my darlin'," said the old man with a look of pride. "Ah! you're better now; stay, don't attempt to rise."

"Yes, yes, uncle," she said, getting up and looking round, "it is time that we should go now; we have a long way to go, you know. Where is the boat?"

"The boat, my precious, is at the bottom of the sea."

As he said this, he pointed to the mast, half of which was seen rising out of the pool where the boat had gone down.

"But you don't need to mind," continued the captain, "for they're goin' to send us in one o' their own boats aboord the floatin' lightship, where we'll get a change o' clothes an' somethin' to eat."

As he spoke, one of the sailors came forward and announced that the boat was ready, so the captain and the major assisted Minnie into the boat, which soon pushed off with part of the workmen from the rock. It was to be sent back for the remainder of the crew, by which time the tide would render it necessary that all should leave.

Ruby purposely kept away from the group while they were embarking, and after they were gone proceeded to resume work.

"You took a smart dive that time, lad," observed Joe Dumsby as they went along.

"Not more than anyone would do for a girl," said Ruby.

"An' such a purty wan, too," said O'Connor. "Ah! av she's not Irish, she should ha' bin."

"Ye're a lucky chap to hae sic a chance," observed John Watt.

"Make up to her, lad," said Forsyth; "I think she couldn't refuse ye after doin' her such service."

"Time enough to chaff after work is over," cried Ruby with a laugh, as he turned up his sleeves, and, seizing the hammer, began, as his friend Dove said, "to work himself dry."

In a few minutes, work was resumed, and for another hour all continued busy as bees, cutting and pounding at the flinty surface of the Bell Rock.

Chapter Thirteen

A Sleepless but a Pleasant Night

The evening which followed the day that has just been described was bright, calm, and beautiful, with the starry host unclouded and distinctly visible to the profoundest depths of space.

As it was intended to send the *Smeaton* to Arbroath next morning for a cargo of stones from the building-yard, the wrecked party were prevailed on to remain all night on board the *Pharos*, instead of going ashore in one of the ship's boats, which could not well be spared at the time.

This arrangement, we need hardly say, gave inexpressible pleasure to Ruby, and was not altogether distasteful to Minnie, although she felt anxious about Mrs Brand, who would naturally be much alarmed at the prolonged absence of herself and the captain. However, "there was no help for it"; and it was wonderful the resignation which she displayed in the circumstances.

It was not Ruby's duty to watch on deck that night, yet, strange to say, Ruby kept watch the whole night long!

There was no occasion whatever for Minnie to go on deck after it was dark, yet, strange to say, Minnie kept coming on deck at intervals *nearly* the whole night long! Sometimes to "look at the stars", sometimes to "get a mouthful of fresh air", frequently to find out what "that strange noise could be that had alarmed her", and at last—especially towards the early hours of morning—for no reason whatever, except that "she could not sleep below."

It was very natural that when Minnie paced the quarterdeck between the stern and the mainmast, and Ruby paced the forepart of the deck between the bows and the mainmast, the two should occasionally meet at the mainmast. It was also very natural that when they did meet, the girl who had been rescued should stop and address a few words of gratitude to the man who had saved her. But it was by no means natural—nay, it was altogether unnatural and unaccountable, that, when it became dark, the said man and the said girl should get into a close and confidential conversation, which lasted for hours, to the amusement of Captain Ogilvy and the major, who quite understood it, and to the amazement of many of the ship's crew, who couldn't understand it at all.

At last Minnie bade Ruby a final good night and went below, and Ruby, who could not persuade himself that it was final, continued to walk the deck until his eyes began to shut and open involuntarily like those of a sick owl. Then he also went below, and, before he fell quite asleep (according to his own impression), was awakened by the bell that called the men to land on the rock and commence work.

It was not only Ruby who found it difficult to rouse himself that morning. The landing-bell was rung at four o'clock, as the tide suited at that early hour, but the men were so fatigued that they would gladly have slept some hours longer. This, however, the nature of the service would not admit of. The building of the Bell Rock Lighthouse was a peculiar service. It may be said to have resembled duty in the trenches in military warfare. At times the work was light enough, but for the most part it was severe and irregular, as the men had to work in all kinds of weather, as long as possible, in the face of unusual difficulties and dangers, and were liable to be called out at all unseasonable hours. But they knew and expected this, and faced the work like men.

After a growl or two, and a few heavy sighs, they all tumbled out of their berths, and, in a very short time, were mustered on deck, where a glass of rum and a biscuit were served to each, being the regular allowance when they had to begin work before breakfast. Then they got into the boats and rowed away.

Ruby's troubles were peculiar on this occasion. He could not bear the thought of leaving the *Pharos* without saying goodbye to Minnie; but as Minnie knew nothing of such early rising, there was no reasonable hope that she would be awake. Then he wished to put a few questions to his uncle which he had forgotten the day before, but his uncle was at that moment buried in profound repose, with his mouth wide open, and a trombone solo proceeding from his nose, which sadly troubled the unfortunates who lay near him.

As there was no way of escape from these difficulties, Ruby, like a wise man, made up his mind to cast them aside, so, after swallowing his allowance, he shouldered his big bellows, heaved a deep sigh, and took his place in one of the boats alongside.

The lassitude which strong men feel when obliged to rise before they have had enough of rest soon wears off. The two boats had not left the *Pharos* twenty yards astern, when Joe Dumsby cried, "Ho! boys, let's have a race."

"Hooray!" shouted O'Connor, whose elastic spirits were always equal to anything, "an' sure Ruby will sing us 'The girl we've left behind us.' Och! an' there she is, av I'm not draymin'."

At that moment a little hand was waved from one of the ports of the floating light. Ruby at once waved his in reply, but as the attention of the men had been directed to the vessel by Ned's remark, each saw the salutation, and, claiming it as a compliment to himself, uttered a loud cheer, which terminated in a burst of laughter, caused by the sight of Ruby's half-angry, half-ashamed expression of face.

As the other boat had shot ahead, however, at the first mention of the word "race", the men forgot this incident in their anxiety to overtake their comrades. In a few seconds both boats were going at full speed, and they kept it up all the way to the rock.

While this was going on, the *Smeaton's* boat was getting ready to take the strangers on board the sloop, and just as the workmen landed on the rock, the *Smeaton* cast loose her sails, and proceeded to Arbroath.

There were a few seals basking on the Bell Rock this morning when the men landed. These at once made off, and were not again seen during the day.

At first, seals were numerous on the rock. Frequently from fifty to sixty of them were counted at one time, and they seemed for a good while unwilling to forsake their old quarters, but when the forge was set up they could stand it no longer. Some of the boldest ventured to sun themselves there occasionally, but when the clatter of the anvil and the wreaths of smoke became matters of daily occurrence, they forsook the rock finally, and sought the peace and quiet which man denied them there in other regions of the deep.

The building of the lighthouse was attended with difficulties at every step. As a short notice of some of these, and an account of the mode in which the great work was carried on, cannot fail to be interesting to all who admire those engineering works which exhibit prominently the triumph of mind over matter, we shall turn aside for a brief space to consider this subject.

Chapter Fourteen

Somewhat Statistical

It has been already said that the Bell Rock rises only a few feet out of the sea at low tide. The foundation of the tower, sunk into the solid rock, was just three feet three inches above low water of the lowest spring-tides, so that the lighthouse may be said with propriety to be founded beneath the waves.

One great point that had to be determined at the commencement of the operations was the best method of landing the stones of the building, this being a delicate and difficult process, in consequence of the weight of the stones and their brittle nature, especially in those parts which were worked to a delicate edge or formed into angular points. As the loss of a single stone, too, would stop the progress of the work until another should be prepared at the workyard in Arbroath and sent off to the rock, it may easily be imagined that this matter of the landing was of the utmost importance, and that much consultation was held in regard to it.

It would seem that engineers, as well as doctors, are apt to differ. Some suggested that each particular stone should be floated to the rock, with a cork buoy attached to it; while others proposed an air-tank, instead of the cork buoy. Others, again, proposed to sail over the rock at high water in a flat-bottomed vessel, and drop the stones one after another when over the spot they were intended to occupy. A few, still more eccentric and daring in their views, suggested that a huge cofferdam or vessel should be built on shore, and as much of the lighthouse built in this as would suffice to raise the building above the level of the highest tides; that then it should be floated off to its station on the rock, which should be previously prepared for its reception; that the cofferdam should be scuttled, and the ponderous mass of masonry, weighing perhaps 1000 tons, allowed to sink at once into its place!

All these plans, however, were rejected by Mr Stevenson, who resolved to carry the stones to the rock in boats constructed for the purpose. These were named praam boats. The stones were therefore cut in conformity with exactly measured moulds in the workyard at Arbroath, and conveyed thence in the sloops already mentioned to the rock, where the vessels were anchored at a distance sufficient to enable them to clear it in case of drifting. The cargoes were then unloaded at the moorings, and laid on the decks of the praam boats, which conveyed them to the rock, where they were laid on small trucks, run along the temporary rails, to their positions, and built in at once.

Each stone of this building was treated with as much care and solicitude as if it were a living creature. After being carefully cut and curiously formed, and conveyed to the neighbourhood of the rock, it was hoisted out of the hold and laid on the vessel's deck, when it was handed over to the landing-master, whose duty it became to transfer it, by means of a combination of ropes and blocks, to the deck of the praam boat, and then deliver it at the rock.

As the sea was seldom calm during the building operations, and frequently in a state of great agitation, lowering the stones on the decks of the praam boats was a difficult matter.

In the act of working the apparatus, one man was placed at each of the guy-tackles. This man assisted also at the purchase-tackles for raising the stones; and one of the ablest and most active of the crew was appointed to hold on the end of the fall-tackle, which often required all his strength and his utmost agility in letting go, for the purpose of lowering the stone at the instant the word "lower" was given. In a rolling sea, much depended on the promptitude with which this part of the operation was performed. For the purpose of securing this, the man who held the tackle placed himself before the mast in a sitting, more frequently in a lying posture, with his feet stretched under the winch and abutting against the mast, as by this means he was enabled to exert his greatest strength.

The signal being given in the hold that the tackle was hooked to the stone and all ready, every man took his post, the stone was carefully, we might almost say tenderly, raised, and gradually got into position over the praam boat; the right moment was intently watched, and the word "lower" given sternly and sharply. The order was obeyed with exact promptitude, and the stone rested on the deck of the praam boat. Six blocks of granite having been thus placed on the boat's deck, she was rowed to a buoy, and moored near the rock until the proper time of the tide for taking her into one of the landing creeks.

We are thus particular in describing the details of this part of the work, in order that the reader may be enabled to form a correct estimate of what may be termed the minor difficulties of the undertaking.

The same care was bestowed upon the landing of every stone of the building; and it is worthy of record, that notwithstanding the difficulty of this process in such peculiar circumstances, not a single stone was lost, or even seriously damaged, during the whole course of the erection of the tower, which occupied four years in building, or rather, we should say, four *seasons*, for no work was or could be done during winter.

A description of the first entire course of the lower part of the tower, which was built solid, will be sufficient to give an idea of the general nature of the whole work.

This course or layer consisted of 123 blocks of stone, those in the interior being sandstone, while the outer casing was of granite. Each stone was fastened to its neighbour above, below, and around by means of dovetails, joggles, oaken trenails, and mortar. Each course was thus built from its centre to its circumference, and as all the courses from the foundation to a height of thirty feet were built in this way, the tower, up to that height, became a mass of solid stone, as strong and immovable as the Bell Rock itself. Above this, or thirty feet from the foundation, the entrance-door was placed, and the hollow part of the tower began.

Thus much, then, as to the tower itself, the upper part of which will be found described in a future chapter. In regard to the subsidiary works, the erection of the beacon house was in itself a work of considerable difficulty, requiring no common effort of engineering skill. The principal beams of this having been towed to the rock by the *Smeaton*, all the stanchions and other material for setting them up were landed, and the workmen set about erecting them as quickly as possible, for if a single day of bad weather should occur before the necessary fixtures could be made, the whole apparatus would be infallibly swept away.

The operation being, perhaps, the most important of the season, and one requiring to be done with the utmost expedition, all hands were, on the day in which its erection was begun, gathered on the rock, besides ten additional men engaged for the purpose, and as many of the seamen from the *Pharos* and other vessels as could be spared. They amounted altogether to fifty-two in number.

About half-past eight o'clock in the morning a derrick, or mast, thirty feet high, was erected, and properly supported with guy-ropes for suspending the block for raising the first principal beam of the beacon, and a winch-machine was bolted down to the rock for working the purchase-tackle. The necessary blocks and tackle were likewise laid to hand and properly arranged. The men were severally allotted in squads to different stations; some were to bring the principal beams to hand, others were to work the tackles, while a third set had the charge of the iron stanchions, bolts, and wedges, so that the whole operation of raising the beams and fixing them to the rock might go forward in such a mariner that some provision might be made, in any stage of the work, for securing what had been accomplished, in case of an adverse change of weather.

The raising of the derrick was the signal for three hearty cheers, for this was a new era in the operations. Even that single spar, could it be preserved, would have been sufficient to have saved the workmen on that day when the *Smeaton* broke adrift and left them in such peril.

This was all, however, that could be accomplished that tide. Next day, the great beams, each fifty feet long, and about sixteen inches square, were towed to the rock about seven in the morning, and the work immediately commenced, although they had gone there so much too early in the tide that the men had to work a considerable time up to their middle in water. Each beam was raised by the tackle affixed to the derrick, until the end of it could be placed or "stepped" into the hole which had been previously prepared for its reception; then two of the great iron stanchions or supports were set into their respective holes on each side of the beam, and a rope passed round them to keep it from slipping, until it could be more permanently fixed.

This having been accomplished, the first beam became the means of raising the second, and when the first and second were fastened at the top, they formed a pair of shears by which the rest were more easily raised to their places. The heads of the beams were then fitted together and secured with ropes in a temporary manner, until the falling of the tide would permit the operations to be resumed.

Thus the work went on, each man labouring with all his might, until this important erection was completed.

The raising of the first beams took place on a Sunday. Indeed, during the progress of the works at the Bell Rock, the men were accustomed to work regularly on Sundays when possible; but it is right to say that it was not done in defiance of, or disregard to, God's command to cease from labour on the Sabbath day, but because of the urgent need of a lighthouse on a rock which, unlighted, would be certain to wreck numerous vessels and destroy many lives in time to come, as it had done in time past. Delay in this matter might cause death and disaster, therefore it was deemed right to carry on the work on Sundays. (See note 1.)

An accident happened during the raising of the last large beam of the beacon, which, although alarming, fortunately caused no damage. Considering the nature of the work, it is amazing, and greatly to the credit of all engaged, that so few accidents occurred during the building of the lighthouse.

When they were in the act of hoisting the sixth and last log, and just about to cant it into its place, the iron hook of the principal purchase-block gave way, and the great beam, measuring fifty feet in length, fell upon the rock with a terrible crash; but although there were fifty-two men around the beacon at the time, not one was touched, and the beam itself received no damage worth mentioning.

Soon after the beacon had been set up, and partially secured to the rock, a severe gale sprang up, as if Ocean were impatient to test the handiwork of human engineers. Gales set in from the eastward, compelling the attending sloops to slip from their moorings, and run for the shelter of Arbroath and Saint Andrews, and raising a sea on the Bell Rock which was described as terrific, the spray rising more than thirty feet in the air above it.

In the midst of all this turmoil the beacon stood securely, and after the weather moderated, permitting the workmen once more to land, it was found that no damage had been done by the tremendous breaches of the sea over the rock.

That the power of the waves had indeed been very great, was evident from the effects observed on the rock itself, and on materials left there. Masses of rock upwards of a ton in weight had been cast up by the sea, and then, in their passage over the Bell Rock, had made deep and indelible ruts. An anchor of a ton weight, which had been lost on one side of the rock, was found to have been washed up and *over* it to the other side. Several large blocks of granite that had been landed and left on a ledge, were found to have been swept away like pebbles, and hurled into a hole at some distance; and the heavy hearth of the smith's forge, with the ponderous anvil, had been washed from their places of supposed security.

From the time of the setting up of the beacon a new era in the work began. Some of the men were now enabled to remain on the rock all day, working at the lighthouse when the tide was low, and betaking themselves to the beacon when it rose, and leaving it at night; for there was much to do before this beacon could be made the habitable abode which it finally became; but it required the strictest attention to the state of the weather, in case of their being overtaken with a gale, which might prevent the possibility of their being taken off the rock.

At last the beacon was so far advanced and secured that it was deemed capable of withstanding any gale that might blow. As yet it was a great ungainly pile of logs, iron stanchions, and bracing-chains, without anything that could afford shelter to man from winds or waves, but with a platform laid from its cross-beams at a considerable height above high-water mark.

The works on the rock were in this state, when two memorable circumstances occurred in the Bell Rock annals, to which we shall devote a separate chapter.

Note 1. It was always arranged, however, to have public worship on Sundays when practicable. And this arrangement was held to during the continuance of the work. Indeed, the manner in which Mr Stevenson writes in regard to the conclusion of the day's work at the beacon, which we have described, shows clearly that he felt himself to be acting in this matter in accordance with the spirit of our Saviour, who wrought many of His works of mercy on the Sabbath day. Mr Stevenson writes thus:—

"All hands having returned to their respective ships, they got a shift of dry clothes, and some refreshment. Being Sunday, they were afterwards convened by signal on board of the lighthouse yacht, when prayers were read, for every heart upon this occasion felt gladness, and every mind was disposed to be thankful for the happy and successful termination of the operations of this day."

It is right to add that the men, although requested, were not constrained to work on Sundays. They were at liberty to decline if they chose. A few conscientiously refused at first, but were afterwards convinced of the necessity of working on all opportunities that offered, and agreed to do so.

Chapter Fifteen

Ruby has a Rise in Life, and a fall

James Dove, the blacksmith, had, for some time past, been watching the advancing of the beacon-works with some interest, and a good deal of impatience. He was tired of working so constantly up to the knees in water, and aspired to a drier and more elevated workshop.

One morning he was told by the foreman that orders had been given for him to remove his forge to the beacon, and this removal, this "flitting", as he called it, was the first of the memorable events referred to in the last chapter.

"Hallo! Ruby, my boy," cried the elated son of Vulcan, as he descended the companion ladder, "we're goin' to flit, lad. We're about to rise in the world, so get up your bellows. It's the last time we shall have to be bothered with them in the boat, I hope."

"That's well," said Ruby, shouldering the unwieldy bellows; "they have worn my shoulders threadbare, and tried my patience almost beyond endurance."

"Well, it's all over now, lad," rejoined the smith. "In future you shall have to blow up in the beacon yonder; so come along."

"Come, Ruby, that ought to comfort the cockles o' yer heart," said O'Connor, who passed up the ladder as he spoke; "the smith won't need to blow you up any more, av you're to blow yourself up in the beacon in futur'. Arrah! there's the bell again. Sorrow wan o' me iver gits to slape, but I'm turned up immadiately to go an' poke away at that rock— faix, it's well named the Bell Rock, for it makes me like to *bell*ow me lungs out wid vexation."

"That pun is *bel*ow contempt," said Joe Dumsby, who came up at the moment.

"That's yer sort, laddies; ye're guid at ringing the changes on that head onyway," cried Watt.

"I say, we're gittin' a *bell*y-full of it," observed Forsyth, with a rueful look. "I hope nobody's goin' to give us another!"

"It'll create a re*bell*ion," said Bremner, "if ye go on like that."

"It'll bring my *bell*ows down on the head o' the next man that speaks!" cried Ruby, with indignation.

"Don't you hear the bell, there?" cried the foreman down the hatchway.

There was a burst of laughter at this unconscious continuation of the joke, and the men sprang up the ladder,—down the side, and into the boats, which were soon racing towards the rock.

The day, though not sunny, was calm and agreeable, nevertheless the landing at the rock was not easily accomplished, owing to the swell caused by a recent gale. After one or two narrow escapes of a ducking, however, the crews landed, and the bellows, instead of being conveyed to their usual place at the forge, were laid at the foot of the beacon.

The carriage of these bellows to and fro almost daily had been a subject of great annoyance to the men, owing to their being so much in the way, and so unmanageably bulky, yet so essential to the progress of the works, that they did not dare to leave them on the rock, lest they should be washed away, and they had to handle them tenderly, lest they should get damaged.

"Now, boys, lend a hand with the forge," cried the smith, hurrying towards his anvil.

Those who were not busy eating dulse responded to the call, and in a short time the ponderous *matériel* of the smithy was conveyed to the beacon, where, in process of time, it was hoisted by means of tackle to its place on the platform to which reference has already been made.

When it was safely set up and the bellows placed in position, Ruby went to the edge of the platform, and, looking down on his comrades below, took off his cap and shouted in the tone of a Stentor, "Now, lads, three cheers for the Dovecot!"

This was received with a roar of laughter and three tremendous cheers.

"Howld on, boys," cried O'Connor, stretching out his hand as if to command silence; "you'll scare the dove from his cot altogether av ye roar like that!"

"Surely they're sendin' us a fire to warm us," observed one of the men, pointing to a boat which had put off from the *Smeaton*, and was approaching the rock by way of *Macurich's Track*.

"What can'd be, I wonder?" said Watt; "I think I can smell somethin'."

"I halways thought you 'ad somethink of an old dog in you," said Dumsby.

"Ay, man!" said the Scot with a leer, "I ken o' war beasts than auld dowgs."

"Do you? come let's 'ear wat they are," said the Englishman.

"Young puppies," answered the other.

"Hurrah! dinner, as I'm a Dutchman," cried Forsyth.

This was indeed the case. Dinner had been cooked on board the *Smeaton* and sent hot to the men; and this,—the first dinner ever eaten on the Bell Rock,—was the second of the memorable events before referred to.

The boat soon ran into the creek and landed the baskets containing the food on *Hope's Wharf*.

The men at once made a rush at the viands, and bore them off exultingly to the flattest part of the rock they could find.

"A regular picnic," cried Dumsby in high glee, for unusual events, of even a trifling kind, had the effect of elating those men more than one might have expected.

"Here's the murphies," cried O'Connor, staggering over the slippery weed with a large smoking tin dish.

"Mind you don't let 'em fall," cried one.

"Have a care," shouted the smith; "if you drop them I'll beat you red-hot, and hammer ye so flat that the biggest flatterer as ever walked won't be able to spread ye out another half-inch."

"Mutton! oh!" exclaimed Forsyth, who had been some time trying to wrench the cover off the basket containing a roast leg, and at last succeeded.

"Here, spread them all out on this rock. You han't forgot the grog, I hope, steward?"

"No fear of him: he's a good feller, is the steward, when he's asleep partiklerly. The grog's here all right."

"Dinna let Dumsby git haud o't, then," cried Watt. "What! hae ye begood a'ready? Patience, man, patience. Is there ony saut?"

"Lots of it, darlin', in the say. Sure this shape must have lost his tail somehow. Och, murther! if there isn't Bobby Selkirk gone an' tumbled into Port Hamilton wid the cabbage, av it's not the carrots!"

"There now, don't talk so much, boys," cried Peter Logan. "Let's drink success to the Bell Rock Lighthouse."

It need scarcely be said that this toast was drunk with enthusiasm, and that it was followed up with "three times three."

"Now for a song. Come, Joe Dumsby, strike up," cried one of the men.

O'Connor, who was one of the most reckless of men in regard to duty and propriety, here shook his head gravely, and took upon himself to read his comrade a lesson.

"Ye shouldn't talk o' sitch things in workin' hours," said he. "Av we wos all foolish, waakehidded cratures like *you*, how d'ye think we'd iver git the lighthouse sot up! Ate yer dinner, lad, and howld yer tongue."

"O Ned, I didn't think your jealousy would show out so strong," retorted his comrade. "Now, then, Dumsby, fire away, if it was only to aggravate him."

Thus pressed, Joe Dumsby took a deep draught of the small-beer with which the men were supplied, and began a song of his own composition.

When the song was finished the meal was also concluded, and the men returned to their labours on the rock; some to continue their work with the picks at the hard stone of the foundation-pit, others to perform miscellaneous jobs about the rock, such as mixing the mortar and removing *débris*, while James Dove and his fast friend Ruby Brand mounted to their airy "cot" on the beacon, from which in a short time began to proceed the volumes of smoke and the clanging sounds that had formerly arisen from "Smith's Ledge."

While they were all thus busily engaged, Ruby observed a boat advancing towards the rock from the floating light. He was blowing the bellows at the time, after a spell at the fore-hammer.

"We seem to be favoured with unusual events to-day, Jamie," said he, wiping his forehead with the corner of his apron with one hand, while he worked the handle of the bellows with the other, "yonder comes another boat; what can it be, think you?"

"Surely it can't be tea!" said the smith with a smile, as he turned the end of a pickaxe in the fire, "it's too soon after dinner for that."

"It looks like the boat of our friends the fishermen, Big Swankie and Davy Spink," said Ruby, shading his eyes with his hand, and gazing earnestly at the boat as it advanced towards them.

"Friends!" repeated the smith, "rascally smugglers, both of them; they're no friends of mine."

"Well, I didn't mean bosom friends," replied Ruby, "but after all, Davy Spink is not such a bad fellow, though I can't say that I'm fond of his comrade."

The two men resumed their hammers at this point in the conversation, and became silent as long as the anvil sounded.

The boat had reached the rock when they ceased, and its occupants were seen to be in earnest conversation with Peter Logan.

There were only two men in the boat besides its owners, Swankie and Spink.

"What can they want?" said Dove, looking down on them as he turned to thrust the iron on which he was engaged into the fire.

As he spoke the foreman looked up.

"Ho! Ruby Brand," he shouted, "come down here; you're wanted."

"Hallo! Ruby," exclaimed the smith, "*more* friends o' yours! Your acquaintance is extensive, lad, but there's no girl in the case this time."

Ruby made no reply, for an indefinable feeling of anxiety filled his breast as he threw down the fore-hammer and prepared to descend.

On reaching the rock he advanced towards the strangers, both of whom were stout, thickset men, with grave, stern countenances. One of them stepped forward and said, "Your name is—"

"Ruby Brand," said the youth promptly, at the same time somewhat proudly, for he knew that he was in the hands of the Philistines.

The man who first spoke hereupon drew a small instrument from his pocket, and tapping Ruby on the shoulder, said—

"I arrest you, Ruby Brand, in the name of the King."

The other man immediately stepped forward and produced a pair of handcuffs.

At sight of these Ruby sprang backward, and the blood rushed violently to his forehead, while his blue eyes glared with the ferocity of those of a tiger.

"Come, lad, it's of no use, you know," said the man, pausing; "if you won't come quietly we must find ways and means to compel you."

"Compel me!" cried Ruby, drawing himself up with a look of defiance and a laugh of contempt, that caused the two men to shrink back in spite of themselves.

"Ruby," said the foreman, gently, stepping forward and laying his hand on the youth's shoulder, "you had better go quietly, for there's no chance of escape from these fellows. I have no doubt it's a mistake, and that you'll come off with flyin' colours, but it's best to go quietly whatever turns up."

While Logan was speaking, Ruby dropped his head on his breast, the officer with the handcuffs advanced, and the youth held out his hands, while the flush of anger deepened into the crimson blush of shame.

It was at this point that Jamie Dove, wondering at the prolonged absence of his friend and assistant, looked down from the platform of the beacon, and beheld what was taking place.

The stentorian roar of amazement and rage that suddenly burst from him, attracted the attention of all the men on the rock, who dropped their tools and looked up in consternation, expecting, no doubt, to behold something terrible.

Their eyes at once followed those of the smith, and no sooner did they see Ruby being led in irons to the boat, which lay in *Port Hamilton*, close to *Sir Ralph the Rover's Ledge*, than they uttered a yell of execration, and rushed with one accord to the rescue.

The officers, who were just about to make their prisoner step into the boat, turned to face the foe,—one, who seemed to be the more courageous of the two, a little in advance of the other.

Ned O'Connor, with that enthusiasm which seems to be inherent in Irish blood, rushed with such irresistible force against this man that he drove him violently back against his comrade, and sent them both head over heels into Port Hamilton. Nay, with such momentum was this act performed, that Ned could not help but follow them, falling on them both as they came to the surface and sinking them a second time, amid screams and yells of laughter.

O'Connor was at once pulled out by his friends. The officers also were quickly landed.

"I ax yer parding, gintlemen," said the former, with an expression of deep regret on his face, "but the say-weed *is* so slippy on them rocks we're almost for iver doin' that sort o' thing be the merest accident. But av yer as fond o' cowld wather as meself ye won't objec' to it, although it do come raither onexpected."

The officers made no reply, but, collaring Ruby, pushed him into the boat.

Again the men made a rush, but Peter Logan stood between them and the boat.

"Lads," said he, holding up his hand, "it's of no use resistin' the law. These are King's officers, and they are only doin' their duty. Sure am I that Ruby Brand is guilty of no crime, so they've only to enquire into it and set him free."

The men hesitated, but did not seem quite disposed to submit without another struggle.

"It's a shame to let them take him," cried the smith.

"So it is. I vote for a rescue," cried Joe Dumsby.

"Hooray! so does I," cried O'Connor, stripping off his waist-coat, and for once in his life agreeing with Joe.

189

"Na, na, lads," cried John Watt, rolling up his sleeves, and baring his brawny arms as if about to engage in a fight, "it'll niver do to interfere wi' the law; but what d'ye say to gie them anither dook?"

Seeing that the men were about to act upon Watt's suggestion, Ruby started up in the boat, and turning to his comrade, said:

"Boys, it's very kind of you to be so anxious to save me but you can't—"

"Faix, but we can, darlin'," interrupted O'Connor.

"No, you can't," repeated Ruby firmly, "because I won't let you. I don't think I need say to you that I am innocent," he added, with a look in which truth evidently shone forth like a sunbeam, "but now that they have put these irons on me I will not consent that they shall be taken off except by the law which put them on."

While he was speaking the boat had been pushed off, and in a few seconds it was beyond the reach of the men.

"Depend upon it, comrades," cried Ruby, as they pulled away, "that I shall be back again to help you to finish the work on the Bell Rock."

"So you will, lad, so you will," cried the foreman.

"My blessin' on ye," shouted O'Connor. "Ach! ye dirty villains, ye low-minded spalpeens," he added, shaking his fist at the officers of justice.

"Don't be long away, Ruby," cried one.

"Never say die," shouted another, earnestly.

"Three cheers for Ruby Brand!" exclaimed Forsyth, "hip! hip! hip!—"

The cheer was given with the most vociferous energy, and then the men stood in melancholy silence on *Ralph the Rover's Ledge*, watching the boat that bore their comrade to the shore.

Chapter Sixteen

New Arrangements—The Captain's Philosophy in Regard to Pipeology

That night our hero was lodged in the common jail of Arbroath. Soon after, he was tried, and, as Captain Ogilvy had prophesied, was acquitted. Thereafter he went to reside for the winter with his mother, occupying the same room as his worthy uncle, as there was not another spare one in the cottage, and sleeping in a hammock, slung parallel with and close to that of the captain.

On the night following his release from prison, Ruby lay on his back in his hammock meditating intently on the future, and gazing at the ceiling, or rather at the place where he knew the ceiling to be, for it was a dark night, and there was no light in the room, the candle having just been extinguished.

We are not strictly correct, however, in saying that there was *no* light in the room, for there was a deep red glowing spot of fire near to Captain Ogilvy's head, which flashed and grew dim at each alternate second of time. It was, in fact, the captain's pipe, a luxury in which that worthy man indulged morning, noon, and night. He usually rested the bowl of the pipe on and a little over the edge of his hammock, and, lying on his back, passed the mouthpiece over the blankets into the corner of his mouth, where four of his teeth seemed to have agreed to form an exactly round hole suited to receive it. At each draw the fire in the bowl glowed so that the captain's nose was faintly illuminated; in the intervals the nose disappeared.

The breaking or letting fall of this pipe was a common incident in the captain's nocturnal history, but he had got used to it, from long habit, and regarded the event each time it occurred with the philosophic composure of one who sees and makes up his mind to endure an inevitable and unavoidable evil.

"Ruby," said the captain, after the candle was extinguished.

"Well, uncle?"

"I've bin thinkin', lad,—"

Here the captain drew a few whiffs to prevent the pipe from going out, in which operation he evidently forgot himself and went on thinking, for he said nothing more.

"Well, uncle, what have you been thinking?"

"Eh! ah, yes, I've bin thinkin', lad (pull), that you'll have to (puff)—there's somethin' wrong with the pipe to-night, it don't draw well (puff)—you'll have to do somethin' or other in the town, for it won't do to leave the old woman, lad, in her delicate state o' health. Had she turned in when you left the kitchen?"

"Oh yes, an hour or more."

"An' Blue Eyes,—

"'The tender bit flower that waves in the breeze,
And scatters its fragrance all over the seas.'

"Has she turned in too?"

"She was just going to when I left," replied Ruby; "but what has that to do with the question?"

"I didn't say as it had anything to do with it, lad. Moreover, there ain't no question between us as I knows on (puff); but what have you to say to stoppin' here all winter?"

"Impossible," said Ruby, with a sigh.

"No so, lad; what's to hinder?—Ah! there she goes."

The pipe fell with a crash to the floor, and burst with a bright shower of sparks, like a little bombshell.

"That's the third, Ruby, since I turned in," said the captain, getting slowly over the side of his hammock, and alighting on the floor heavily. "I won't git up again if it goes another time."

After knocking off the chimney-piece five or six articles which appeared to be made of tin from the noise they made in falling, the captain succeeded in getting hold of another pipe and the tinder-box, for in those days flint and steel were the implements generally used in procuring a light. With much trouble he re-lit the pipe.

"Now, Ruby, lad, hold it till I tumble in."

"But I can't see the stem, uncle."

"What a speech for a seaman to make! Don't you see the fire in the bowl?"

"Yes, of course."

"Well, just make a grab two inches astarn of the bowl and you'll hook the stem."

The captain was looking earnestly into the bowl while he spoke, stuffing down the burning tobacco with the end of his little finger. Ruby, acting in rather too prompt obedience to the instructions, made a "grab" as directed, and caught his uncle by the nose.

A yell and an apology followed of course, in the midst of which the fourth pipe was demolished.

"Oh! uncle, what a pity!"

"Ah! Ruby, that comes o' inconsiderate youth, which philosophers tell us is the nat'ral consequence of unavoidable necessity, for you can't put a young head on old shoulders, d'ye see?"

From the tone in which this was said Ruby knew that the captain was shaking his head gravely, and from the noise of articles being kicked about and falling, he became aware that the unconquerable man was filling a fifth pipe.

This one was more successfully managed, and the captain once more got into his hammock, and began to enjoy himself.

"Well, Ruby, where was I? O ay; what's to hinder you goin' and gettin' employed in the Bell Rock workyard? There's plenty to do, and good wages there."

It may be as well to inform the reader here, that although the operations at the Bell Rock had come to an end for the season about the beginning of October, the work of hewing the stones for the lighthouse was carried on briskly during the winter at the workyard on shore; and as the tools, etcetera, required constant sharpening and mending, a blacksmith could not be dispensed with.

"Do you think I can get in again?" enquired Ruby.

"No doubt of it, lad. But the question is, are ye willin' to go if they'll take you?"

"Quite willing, uncle."

"Good: then that's all square, an' I knows how to lay my course—up anchor to-morrow mornin', crowd all sail, bear down on the workyard, bring-to off the countin'-room, and open fire on the superintendent."

The captain paused at this point, and opened fire with his pipe for some minutes.

"Now," he continued, "there's another thing I want to ax you. I'm goin' to-morrow afternoon to take a cruise along the cliffs to the east'ard in the preventive boat, just to keep up my sea legs. They've got scent o' some smugglin' business that's goin' on, an' my friend Leftenant Lindsay has asked me to go. Now, Ruby, if you want a short cruise of an hour or so you may come with me."

Ruby smiled at the manner in which this offer was made, and replied:

"With pleasure, uncle."

"So, then, that's settled too. Good night, nephy."

The captain turned on his side, and dropped the pipe on the floor, where it was shivered to atoms.

It must not be supposed that this was accidental.

It was done on purpose. Captain Ogilvy had found from experience that it was not possible to stretch out his arm to its full extent and lay the pipe on the chimney-piece, without waking himself up just at that critical moment when sleep was consenting to be wooed. He also found that on the average he broke one in every four pipes that he thus attempted to deposit. Being a philosophical and practical man, he came to the conclusion that it would be worth while to pay something for the comfort of being undisturbed at the minute of time that lay between the conclusion of smoking and the commencement of repose. He therefore got a sheet of foolscap and a pencil, and spent a whole forenoon in abstruse calculations. He ascertained the exact value of three hundred and sixty-five clay pipes. From this he deducted a fourth for breakage that would have certainly occurred in the old system of laying the pipes down every night, and which, therefore, he felt, in a confused sort of way, ought not to be charged in the estimates of a new system. Then he added a small sum to the result for probable extra breakages, such as had occurred that night, and found that the total was not too high a price for a man in his circumstances to pay for the blessing he wished to obtain.

From that night forward he deliberately dropped his pipe every night over the side of his hammock before going to sleep.

The captain, in commenting on this subject, was wont to observe that everything in life, no matter how small, afforded matter of thought to philosophical men. He had himself found a pleasing subject of study each morning in the fact that some of the pipes survived the fall of the previous night. This led him to consider the nature of clay pipes in general, and to test them in various ways. It is true he did not say that anything of importance resulted from his peculiar studies, but he argued that a true philosopher looks for facts, and leaves results alone. One discovery he undoubtedly did make, which was, that the pipes obtained from a certain maker in the town *invariably* broke, while those obtained from another maker broke only occasionally. Hence he came to the conclusion that one maker was an honest man, the other a doubtful character, and wisely bestowed his custom in accordance with that opinion.

About one minute after the falling of the pipe Ruby Brand fell asleep, and about two minutes after that Captain Ogilvy began to snore, both of which conditions were maintained respectively and uninterruptedly until the birds began to whistle and the sun began to shine.

Chapter Seventeen

A Meeting with Old Friends, and an Excursion

Next morning the captain and his nephew "bore down", as the former expressed it, on the workyard, and Ruby was readily accepted, his good qualities having already been well tested at the Bell Rock.

"Now, boy, we'll go and see about the little preventive craft," said the captain on quitting the office.

"But first," said Ruby, "let me go and tell my old comrade Dove that I am to be with him again."

There was no need to enquire the way to the forge, the sound of the anvil being distinctly heard above all the other sounds of that busy spot.

The workyard at Arbroath, where the stones for the lighthouse were collected and hewn into shape before being sent off to the rock, was an enclosed piece of ground, extending to about three-quarters of an acre, conveniently situated on the northern side of the Lady Lane, or Street, leading from the western side of the harbour.

Here were built a row of barracks for the workmen, and several apartments connected with the engineer's office, mould-makers' department, stores, workshops for smiths and joiners, stables, etcetera, extending 150 feet along the north side of the yard. All of these were fully occupied, there being upwards of forty men employed permanently.

Sheds of timber were also constructed to protect the workmen in wet weather; and a kiln was built for burning lime. In the centre of the yard stood a circular platform of masonry on which the stones were placed when dressed, so that each stone was tested and marked, and each "course" or layer of the lighthouse fitted up and tried, before being shipped to the rock.

The platform measured 44 feet in diameter. It was founded with large broad stones at a depth of about 2 feet 6 inches, and built to within 10 inches of the surface with rubble work, on which a course of neatly dressed and well-jointed masonry was laid, of the red sandstone from the quarries to the eastward of Arbroath, which brought the platform on a level with the surface of the ground. Here the dressed part of the first entire course, or layer, of the lighthouse was lying, and the platform was so substantially built as to be capable of supporting any number of courses which it might be found convenient to lay upon it in the further progress of the work.

Passing this platform, the captain and Ruby threaded their way through a mass of workyard *débris* until they came to the building from which the sounds of the anvil proceeded. For a few minutes they stood looking at our old friend Jamie Dove, who, with bared arms, was causing the sparks to fly, and the glowing metal to yield, as vigorously as of old. Presently he ceased hammering, and turning to the fire thrust the metal into it. Then he wiped his brow, and glanced towards the door.

"What! eh! Ruby Brand?" he shouted in surprise.

"Och! or his ghost!" cried Ned O'Connor, who had been appointed to Ruby's vacant situation.

"A pretty solid ghost you'll find me," said Ruby with a laugh, as he stepped forward and seized the smith by the hand.

"Musha! but it's thrue," cried O'Connor, quitting the bellows, and seizing Ruby's disengaged hand, which he shook almost as vehemently as the smith did the other.

"Now, then, don't dislocate him altogether," cried the captain, who was much delighted with this warm reception; "he's goin' to jine you, boys, so have mercy on his old timbers."

"Jine us!" cried the smith.

"Ay, been appointed to the old berth," said Ruby, "so I'll have to unship *you*, Ned."

"The sooner the better; faix, I niver had much notion o' this fiery style o' life; it's only fit for sallymanders and bottle-imps. But when d'ye begin work, lad?"

"To-morrow, I believe. At least, I was told to call at the office to-morrow. To-day I have an engagement."

"Ay, an' it's time we was under weigh," said Captain Ogilvy, taking his nephew by the arm. "Come along, lad, an' don't keep them waiting."

So saying they bade the smith goodbye, and, leaving the forge, walked smartly towards that part of the harbour where the boats lay.

"Ruby," said the captain, as they went along, "it's lucky it's such a fine day, for Minnie is going with us."

Ruby said nothing, but the deep flush of pleasure that overspread his countenance proved that he was not indifferent to the news.

"You see she's bin out of sorts," continued the captain, "for some time back; and no wonder, poor thing, seein' that your mother has been so anxious about you, and required more than usual care, so I've prevailed on the leftenant to let her go. She'll get good by our afternoon's sail, and we won't be the worse of her company. What say ye to that, nephy?"

Ruby said that he was glad to hear it, but he thought a great deal more than he said, and among other things he thought that the lieutenant might perhaps be rather in the way; but as his presence was unavoidable he made up his mind to try to believe that he, the lieutenant, would in all probability be an engaged man already. As to the possibility of his seeing Minnie and being indifferent to her (in the event of his being a free man), he felt that such an idea was preposterous! Suddenly a thought flashed across him and induced a question—

"Is the lieutenant married, uncle?"

"Not as I know of, lad; why d'ye ask?"

"Because—because—married men are so much pleasanter than—"

Ruby stopped short, for he just then remembered that his uncle was a bachelor.

"'Pon my word, youngster! go on, why d'ye stop in your purlite remark?"

"Because," said Ruby, laughing, "I meant to say that *young* married men were so much more agreeable than *young* bachelors."

"Humph!" ejaculated the captain, who did not see much force in the observation, "and how d'ye know the leftenant's a *young* man? I didn't say he was young; mayhap he's old. But here he is, so you'll judge for yourself."

At the moment a tall, deeply-bronzed man of about thirty years of age walked up and greeted Captain Ogilvy familiarly as his "buck", enquiring, at the same time, how his "old timbers" were, and where the "bit of baggage" was.

"She's to be at the end o' the pier in five minutes," said the captain, drawing out and consulting a watch that was large enough to have been mistaken for a small eight-day clock. "This is my nephy, Ruby. Ruby Brand— Leftenant Lindsay. True blues, both of ye—

"'When shall we three meet again? Where the stormy winds do blow, do blow, do blow,
And the thunder, lightenin', and the rain, Riots up above, and also down below, below, below.'

"Ah! here comes the pretty little craft."

Minnie appeared as he spoke, and walked towards them with a modest, yet decided air that was positively bewitching.

She was dressed in homely garments, but that served to enhance the beauty of her figure, and she had on the plainest of little bonnets, but that only tended to make her face more lovely. Ruby thought it was perfection. He glanced at Lieutenant Lindsay, and perceiving that he thought so too (as how could he think otherwise?) a pang of jealousy shot into his breast. But it passed away when the lieutenant, after politely assisting Minnie into the boat, sat down beside the captain and began to talk earnestly to him, leaving Minnie entirely to her lover. We may remark here, that the title of "leftenant", bestowed on Lindsay by the captain was entirely complimentary.

The crew of the boat rowed out of the harbour, and the lieutenant steered eastward, towards the cliffs that have been mentioned in an earlier part of our tale.

The day turned out to be one of those magnificent and exceptional days which appear to have been cut out of summer and interpolated into autumn. It was bright, warm, and calm, so calm that the boat's sail was useless, and the crew had to row; but this was, in Minnie's estimation, no disadvantage, for it gave her time to see the caves and picturesque inlets which abound all along that rocky coast. It also gave her time to—but no matter.

"O how very much I should like to have a little boat," said Minnie, with enthusiasm, "and spend a long day rowing in and out among these wild rocks, and exploring the caves! Wouldn't it be delightful, Ruby?"

Ruby admitted that it would, and added, "You shall have such a day, Minnie, if we live long."

"Have you ever been in the *Forbidden Cave*?" enquired Minnie.

"I'll warrant you he has," cried the captain, who overheard the question; "you may be sure that wherever Ruby is forbidden to go, there he'll be sure to go!"

"Ay, is he so self-willed?" asked the lieutenant, with a smile, and a glance at Minnie.

"A mule; a positive mule," said the captain.

"Come, uncle, you know that I don't deserve such a character, and it's too bad to give it to me to-day. Did I not agree to come on this excursion at once, when you asked me?"

"Ay, but you wouldn't if I had *ordered* you," returned the captain.

"I rather think he would," observed the lieutenant, with another smile, and another glance at Minnie.

Both smiles and glances were observed and noticed by Ruby, whose heart felt another pang shoot through it; but this, like the former, subsided when the lieutenant again addressed the captain, and devoted himself to him so exclusively, that Ruby began to feel a touch of indignation at his want of appreciation of *such* a girl as Minnie.

"He's a stupid ass," thought Ruby to himself, and then, turning to Minnie, directed her attention to a curious natural arch on the cliffs, and sought to forget all the rest of the world.

In this effort he was successful, and had gradually worked himself into the firm belief that the world was paradise, and that he and Minnie were its sole occupants—a second edition, as it were, of Adam and Eve—when the lieutenant rudely dispelled the sweet dream by saying sharply to the man at the bow-oar—

"Is that the boat, Baker? You ought to know it pretty well."

"I think it is, sir," answered the man, resting on his oar a moment, and glancing over his shoulder; "but I can't be sure at this distance."

"Well, pull easy," said the lieutenant; "you see, it won't do to scare them, Captain Ogilvy, and they'll think we're a pleasure party when they see a woman in the boat."

Ruby thought they would not be far wrong in supposing them a pleasure party. He objected, mentally, however, to Minnie being styled a "woman"—not that he would have had her called a man, but he thought that *girl* would

208

have been more suitable—angel, perhaps, the most appropriate term of all.

"Come, captain, I think I will join you in a pipe," said the lieutenant, pulling out a tin case, in which he kept the blackest of little cutty pipes. "In days of old our ancestors loved to fight—now we degenerate souls love to smoke the pipe of peace."

"I did not know that your ancestors were enemies," said Minnie to the captain.

"Enemies, lass! ay, that they were. What! have ye never heard tell o' the great fight between the Ogilvys and Lindsays?"

"Never," said Minnie.

"Then, my girl, your education has been neglected, but I'll do what I can to remedy that defect."

Here the captain rekindled his pipe (which was in the habit of going out, and requiring to be relighted), and, clearing his throat with the emphasis of one who is about to communicate something of importance, held forth as follows.

Chapter Eighteen

The Battle of Arbroath, and Other Warlike Matters

"It was in the year 1445—that's not far short o' four hundred years ago—ah! *tempus fugit*, which is a Latin quotation, my girl, from Horace Walpole, I believe, an' signifies time and tide waits for no man; that's what they calls a free translation, you must know; well, it was in the winter o' 1445 that a certain Alexander Ogilvy of Inverquharity, was chosen to act as Chief Justiciar in these parts—I suppose that means a kind of upper bailiff, a sort o' bo's'n's mate, to compare great things with small. He was set up in place of one o' the Lindsay family, who, it seems, was rather extravagant, though whether his extravagance lay in wearin' a beard (for he was called Earl Beardie), or in spendin' too much cash, I can't take upon me for to say. Anyhow, Beardie refused to haul down his colours, so the Ogilvys mustered their men and friends, and the Lindsays did the same, and they went at it, hammer and tongs, and fowt what ye may call the Battle of Arbroath, for it was close to the old town where they fell to.

"It was a most bloody affair. The two families were connected with many o' the richest and greatest people in the land, and these went to lend a hand when they beat to quarters, and there was no end o' barbed horses, as they call them—which means critters with steel spikes in their noses, I'm told—and lots of embroidered banners and flags, though I never heard that anyone hoisted the Union Jack; but, however that may be, they fowt like bluejackets, for five hundred men were left dead on the field, an' among them a lot o' the great folk.

"But I'm sorry to say that the Ogilvys were licked, though I say it that shouldn't," continued the captain, with a sigh, as he relighted his pipe. "Howsever,—

"'Never ventur', never win,
 Blaze away an' don't give in,'

"As Milton remarks in his preface to the *Pilgrim's Progress*."

"True, captain," said the lieutenant, "and you know that he who fights and runs away, shall live to fight another day."

"Leftenant," said the captain gravely, "your quotation, besides bein' a kind o' desecration, is not applicable; 'cause the Ogilvys did *not* run away. They fowt on that occasion like born imps, an' they would ha' certainly won the day, if they hadn't been, every man jack of 'em, cut to pieces before the battle was finished."

"Well said, uncle," exclaimed Ruby, with a laugh. "No doubt the Ogilvys would lick the Lindsays *now* if they had a chance."

"I believe they would," said the lieutenant, "for they have become a race of heroes since the great day of the Battle of Arbroath. No doubt, Miss Gray," continued the lieutenant, turning to Minnie with an arch smile, "no doubt you have heard of that more recent event, the threatened attack on Arbroath by the French fire-eater, Captain Fall, and the heroic part played on that occasion by an Ogilvy—an uncle, I am told, of my good friend here?"

"I have heard of Captain Fall, of course," replied Minnie, "for it was not many years before I was born that his visit took place, and Mrs Brand has often told me of the consternation into which the town was thrown by his doings; but I never heard of the deeds of the Ogilvy to whom you refer."

"No? Now, that *is* surprising! How comes it, captain, that you have kept so silent on this subject?"

"'Cause it ain't true," replied the captain stoutly, yet with a peculiar curl about the corners of his mouth, that implied something in the mind beyond what he expressed with the lips.

"Ah! I see—modesty," said Lindsay. "Your uncle is innately modest, Miss Gray, and never speaks of anything that bears the slightest resemblance to boasting. See, the grave solemnity with which he smokes while I say this proves the truth of my assertion. Well, since he has never told you, I will tell yell myself. You have no objection, captain?"

The captain sent a volume of smoke from his lips, and followed it up with— "Fire away, shipmet."

The lieutenant, having drawn a few whiffs in order to ensure the continued combustion of his pipe, related the following anecdote, which is now matter of history, as anyone may find by consulting the archives of Arbroath.

"In the year 1781, on a fine evening of the month of May, the seamen of Arbroath who chanced to be loitering about the harbour observed a strange vessel manoeuvring in the offing. They watched and commented on the motions of the stranger with considerable interest, for the wary skill displayed by her commander proved that he was unacquainted with the navigation of the coast, and from the cut of her jib they knew that the craft was a foreigner. After a time she took up a position, and cast anchor in the bay, directly opposite the town.

"At that time we were, as we still are, and as it really appears likely to me we ever shall be, at war with France; but as the scene of the war was far removed from Arbroath, it never occurred to the good people that the smell of powder could reach their peaceful town. That idea was somewhat rudely forced upon them when the French flag was run up to the mizzentop, and a white puff of smoke burst from the vessel, which was followed by a shot, that went hissing over their heads, and plumped right into the middle of the town!

"That shot knocked over fifteen chimney-pots and two weathercocks in Market-gate, went slap through a house in the suburbs, and finally stuck in the carcass of an old horse belonging to the Provost of the town, which didn't survive the shock—the horse, I mean, not the Provost.

"It is said that there was an old gentleman lying in bed in a room of the house that the shot went through. He was a sort of 'hipped' character, and believed that he could not walk, if he were to try ever so much. He was looking quietly at the face of a great Dutch clock when the shot entered and knocked the clock inside out, sending its contents in a shower over the old gentleman, who jumped up and rushed out of the house like a maniac! He was cured completely from that hour. At least, so it's said, but I don't vouch for the truth of the story.

"However, certain it is that the shot was fired, and was followed up by two or three more; after which the Frenchman ceased firing, and a boat was seen to quit the side of the craft, bearing a flag of truce.

"The consternation into which the town was thrown is said to have been tremendous."

"That's false," interrupted the captain, removing his pipe while he spoke. "The word ain't appropriate. The men of Arbroath doesn't know nothin' about no such word as 'consternation.' They was *surprised*, if ye choose, an' powerfully enraged mayhap, but they wasn't consternated by no means."

"Well, I don't insist on the point," said the lieutenant, "but chroniclers write so—

"Chroniclers write lies sometimes," interrupted the captain curtly.

"Perhaps they do; but you will admit, I dare say, that the women and children were thrown into a great state of alarm."

"I'm not so sure of that," interposed Ruby. "In a town where the men were so bold, the women and children would be apt to feel very much at their ease. At all events, I am acquainted with *some* women who are not easily frightened."

"Really, I think it is not fair to interrupt the story in this way," said Minnie, with a laugh.

"Right, lass, right," said the captain. "Come, leftenant, spin away at yer yarn, and don't ventur' too much commentary thereon, 'cause it's apt to lead to error, an' ye know, as the poet says—

"'Errors in the heart breed errors in the brain,
An' these are apt to twist ye wrong again.'

"I'm not 'xactly sure o' the precise words in this case, but that's the sentiment, and everybody knows that sentiment is everything in poetry, whether ye understand it or not. Fire away, leftenant, an' don't be long-winded if ye can help it."

"Well, to return to the point," resumed Lindsay. "The town was certainly thrown into a tremendous state of *some* sort, for the people had no arms of any kind wherewith to defend themselves. There were no regular soldiers, no militia, and no volunteers. Everybody ran wildly about in every direction, not knowing what to do. There was no leader, and, in short, the town was very like a shoal of small fish in a pool when a boy wades in and makes a dash amongst them.

"At last a little order was restored by the Provost, who was a sensible old man, and an old soldier to boot, but too infirm to take as active a part in such an emergency as he would have done had he been a dozen years younger. He, with several of the principal men of the town, went down to the beach to receive the bearers of the flag of truce.

"The boat was manned by a crew of five or six seamen, armed with cutlasses and arquebusses. As soon as its keel grated on the sand a smart little officer leaped ashore, and presented to the Provost a letter from Captain Fall, which ran somewhat in this fashion:—

"'At Sea, *May twenty-third*.

"'Gentlemen,—I send these two words to inform you, that I will have you to bring-to the French colour in less than a quarter of an hour, or I set the town on fire directly. Such is the order of my master, the King of France, I am sent by. Send directly the Mair and chiefs of the town to make some agreement with me, or I'll make my duty. It is the will of yours, — **G. Fall**.

"'To Monsieur Mair of the town called Arbrought, or in his absence to the chief man after him in Scotland.'

"On reading this the Provost bowed respectfully to the officer, and begged of him to wait a few minutes while he should consult with his chief men. This was agreed to, and the Provost said to his friends, as he walked to a neighbouring house—

"'Ye see, freens, this whipper-snapper o' a tade-eater has gotten the whup hand o' us; but we'll be upsides wi' him. The main thing is to get delay, so cut away, Tam Cargill, and tak' horse to Montrose for the sodgers. Spare na the spur, lad, an' gar them to understan' that the case is urgent.'

"While Tam Cargill started away on his mission, the Provost, whose chief aim was to gain time and cause delay, penned an epistle to the Frenchman, in which he stated that he had neglected to name the terms on which he would consent to spare the town, and that he would consider it extremely obliging if he would, as speedily as possible, return an answer, stating them, in order that they might be laid before the chief men of the place."

"When the Provost, who was a grave, dignified old man, with a strong dash of humour in him, handed this note to the French officer, he did so with a humble obeisance that appeared to afford much gratification to the little man. As the latter jumped into the boat and ordered the men to push off, the Provost turned slowly to his brother magistrates with a wink and a quiet smile that convulsed them with suppressed laughter, and did more to encourage any of the wavering or timid inhabitants than if he had harangued them heroically for an hour.

"Some time after the boat returned with a reply, which ran thus:—

"'At Sea, *eight o'clock in the Afternoon.'*

"'Gentlemen,—I received just now your answer, by which you say I ask no terms. I thought it was useless, since I asked you to come aboard for agreement. But here are my terms:— I will have 30,000 pounds sterling at least, and six of the chiefs men of the town for otage. Be speedy, or I shot your town away directly, and I set fire to it. I am, gentlemen, your servant, — **G. Fall**.

"'I sent some of my crew to you, but if some harm happens to them, you'll be sure we'll hang up the mainyard all the prisoners we have aboard.

"'To Monsieurs the chiefs men of Arbrought in Scotland.'

"I'm not quite certain," continued the lieutenant, "what were the exact words of the Provost's reply to this letter, but they conveyed a distinct and contemptuous refusal to accede to any terms, and, I believe, invited Fall to come ashore, where, if he did not get precisely what he had asked, he would be certain to receive a great deal more than he wanted.

"The enraged and disappointed Frenchman at once began a heavy fire upon the town, and continued it for a long time, but fortunately it did little or no harm, as the town lay in a somewhat low position, and Fall's guns being too much elevated, the shot passed over it.

"Next day another letter was sent to the Provost by some fishermen, who were captured while fishing off the Bell Rock. This letter was as tremendous as the two former. I can give it to you, word for word, from memory.

"'At Sea, *May* 24th.'

"'Gentlemen,—See whether you will come to some terms with me, or I come in presently with my cutter into the arbour, and I will cast down the town all over. Make haste, because I have no time to spare. I give you a quarter of an hour to your decision, and after I'll make my duty. I think it would be better for you, gentlemen, to come some of you aboard presently, to settle the affairs of your town. You'll sure no to be hurt. I give you my parole of honour. I am your, **G. Fall**.'

"When the Provost received this he looked round and said, 'Now, gentlemen all, we'll hae to fight. Send me Ogilvy.'

"'Here I am, Provost,' cried a stout, active young fellow; something like what the captain must have been when he was young, I should think!"

"Ahem!" coughed the captain.

"Well," continued Lindsay, "the Provost said, 'Now, Ogilvy, you're a smart cheel, an' ken aboot war and strategy and the like: I charge ye to organise the men o' the toon without delay, and tak' what steps ye think adveesable. Meanwhile, I'll away and ripe oot a' the airms and guns I can find. Haste ye, lad, an' mak' as muckle noise aboot it as ye can.'

"'Trust me,' said Ogilvy, who appeared to have been one of those men who regard a fight as a piece of good fun.

"Turning to the multitude, who had heard the commission given, and were ready for anything, he shouted, 'Now, boys, ye heard the Provost. I need not ask if you are all ready to fight—'

"A deafening cheer interrupted the speaker, who, when it ceased, proceeded—

"'Well, then, I've but one piece of advice to give ye: *Obey orders at once*. When I tell ye to halt, stop dead like lampposts; when I say, "Charge!" go at them like wild cats, and drive the Frenchmen into the sea!' 'Hurrah!' yelled the crowd, for they were wild with excitement and rage, and only wanted a leader to organise them and make them formidable. When the cheer ceased, Ogilvy cried, 'Now, then, every man who knows how to beat a kettledrum and blow a trumpet come here.'

"About twenty men answered to the summons, and to these Ogilvy said aloud, in order that all might hear, 'Go, get you all the trumpets, drums, horns, bugles, and trombones in the town; beat the drums till they split, and blow the bugles till they burst, and don't give in till ye can't go on. The rest of you,' he added, turning to the crowd, 'go, get arms, guns, swords, pistols, scythes, pitchforks, pokers—any thing, everything—and meet me at the head of Market-gate—away!'

"No king of necromancers ever dispersed his legions more rapidly than did Ogilvy on that occasion. They gave one final cheer, and scattered like chaff before the wind, leaving their commander alone, with a select few, whom he kept by him as a sort of staff to consult with and despatch with orders.

"The noise that instantly ensued in the town was something pandemoniacal. Only three drums were found, but tin kettles and pans were not wanting, and these, superintended by Hugh Barr, the town drummer, did great execution. Three key-bugles, an old French horn, and a tin trumpet of a mail-coach guard, were sounded at intervals in every quarter of the town, while the men were marshalled, and made to march hither and thither in detached bodies, as if all were busily engaged in making preparations for a formidable defence.

"In one somewhat elevated position a number of men were set to work with spades, picks, and shovels, to throw up an earthwork. When it had assumed sufficiently large dimensions to attract the attention of the French, a body of men, with blue jackets, and caps with bits of red flannel hanging down the sides, were marched up behind it at the double, and posted there.

"Meanwhile Ogilvy had prepared a dummy field piece, by dismounting a cart from its wheels and fixing on the axle a great old wooden pump, not unlike a big gun in shape; another cart was attached to this to represent a limber; four horses were harnessed to the affair; two men mounted these, and, amid a tremendous flourish of trumpets and beating of drums, the artillery went crashing along the streets and up the eminence crowned by the earthwork, where they wheeled the gun into position.

"The artillerymen sprang at the old pump like true Britons, and began to sponge it out as if they had been bred to gunnery from childhood, while the limber was detached and galloped to the rear. In this operation the cart was smashed to pieces, and the two hindmost horses were thrown; but this mattered little, as they had got round a corner, and the French did not see it.

"Fall and his brave men seem to have been upset altogether by these warlike demonstrations, for the moment the big gun made its appearance the sails were shaken loose, and the French privateer sheered off; capturing as he left the bay, however, several small vessels, which he carried off as prizes to France. And so," concluded the lieutenant,

"Captain Fall sailed away, and never was heard of more."

"Well told; well told, leftenant," cried the captain, whose eyes sparkled at the concluding account of the defensive operations, "and true every word of it."

"That's good testimony to my truthfulness, then," said Lindsay, laughing, "for you were there yourself!"

"There yourself, uncle?" repeated Minnie, with a glance of surprise that quickly changed into a look of intelligence, as she exclaimed, with a merry laugh, "Ah! I see. It was *you*, uncle, who did it all; who commanded on that occasion—"

"My child," said the captain, resuming his pipe with an expression of mild reproof on his countenance, "don't go for to pry too deep into things o' the past. I *may* have been a fire-eater once—I *may* have been a gay young feller as could—; but no matter. Avast musin'! As Lord Bacon says—

"'The light of other days is faded,
An' all their glory's past;
My boots no longer look as they did,
But, like my coat, are goin' fast.'

"But I say, leftenant, how long do you mean to keep pullin' about here, without an enemy, or, as far as I can see, an object in view? Don't you think we might land, and let Minnie see some of the caves?"

"With all my heart, captain, and here is a convenient bay to run the boat ashore."

As he spoke the boat shot past one of those bold promontories of red sandstone which project along that coast in wild picturesque forms, terminating in some instances in detached headlands, elsewhere in natural arches. The cliffs were so close to the boat that they could have been touched by the oars, while the rocks, rising to a considerable height, almost overhung them. Just beyond this a beautiful bay opened up to view, with a narrow strip of yellow shingle round the base of the cliffs, which here lost for a short distance their rugged character, though not their height, and were covered with herbage. A zigzag path led to the top, and the whole neighbourhood was full of ocean-worn coves and gullies, some of them dry, and many filled with water, while others were filled at high tide, and left empty when the tides fell.

"O how beautiful! and what a place for smugglers!" was Minnie's enthusiastic exclamation on first catching sight of the bay.

"The smugglers and you would appear to be of one mind," said Ruby, "for they are particularly fond of this place."

"So fond of it," said the lieutenant, "that I mean to wait for them here in anticipation of a moonlight visit this night, if my fair passenger will consent to wander in such wild places at such late hours, guarded from the night air by my boat-cloak, and assured of the protection of my stout boatmen in case of any danger, although there is little prospect of our meeting with any greater danger than a breeze or a shower of rain."

Minnie said that she would like nothing better; that she did not mind the night air; and, as to danger from men, she felt that she should be well cared for in present circumstances.

As she uttered the last words she naturally glanced at Ruby, for Minnie was of a dependent and trusting nature; but as Ruby happened to be regarding her intently, though quite accidentally, at the moment, she dropped her eyes and blushed.

It is wonderful the power of a little glance at times. The glance referred to made Ruby perfectly happy. It conveyed to him the assurance that Minnie regarded the protection of the entire boat's crew, including the lieutenant, as quite unnecessary, and that she deemed his single arm all that she required or wanted.

The sun was just dipping behind the tall cliffs, and his parting rays were kissing the top of Minnie's head as if they positively could not help it, and had recklessly made up their mind to do it, come what might!

Ruby looked at the golden light kissing the golden hair, and he felt—

Oh! you know, reader; if you have ever been in similar circumstances, you *understand* what he felt; if you have not, no words from me, or from any other man, can ever convey to you the most distant idea of *what* Ruby felt on that occasion!

On reaching the shore they all went up to the green banks at the foot of the cliffs, and turned round to watch the men as they pulled the boat to a convenient point for re-embarking at a moment's notice.

"You see," said the lieutenant, pursuing a conversation which he had been holding with the captain, "I have been told that Big Swankie, and his mate Davy Spink (who, it seems, is not over-friendly with him just now), mean to visit one of the luggers which is expected to come in to-night, before the moon rises, and bring off some kegs of Auchmithie water, which, no doubt, they will try to hide in Dickmont's Den. I shall lie snugly here on the watch, and hope to nab them before they reach that celebrated old smuggler's abode."

"Well, I'll stay about here," said the captain, "and show Minnie the caves. I would like to have taken her to see the Gaylet Pot, which is one o' the queerest hereabouts; but I'm too old for such rough work now."

"But *I* am not too old for it," interposed Ruby, "so if Minnie would like to go—"

"But I won't desert *you*, uncle," said Minnie hastily.

"Nay, lass, call it not desertion. I can smoke my pipe here, an' contemplate. I'm fond of contemplation—

"'By the starry light of the summer night,
  On the banks of the blue Moselle,'

"Though, for the matter o' that, moonlight'll do, if there's no stars. I think it's good for the mind, Minnie, and keeps all taut. Contemplation is just like takin' an extra pull on the lee braces. So you may go with Ruby, lass."

Thus advised, and being further urged by Ruby himself, and being moreover exceedingly anxious to see this cave, Minnie consented; so the two set off together, and, climbing to the summit of the cliffs, followed the narrow footpath that runs close to their giddy edge all along the coast.

In less than half an hour they reached the Giel or Gaylet Pot.

Chapter Nineteen

An Adventure—Secrets Revealed, and a Prize

The Giel or Gaylet Pot, down into which Ruby, with great care and circumspection, led Minnie, is one of the most curious of Nature's freaks among the cliffs of Arbroath.

In some places there is a small scrap of pebbly beach at the base of those perpendicular cliffs; in most places there is none—the cliffs presenting to the sea almost a dead wall, where neither ship nor boat could find refuge from the storm.

The country, inland, however, does not partake of the rugged nature of the cliffs. It slopes gradually towards them—so gradually that it may be termed flat, and if a stranger were to walk towards the sea over the fields in a dark night, the first intimation he would receive of his dangerous position would be when his foot descended into the terrible abyss that would receive his shattered frame a hundred feet below.

In one of the fields there is a hole about a hundred yards across, and as deep as the cliffs in that part are high. It is about fifty or eighty yards from the edge of the cliffs, and resembles an old quarry; but it is cut so sharply out of the flat field that it shows no sign of its existence until the traveller is close upon it. The rocky sides, too, are so steep, that at first sight it seems as if no man could descend into it. But the most peculiar point about this hole is, that at the foot of it there is the opening of a cavern, through which the sea rolls into the hole, and breaks in wavelets on a miniature shore. The sea has forced its way inland and underground until it has burst into the bottom of this hole, which is not inaptly compared to a pot with water boiling at the bottom of it. When a spectator looks into the cave, standing at the bottom of the "Pot", he sees the seaward opening at the other end—a bright spot of light in the dark interior.

"You won't get nervous, Minnie?" said Ruby, pausing when about halfway down the steep declivity, where the track, or rather the place of descent, became still more steep and difficult; "a slip here would be dangerous."

"I have no fear, Ruby, as long as you keep by me."

In a few minutes they reached the bottom, and, looking up, the sky appeared above them like a blue circular ceiling, with the edges of the Gaylet Pot sharply defined against it.

Proceeding over a mass of fallen rock, they reached the pebbly strand at the cave's inner mouth.

"I can see the interior now, as my eyes become accustomed to the dim light," said Minnie, gazing up wistfully into the vaulted roof, where the edges of projecting rocks seemed to peer out of darkness. "Surely this must be a place for smugglers to come to!"

"They don't often come here. The place is not so suitable as many of the other caves are."

From the low, subdued tones in which they both spoke, it was evident that the place inspired them with feelings of awe.

"Come, Minnie," said Ruby, at length, in a more cheerful tone, "let us go into this cave and explore it."

"But the water may be deep," objected Minnie; "besides, I do not like to wade, even though it be shallow."

"Nay, sweet one; do you think I would ask you to wet your pretty feet? There is very little wading required. See, I have only to raise you in my arms and take two steps into the water, and a third step to the left round that projecting rock, where I can set you down on another beach inside the cave. Your eyes will soon get used to the subdued light, and then you will see things much more clearly than you would think it possible viewed from this point."

Minnie did not require much pressing. She had perfect confidence in her lover, and was naturally fearless in disposition, so she was soon placed on the subterranean beach of the Gaylet Cave, and for some time wandered about in the dimly-lighted place, leaning on Ruby's arm.

Gradually their eyes became accustomed to the place, and then its mysterious beauty and wildness began to have full effect on their minds, inducing them to remain for a long time, silent, as they sat side by side on a piece of fallen rock.

They sat looking in the direction of the seaward entrance to the cavern, where the light glowed brightly on the rocks, gradually losing its brilliancy as it penetrated the cave, until it became quite dim in the centre. No part of the main cave was quite dark, but the offshoot, in which the lovers sat, was almost dark. To anyone viewing it from the outer cave it would have appeared completely so.

"Is that a sea-gull at the outlet?" enquired Minnie, after a long pause.

Ruby looked intently for a moment in the direction indicated.

"Minnie," he said quickly, and in a tone of surprise, "that is a large gull, if it be one at all, and uses oars instead of wings. Who can it be? Smugglers never come here that I am aware of, and Lindsay is not a likely man to waste his time in pulling about when he has other work to do."

"Perhaps it may be some fishermen from Auchmithie," suggested Minnie, "who are fond of exploring, like you and me."

"Mayhap it is, but we shall soon see, for here they come. We must keep out of sight, my girl."

Ruby rose and led Minnie into the recesses of the cavern, where they were speedily shrouded in profound darkness, and could not be seen by anyone, although they themselves could observe all that occurred in the space in front of them.

The boat, which had entered the cavern by its seaward mouth, was a small one, manned by two fishermen, who were silent as they rowed under the arched roof; but it was evident that their silence did not proceed from caution, for they made no effort to prevent or check the noise of the oars.

In a few seconds the keel grated on the pebbles, and one of the men leaped out.

"Noo, Davy," he said, in a voice that sounded deep and hollow under that vaulted roof, "oot wi' the kegs. Haste ye, man."

"'Tis Big Swankie," whispered Ruby.

"There's nae hurry," objected the other fisherman, who, we need scarcely inform the reader, was our friend, Davy Spink.

"Nae hurry!" repeated his comrade angrily. "That's aye yer cry. Half o' oor ventures hae failed because ye object to hurry."

"Hoot, man! that's enough o't," said Spink, in the nettled tone of a man who has been a good deal worried. Indeed, the tones of both showed that these few sentences were but the continuation of a quarrel which had begun elsewhere.

"It's plain to me that we must pairt, freen'," said Swankie in a dogged manner, as he lifted a keg out of the boat and placed it on the ground.

"Ay," exclaimed Spink, with something of a sneer, "an' d'ye think I'll pairt without a diveesion o' the siller tea-pots and things that ye daurna sell for fear o' bein' fund out?"

"I wonder ye dinna claim half o' the jewels and things as weel," retorted Swankie; "ye hae mair right to *them*, seein' ye had a hand in findin' them."

"*Me* a hand in findin' them," exclaimed Spink, with sudden indignation. "Was it *me* that fand the deed body o' the auld man on the Bell Rock? Na, na, freend. I hae naething to do wi' deed men's jewels."

234

"Have ye no?" retorted the other. "It's strange, then, that ye should entertain such sma' objections to deed men's siller."

"Weel-a-weel, Swankie, the less we say on thae matters the better. Here, tak' haud o' the tither keg."

The conversation ceased at this stage abruptly. Evidently each had touched on the other's weak point, so both tacitly agreed to drop the subject.

Presently Big Swankie took out a flint and steel, and proceeded to strike a light. It was some some time before the tinder would catch. At each stroke of the steel a shower of brilliant sparks lit up his countenance for an instant, and this momentary glance showed that its expression was not prepossessing by any means.

Ruby drew Minnie farther into the recess which concealed them, and awaited the result with some anxiety, for he felt that the amount of knowledge with which he had become possessed thus unintentionally, small though it was, was sufficient to justify the smugglers in regarding him as a dangerous enemy.

He had scarcely drawn himself quite within the shadow of the recess, when Swankie succeeded in kindling a torch, which filled the cavern with a lurid light, and revealed its various forms, rendering it, if possible, more mysterious and unearthly than ever.

"Here, Spink," cried Swankie, who was gradually getting into better humour, "haud the light, and gie me the spade."

"Ye better put them behind the rock, far in," suggested Spink.

The other seemed to entertain this idea for a moment, for he raised the torch above his head, and, advancing into the cave, carefully examined the rocks at the inner end.

Step by step he drew near to the place where Ruby and Minnie were concealed, muttering to himself, as he looked at each spot that might possibly suit his purpose, "Na, na, the waves wad wash the kegs oot o' that if it cam' on to blaw."

He made another step forward, and the light fell almost on the head of Ruby, who felt Minnie's arm tremble. He clenched his hands with that feeling of resolve that comes over a man when he has made up his mind to fight.

Just then an exclamation of surprise escaped from his comrade.

"Losh! man, what have we here?" he cried, picking up a small object that glittered in the light.

Minnie's heart sank, for she could see that the thing was a small brooch which she was in the habit of wearing in her neckerchief, and which must have been detached when Ruby carried her into the cave.

She felt assured that this would lead to their discovery; but it had quite the opposite effect, for it caused Swankie to turn round and examine the trinket with much curiosity.

A long discussion as to how it could have come there immediately ensued between the smugglers, in the midst of which a wavelet washed against Swankie's feet, reminding him that the tide was rising, and that he had no time to lose.

"There's nae place behint the rocks," said he quickly, putting the brooch in his pocket, "so we'll just hide the kegs amang the stanes. Lucky for us that we got the rest o' the cargo run ashore at Auchmithie. This'll lie snugly here, and we'll pull past the leftenant, who thinks we havena seen him, with oor heeds up and oor tongues in oor cheeks."

They both chuckled heartily at the idea of disappointing the preventive officer, and while one held the torch the other dug a hole in the beach deep enough to contain the two kegs.

"In ye go, my beauties," said Swankie, covering them up. "Mony's the time I've buried ye."

"Ay, an' mony's the time ye've helped at their resurrection," added Spink, with a laugh.

"Noo, we'll away an' have a look at the kegs in the Forbidden Cave," said Swankie, "see that they're a' richt, an' then have our game wi' the land-sharks."

Next moment the torch was dashed against the stones and extinguished, and the two men, leaping into their boat, rowed away. As they passed through the outer cavern, Ruby heard them arrange to go back to Auchmithie. Their voices were too indistinct to enable him to ascertain their object in doing so, but he knew enough of the smugglers to enable him to guess that it was for the purpose of warning some of their friends of the presence of the preventive boat, which their words proved that they had seen.

"Now, Minnie," said he, starting up as soon as the boat had disappeared, "this is what I call good luck, for not only shall we be able to return with something to the boat, but we shall be able to intercept big Swankie and his comrade, and offer them a glass of their own gin!"

"Yes, and I shall be able to boast of having had quite a little adventure," said Minnie, who, now that her anxiety was ever, began to feel elated.

They did not waste time in conversation, however, for the digging up of two kegs from a gravelly beach with fingers instead of a spade was not a quick or easy thing to do; so Ruby found as he went down on his knees in that dark place and began the work.

"Can I help you?" asked his fair companion after a time.

"Help me! What? Chafe and tear your little hands with work that all but skins mine? Nay, truly. But here comes one, and the other will soon follow. Yo, heave, *Ho*!"

With the well-known nautical shout Ruby put forth an herculean effort, and tore the kegs out of the earth. After a short pause he carried Minnie out of the cavern, and led her to the field above by the same path by which they had descended.

Then he returned for the kegs of gin. They were very heavy, but not too heavy for the strength of the young giant, who was soon hastening with rapid strides towards the bay, where they had left their friends. He bore a keg under each arm, and Minnie tripped lightly by his side,—and laughingly, too, for she enjoyed the thought of the discomfiture that was in store for the smugglers.

Chapter Twenty

The Smugglers are "Treated" to Gin and Astonishment

They found the lieutenant and Captain Ogilvy stretched on the grass, smoking their pipes together. The daylight had almost deepened into night, and a few stars were beginning to twinkle in the sky.

"Hey! what have we here—smugglers?" cried the captain, springing up rather quickly, as Ruby came unexpectedly on them.

"Just so, uncle," said Minnie, with a laugh. "We have here some gin, smuggled all the way from Holland, and have come to ask your opinion of it."

"Why, Ruby, how came you by this?" enquired Lindsay in amazement, as he examined the kegs with critical care.

"Suppose I should say that I have been taken into confidence by the smugglers and then betrayed them."

"I should reply that the one idea was improbable, and the other impossible," returned the lieutenant.

"Well, I have at all events found out their secrets, and now I reveal them."

In a few words Ruby acquainted his friends with all that has just been narrated.

The moment he had finished, the lieutenant ordered his men to launch the boat. The kegs were put into the stern-sheets, the party embarked, and, pushing off, they rowed gently out of the bay, and crept slowly along the shore, under the deep shadow of the cliffs.

"How dark it is getting!" said Minnie, after they had rowed for some time in silence.

"The moon will soon be up," said the lieutenant. "Meanwhile I'll cast a little light on the subject by having a pipe. Will you join me, captain?"

This was a temptation which the captain never resisted; indeed, he did not regard it as a temptation at all, and would have smiled at the idea of resistance.

"Minnie, lass," said he, as he complacently filled the blackened bowl, and calmly stuffed down the glowing tobacco with the end of that marvellously callous little fingers, "it's a wonderful thing that baccy. I don't know what man would do without it."

"Quite as well as woman does, I should think," replied Minnie.

"I'm not so sure of that, lass. It's more nat'ral for man to smoke than for woman. Ye see, woman, lovely woman, should be 'all my fancy painted her, both lovely and divine.' It would never do to have baccy perfumes hangin' about her rosy lips."

"But, uncle, why should man have the disagreeable perfumes you speak of hanging about *his* lips?"

"I don't know, lass. It's all a matter o' feeling. ''Twere vain to tell thee all I feel, how much my heart would wish to say;' but of this I'm certain sure, that I'd never git along without my pipe. It's like compass, helm, and ballast all in one. Is that the moon, leftenant?"

The captain pointed to a faint gleam of light on the horizon, which he knew well enough to be the moon; but he wished to change the subject.

"Ay is it, and there comes a boat. Steady, men! lay on your oars a bit."

This was said earnestly. In one instant all were silent, and the boat lay as motionless as the shadows of the cliffs among which it was involved.

Presently the sound of oars was heard. Almost at the same moment, the upper edge of the moon rose above the horizon, and covered the sea with rippling silver. Ere long a boat shot into this stream of light, and rowed swiftly in the direction of Arbroath.

"There are only two men in it," whispered the lieutenant.

"Ay, these are my good friends Swankie and Spink, who know a deal more about other improper callings besides smuggling, if I did not greatly mistake their words," cried Ruby.

"Give way, lads!" cried the lieutenant.

The boat sprang at the word from her position under the cliffs, and was soon out upon the sea in full chase of the smugglers, who bent to their oars more lustily, evidently intending to trust to their speed.

"Strange," said the lieutenant, as the distance between the two began sensibly to decrease, "if these be smugglers, with an empty boat, as you lead me to suppose they are, they would only be too glad to stop and let us see that they had nothing aboard that we could touch. It leads me to think that you are mistaken, Ruby Brand, and that these are not your friends."

"Nay, the same fact convinces me that they are the very men we seek; for they said they meant to have some game with you, and what more amusing than to give you a long, hard chase for nothing?"

"True; you are right. Well, we will turn the tables on them. Take the helm for a minute, while I tap one of the kegs."

The tapping was soon accomplished, and a quantity of the spirit was drawn off into the captain's pocket-flask.

"Taste it, captain, and let's have your opinion." Captain Ogilvy complied. He put the flask to his lips, and, on removing it, smacked them, and looked at the party with that extremely grave, almost solemn expression, which is usually assumed by a man when strong liquid is being put to the delicate test of his palate.

"Oh!" exclaimed the captain, opening his eyes very wide indeed.

What "oh" meant, was rather doubtful at first; but when the captain put the flask again to his lips, and took another pull, a good deal longer than the first, much, if not all of the doubt was removed.

"Prime! nectar!" he murmured, in a species of subdued ecstasy, at the end of the second draught.

"Evidently the right stuff," said Lindsay, laughing.

"Liquid   streams—celestial   nectar,
   Darted through the ambient sky,—"

Said the captain; "liquid, ay, liquid is the word."

He was about to test the liquid again:—

"Stop! stop! fair play, captain; it's my turn now," cried the lieutenant, snatching the flask from his friend's grasp, and applying it to his own lips.

Both the lieutenant and Ruby pronounced the gin perfect, and as Minnie positively refused either to taste or to pronounce judgment, the flask was returned to its owner's pocket.

They were now close on the smugglers, whom they hailed, and commanded to lay on their oars.

The order was at once obeyed, and the boats were speedily rubbing sides together.

"I should like to examine your boat, friends," said the lieutenant as he stepped across the gunwales.

"Oh! sir, I'm thankfu' to find you're not smugglers," said Swankie, with an assumed air of mingled respect and alarm.

"If we'd only know'd ye was preventives we'd ha' backed oars at once. There's nothin' here; ye may seek as long's ye please."

The hypocritical rascal winked slyly to his comrade as he said this. Meanwhile Lindsay and one of the men examined the contents of the boat, and, finding nothing contraband, the former said—

"So, you're honest men, I find. Fishermen, doubtless?"

"Ay, some o' yer crew ken us brawly," said Davy Spink with a grin.

"Well, I won't detain you," rejoined the lieutenant; "it's quite a pleasure to chase honest men on the high seas in these times of war and smuggling. But it's too bad to have given you such a fright, lads, for nothing. What say you to a glass of gin?"

Big Swankie and his comrade glanced at each other in surprise. They evidently thought this an unaccountably polite Government officer, and were puzzled. However, they could do no less than accept such a generous offer.

"Thank'ee, sir," said Big Swankie, spitting out his quid and significantly wiping his mouth. "I hae nae objection. Doubtless it'll be the best that the like o' you carries in yer bottle."

"The best, certainly," said the lieutenant, as he poured out a bumper, and handed it to the smuggler. "It was smuggled, of course, and you see His Majesty is kind enough to give his servants a little of what they rescue from the rascals, to drink his health."

"Weel, I drink to the King," said Swankie, "an' confusion to all his enemies, 'specially to smugglers."

He tossed off the gin with infinite gusto, and handed back the cup with a smack of the lips and a look that plainly said, "More, if you please!"

But the hint was not taken. Another bumper was filled and handed to Davy Spink, who had been eyeing the crew of the boat with great suspicion. He accepted the cup, nodded curtly, and said—

"Here's t'ye, gentlemen, no forgettin' the fair leddy in the stern-sheets."

While he was drinking the gin the lieutenant turned to his men—

"Get out the keg, lads, from which that came, and refill the flask. Hold it well up in the moonlight, and see that ye don't spill a single drop, as you value your lives. Hey! my man, what ails you? Does the gin disagree with your stomach, or have you never seen a smuggled keg of spirits before, that you stare at it as if it were a keg of ghosts!"

The latter part of this speech was addressed to Swankie, who no sooner beheld the keg than his eyes opened up until they resembled two great oysters. His mouth slowly followed suit. Davy Spink's attention having been attracted, he became subject to similar alterations of visage.

"Hallo!" cried the captain, while the whole crew burst into a laugh, "you must have given them poison. Have you a stomach-pump, doctor?" he said, turning hastily to Ruby.

"No, nothing but a penknife and a tobacco-stopper. If they're of any use to you—"

He was interrupted by a loud laugh from Big Swankie, who quickly recovered his presence of mind, and declared that he had never tasted such capital stuff in his life.

"Have ye much o't, sir?"

"O yes, a good deal. I have *two* kegs of it" (the lieutenant grinned very hard at this point), "and we expect to get a little more to-night."

"Ha!" exclaimed Davy Spink, "there's no doot plenty o't in the coves hereaway, for they're an awfu' smugglin' set. Whan did ye find the twa kegs, noo, if I may ask?"

"Oh, certainly. I got them not more than an hour ago."

The smugglers glanced at each other and were struck dumb; but they were now too much on their guard to let any further evidence of surprise escape them.

"Weel, I wush ye success, sirs," said Swankie, sitting down to his oar. "It's likely ye'll come across mair if ye try Dickmont's Den. There's usually somethin' hidden thereaboots."

"Thank you, friend, for the hint," said the lieutenant, as he took his place at the tiller-ropes, "but I shall have a look at the Gaylet Cove, I think, this evening."

"What! the Gaylet Cove?" cried Spink. "Ye might as weel look for kegs at the bottom o' the deep sea."

"Perhaps so; nevertheless, I have taken a fancy to go there. If I find nothing, I will take a look into the *Forbidden Cave*."

"The Forbidden Cave!" almost howled Swankie. "Wha iver heard o' smugglers hidin' onything there? The air in't wad pushen a rotten."

"Perhaps it would, yet I mean to try."

"Weel-a-weel, ye may try, but ye might as weel seek for kegs o' gin on the Bell Rock."

"Ha! it's not the first time that strange things have been found on the Bell Rock," said Ruby suddenly. "I have heard of *jewels*, even, being discovered there."

"Give way, men; shove off," cried the lieutenant. "A pleasant pull to you, lads. Good night."

The two boats parted, and while the lieutenant and his friends made for the shore, the smugglers rowed towards Arbroath in a state of mingled amazement and despair at what they had heard and seen.

"It was Ruby Brand that spoke last, Davy."

"Ay; he was i' the shadow o' Captain Ogilvy and I couldna see his face, but I thought it like his voice when he first spoke."

"Hoo *can* he hae come to ken aboot the jewels?"

"That's mair than I can tell."

"I'll bury them," said Swankie, "an' then it'll puzzle onybody to tell whaur they are."

"Ye'll please yoursell," said Spink.

Swankie was too angry to make any reply, or to enter into further conversation with his comrade about the kegs of gin, so they continued their way in silence.

Meanwhile, as Lieutenant Lindsay and his men had a night of work before them, the captain suggested that Minnie, Ruby, and himself should be landed within a mile of the town, and left to find their way thither on foot. This was agreed to; and while the one party walked home by the romantic pathway at the top of the cliffs, the other rowed away to explore the dark recesses of the Forbidden Cave.

Chapter Twenty One

The Bell Rock Again—A Dreary Night in a Strange Habitation

During that winter Ruby Brand wrought diligently in the workyard at the lighthouse materials, and, by living economically, began to save a small sum of money, which he laid carefully by with a view to his marriage with Minnie Gray.

Being an impulsive man, Ruby would have married Minnie, then and there, without looking too earnestly to the future. But his mother had advised him to wait till he should have laid by a little for a "rainy day." The captain had recommended patience, tobacco, and philosophy, and had enforced his recommendations with sundry apt quotations from dead and living novelists, dramatists, and poets. Minnie herself, poor girl, felt that she ought not to run counter to the wishes of her best and dearest friends, so she too advised delay for a "little time"; and Ruby was fain to content himself with bewailing his hard lot internally, and knocking Jamie Dove's bellows, anvils, and sledge-hammers about in a way that induced that son of Vulcan to believe his assistant had gone mad!

As for big Swankie, he hid his ill-gotten gains under the floor of his tumble-down cottage, and went about his evil courses as usual in company with his comrade Davy Spink, who continued to fight and make it up with him as of yore.

It must not be supposed that Ruby forgot the conversation he had overheard in the Gaylet Cove. He and Minnie and his uncle had frequent discussions in regard to it, but to little purpose; for although Swankie and Spink had discovered old Mr Brand's body on the Bell Rock, it did not follow that any jewels or money they had found there were necessarily his. Still Ruby could not divest his mind of the feeling that there was some connexion between the two, and he was convinced, from what had fallen from Davy Spink about "silver teapots and things", that Swankie was the man of whose bad deeds he himself had been suspected.

As there seemed no possibility of bringing the matter home to him, however, he resolved to dismiss the whole affair from his mind in the meantime.

Things were very much in this state when, in the spring, the operations at the Bell Rock were resumed.

Jamie Dove, Ruby, Robert Selkirk, and several of the principal workmen, accompanied the engineers on their first visit to the rock, and they sailed towards the scene of their former labours with deep and peculiar interest, such as one might feel on renewing acquaintance with an old friend who had passed through many hard and trying struggles since the last time of meeting.

The storms of winter had raged round the Bell Rock as usual—as they had done, in fact, since the world began; but that winter the handiwork of man had also been exposed to the fury of the elements there. It was known that the beacon had survived the storms, for it could be seen by telescope from the shore in clear weather—like a little speck on the seaward horizon. Now they were about to revisit the old haunt, and have a close inspection of the damage that it was supposed must certainly have been done.

To the credit of the able engineer who planned and carried out the whole works, the beacon was found to have resisted winds and waves successfully.

It was on a bitterly cold morning about the end of March that the first visit of the season was paid to the Bell Rock. Mr Stevenson and his party of engineers and artificers sailed in the lighthouse yacht; and, on coming within a proper distance of the rock, two boats were lowered and pushed off. The sea ran with such force upon the rock that it seemed doubtful whether a landing could be effected. About half-past eight, when the rock was fairly above water, several attempts were made to land, but the breach of the sea was still so great that they were driven back.

On the eastern side the sea separated into two distinct waves, which came with a sweep round the western side, where they met, and rose in a burst of spray to a considerable height. Watching, however, for what the sailors termed a *smooth*, and catching a favourable opportunity, they rowed between the two seas dexterously, and made a successful landing at the western creek.

The sturdy beacon was then closely examined. It had been painted white at the end of the previous season, but the lower parts of the posts were found to have become green—the sea having clothed them with a soft garment of weed. The sea-birds had evidently imagined that it was put up expressly for their benefit; for a number of cormorants and large herring-gulls had taken up their quarters on it—finding it, no doubt, conveniently near to their fishing-grounds.

A critical inspection of all its parts showed that everything about it was in a most satisfactory state. There was not the slightest indication of working or shifting in the great iron stanchions with which the beams were fixed, nor of any of the joints or places of connexion; and, excepting some of the bracing-chains which had been loosened, everything wars found in the same entire state in which it had been left the previous season.

Only those who know what that beacon had been subjected to can form a correct estimate of the importance of this discovery, and the amount of satisfaction it afforded to those most interested in the works at the Bell Rock. To say that the party congratulated themselves would be far short of the reality. They hailed the event with cheers, and their looks seemed to indicate that some piece of immense and unexpected good fortune had befallen each individual.

From that moment Mr Stevenson saw the practicability and propriety of fitting up the beacon, not only as a place of refuge in case of accidents to the boats in landing, but as a residence for the men during the working months.

From that moment, too, poor Jamie Dove began to see the dawn of happier days; for when the beacon should be fitted up as a residence he would bid farewell to the hated floating light, and take up his abode, as he expressed it, "on land."

"On land!" It is probable that this Jamie Dove was the first man, since the world began, who had entertained the till then absurdly preposterous notion that the fatal Bell Rock was "land," or that it could be made a place of even temporary residence.

A hundred years ago men would have laughed at the bare idea. Fifty years ago that idea was realised; for more than half a century that sunken reef has been, and still is, the safe and comfortable home of man!

Forgive, reader, our tendency to anticipate. Let us proceed with our inspection.

Having ascertained that the foundations of the beacon were all right, the engineers next ascended to the upper parts, where they found the cross-beams and their fixtures in an equally satisfactory condition.

On the top a strong chest had been fixed the preceding season, in which had been placed a quantity of sea-biscuits and several bottles of water, in case of accident to the boats, or in the event of shipwreck occurring on the rock. The biscuit, having been carefully placed in tin canisters, was found in good condition, but several of the water-bottles had burst, in consequence, it was supposed, of frost during the winter. Twelve of the bottles, however, remained entire, so that the Bell Rock may be said to have been transformed, even at that date, from a point of destruction into a place of comparative safety.

While the party were thus employed, the landing-master reminded them that the sea was running high, and that it would be necessary to set off while the rock afforded anything like shelter to the boats, which by that time had been made fast to the beacon and rode with much agitation, each requiring two men with boat-hooks to keep them from striking each other, or ranging up against the beacon. But under these circumstances the greatest confidence was felt by everyone, from the security afforded by that temporary erection; for, supposing that the wind had suddenly increased to a gale, and that it had been found inadvisable to go into the boats; or supposing they had drifted or sprung a leak from striking upon the rocks, in any of these possible, and not at all improbable, cases, they had now something to lay hold of, and, though occupying the dreary habitation of the gull and the cormorant, affording only bread and water, yet *life* would be preserved, and, under the circumstances, they would have been supported by the hope of being ultimately relieved.

Soon after this the works at the Bell Rock were resumed, with, if possible, greater vigour than before, and ere long the "house" was fixed to the top of the beacon, and the engineer and his men took up their abode there.

Think of this, reader. Six great wooden beams were fastened to a rock, over which the waves roared twice every day, and on the top of these a pleasant little marine residence was nailed, as one might nail a dovecot on the top of a pole!

This residence was ultimately fitted up in such a way as to become a comparatively comfortable and commodious abode. It contained four storeys. The first was the mortar-gallery, where the mortar for the lighthouse was mixed as required; it also supported the forge. The second was the cook-room. The third the apartment of the engineer and his assistants; and the fourth was the artificers' barrack-room. This house was of course built of wood, but it was firmly put together, for it had to pass through many a terrific ordeal.

In order to give some idea of the interior, we shall describe the cabin of Mr Stevenson. It measured four feet three inches in breadth on the floor, and though, from the oblique direction of the beams of the beacon, it widened towards the top, yet it did not admit of the full extension of the occupant's arms when he stood on the floor. Its length was little more than sufficient to admit of a cot-bed being suspended during the night. This cot was arranged so as to be triced up to the roof during the day, thus leaving free room for occasional visitors, and for comparatively free motion. A folding table was attached with hinges immediately under the small window of the apartment. The remainder of the space was fitted up with books, barometer, thermometer, portmanteau, and two or three camp-stools.

The walls were covered with green cloth, formed into panels with red tape, a substance which, by the way, might have had an *accidental* connexion with the Bell Rock Lighthouse, but which could not, by any possibility, have influenced it as a *principle*, otherwise that building would probably never have been built, or, if built, would certainly not have stood until the present day! The bed was festooned with yellow cotton stuff, and the diet being plain, the paraphernalia of the table was proportionally simple.

It would have been interesting to know the individual books required and used by the celebrated engineer in his singular abode, but his record leaves no detailed account of these. It does, however, contain a sentence in regard to one volume which we deem it just to his character to quote. He writes thus:—

"If, in speculating upon the abstract wants of man in such a state of exclusion, one were reduced to a single book, the Sacred Volume, whether considered for the striking diversity of its story, the morality of its doctrine, or the important truths of its gospel, would have proved by far the greatest treasure."

It may be easily imagined that in a place where the accommodation of the principal engineer was so limited, that of the men was not extensive. Accordingly, we find that the barrack-room contained beds for twenty-one men.

But the completion of the beacon house, as we have described it, was not accomplished in one season. At first it was only used as a smith's workshop, and then as a temporary residence in fine weather.

One of the first men who remained all night upon it was our friend Bremner. He became so tired of the floating light that he earnestly solicited, and obtained, permission to remain on the beacon.

At the time it was only in a partially sheltered state. The joiners had just completed the covering of the roof with a quantity of tarpaulin, which the seamen had laid over with successive coats of hot tar, and the sides of the erection had been painted with three coats of white lead. Between the timber framing of the habitable part, the interstices were stuffed with moss, but the green baize cloth with which it was afterwards lined had not been put on when Bremner took possession.

It was a splendid summer evening when the bold man made his request, and obtained permission to remain. None of the others would join him. When the boats pushed off and left him the solitary occupant of the rock, he felt a sensation of uneasiness, but, having formed his resolution, he stuck by it, and bade his comrades good night cheerfully.

"Good night, and good*bye*," cried Forsyth, as he took his seat at the oar.

"Farewell, dear," cried O'Connor, wiping his eyes with a *very* ragged pocket handkerchief.

"You won't forget me?" retorted Bremner.

"Never," replied Dumsby, with fervour.

"Av the beacon should be carried away, darlin'," cried O'Connor, "howld tight to the provision-chest, p'raps ye'll be washed ashore."

"I'll drink your health in water, Paddy," replied Bremner.

"Faix, I hope it won't be salt wather," retorted Ned.

They continued to shout good wishes, warnings, and advice to their comrade until out of hearing, and then waved adieu to him until he was lost to view.

We have said that Bremner was alone, yet he was not entirely so; he had a comrade with him, in the shape of his little black dog, to which reference has already been made. This creature was of that very thin and tight-skinned description of dog, that trembles at all times as if afflicted with chronic cold, summer and winter. Its thin tail was always between its extremely thin legs, as though it lived in a perpetual condition of wrong-doing, and were in constant dread of deserved punishment. Yet no dog ever belied its looks more than did this one, for it was a good dog, and a warm-hearted dog, and never did a wicked thing, and never was punished, so that its excessive humility and apparent fear and trembling were quite unaccountable. Like all dogs of its class it was passionately affectionate, and intensely grateful for the smallest favour. In fact, it seemed to be rather thankful than otherwise for a kick when it chanced to receive one, and a pat on the head, or a kind word made it all but jump out of its black skin for very joy.

Bremner called it "Pup." It had no other name, and didn't seem to wish for one. On the present occasion it was evidently much perplexed, and very unhappy, for it looked at the boat, and then wistfully into its master's face, as if to say, "This is awful; have you resolved that we shall perish together?"

"Now, Pup," said Bremner, when the boat disappeared in the shades of evening, "you and I are left alone on the Bell Rock!"

There was a touch of sad uncertainty in the wag of the tail with which Pup received this remark.

"But cheer up, Pup," cried Bremner with a sudden burst of animation that induced the creature to wriggle and dance on its hind legs for at least a minute, "you and I shall have a jolly night together on the beacon; so come along."

Like many a night that begins well, that particular night ended ill. Even while the man spoke, a swell began to rise, and, as the tide had by that time risen a few feet, an occasional billow swept over the rocks and almost washed the feet of Bremner as he made his way over the ledges. In five minutes the sea was rolling all round the foot of the beacon, and Bremner and his friend were safely ensconced on the mortar-gallery.

There was no storm that night, nevertheless there was one of those heavy ground swells that are of common occurrence in the German Ocean.

It is supposed that this swell is caused by distant westerly gales in the Atlantic, which force an undue quantity of water into the North Sea, and thus produce the apparent paradox of great rolling breakers in calm weather.

On this night there was no wind at all, but there was a higher swell than usual, so that each great billow passed over the rock with a roar that was rendered more than usually terrible, in consequence of the utter absence of all other sounds.

At first Bremner watched the rising tide, and as he sat up there in the dark he felt himself dreadfully forsaken and desolate, and began to comment on things in general to his dog, by way of inducing a more sociable and cheery state of mind.

"Pup, this is a lugubrious state o' things. Wot d'ye think o't?"

Pup did not say, but he expressed such violent joy at being noticed, that he nearly fell off the platform of the mortar-gallery in one of his extravagant gyrations.

"That won't do, Pup," said Bremner, shaking his head at the creature, whose countenance expressed deep contrition. "Don't go on like that, else you'll fall into the sea and be drownded, and then I shall be left alone. What a dark night it is, to be sure! I doubt if it was wise of me to stop here. Suppose the beacon were to be washed away?"

Bremner paused, and Pup wagged his tail interrogatively, as though to say, "What then?"

"Ah! it's of no use supposin'," continued the man slowly. "The beacon has stood it out all winter, and it ain't likely it's goin' to be washed away to-night. But suppose I was to be took bad?"

Again the dog seemed to demand, "What then?"

"Well, that's not very likely either, for I never was took bad in my life since I took the measles, and that's more than twenty years ago. Come, Pup, don't let us look at the black side o' things, let us try to be cheerful, my dog. Hallo!"

The exclamation was caused by the appearance of a green billow, which in the uncertain light seemed to advance in a threatening attitude towards the beacon as if to overwhelm it, but it fell at some distance, and only rolled in a churning sea of milky foam among the posts, and sprang up and licked the beams, as a serpent might do before swallowing them.

"Come, it was the light deceived me. If I go for to start at every wave like that I'll have a poor night of it, for the tide has a long way to rise yet. Let's go and have a bit supper, lad."

Bremner rose from the anvil, on which he had seated himself, and went up the ladder into the cook-house above. Here all was pitch dark, owing to the place being enclosed all round, which the mortar-gallery was not, but a light was soon struck, a lamp trimmed, and the fire in the stove kindled.

Bremner now busied himself in silently preparing a cup of tea, which, with a quantity of sea-biscuit, a little cold salt pork, and a hunk of stale bread, constituted his supper. Pup watched his every movement with an expression of earnest solicitude, combined with goodwill, in his sharp intelligent eyes.

When supper was ready Pup had his share, then, feeling that the duties of the day were now satisfactorily accomplished, he coiled himself up at his master's feet, and went to sleep. His master rolled himself up in a rug, and lying down before the fire, also tried to sleep, but without success for a long time.

As he lay there counting the number of seconds of awful silence that elapsed between the fall of each successive billow, and listening to the crash and the roar as wave after wave rushed underneath him, and caused his habitation to tremble, he could not avoid feeling alarmed in some degree. Do what he would, the thought of the wrecks that had taken place there, the shrieks that must have often rung above these rocks, and the dead and mangled bodies that must have lain among them, *would* obtrude upon him and banish sleep from his eyes.

At last he became somewhat accustomed to the rush of waters and the tremulous motion of the beacon. His frame, too, exhausted by a day of hard toil, refused to support itself, and he sank into slumber. But it was not unbroken. A falling cinder from the sinking fire would awaken him with a start; a larger wave than usual would cause him to spring up and look round in alarm; or a shrieking sea-bird, as it swooped past, would induce a dream, in which the cries of drowning men arose, causing him to awake with a cry that set Pup barking furiously.

Frequently during that night, after some such dream, Bremner would get up and descend to the mortar-gallery to see that all was right there. He found the waves always hissing below, but the starry sky was calm and peaceful above, so he returned to his couch comforted a little, and fell again into a troubled sleep, to be again awakened by frightful dreams of dreadful sights, and scenes of death and danger on the sea.

Thus the hours wore slowly away. As the tide fell the noise of waves retired a little from the beacon, and the wearied man and dog sank gradually at last into deep, untroubled slumber.

So deep was it, that they did not hear the increasing noise of the gulls as they wheeled round the beacon after having breakfasted near it; so deep, that they did not feel the sun as it streamed through an opening in the woodwork and glared on their respective faces; so deep, that they were ignorant of the arrival of the boats with the workmen, and were dead to the shouts of their companions, until one of them, Jamie Dove, put his head up the hatchway and uttered one of his loudest roars, close to their ears.

Then indeed Bremner rose up and looked bewildered, and Pup, starting up, barked as furiously as if its own little black body had miraculously become the concentrated essence of all the other noisy dogs in the wide world rolled into one!

Chapter Twenty Two

Life in the Beacon—Story of the Eddystone Lighthouse

Some time after this a number of the men took up their permanent abode in the beacon house, and the work was carried on by night as well as by day, when the state of the tide and the weather permitted.

Immense numbers of fish called poddlies were discovered to be swimming about at high water. So numerous were they, that the rock was sometimes hidden by the shoals of them. Fishing for these thenceforth became a pastime among the men, who not only supplied their own table with fresh fish, but at times sent presents of them to their friends in the vessels.

All the men who dwelt on the beacon were volunteers, for Mr Stevenson felt that it would be cruel to compel men to live at such a post of danger. Those who chose, therefore, remained in the lightship or the tender, and those who preferred it went to the beacon. It is scarcely necessary to add, that among the latter were found all the "sea-sick men!"

These bold artificers were not long of having their courage tested. Soon after their removal to the beacon they experienced some very rough weather, which shook the posts violently, and caused them to twist in a most unpleasant way.

But it was not until some time after that a storm arose, which caused the stoutest-hearted of them all to quail more than once.

It began on the night of as fine a day as they had had the whole season.

In order that the reader may form a just conception of what we are about to describe, it may not be amiss to note the state of things at the rock, and the employment of the men at the time.

A second forge had been put up on the higher platform of the beacon, but the night before that of which we write, the lower platform had been burst up by a wave, and the mortar and forge thereon, with all the implements, were cast down. The damaged forge was therefore set up for the time on its old site, near the foundation-pit of the lighthouse, while the carpenters were busy repairing the mortar-gallery.

The smiths were as usual busy sharpening picks and irons, and making bats and stanchions, and other iron work connected with the building operations. The landing-master's crew were occupied in assisting the millwrights to lay the railways to hand, and joiners were kept almost constantly employed in fitting picks to their handles, which latter were very frequently broken.

Nearly all the miscellaneous work was done by seamen. There was no such character on the Bell Rock as the common labourer. The sailors cheerfully undertook the work usually performed by such men, and they did it admirably.

In consequence of the men being able to remain on the beacon, the work went on literally "by double tides"; and at night the rock was often ablaze with torches, while the artificers wrought until the waves drove them away.

On the night in question there was a low spring-tide, so that a night-tide's work of five hours was secured. This was one of the longest spells they had had since the beginning of the operations.

The stars shone brightly in a very dark sky. Not a breath of air was felt. Even the smoke of the forge fire rose perpendicularly a short way, until an imperceptible zephyr wafted it gently to the west. Yet there was a heavy swell rolling in from the eastward, which caused enormous waves to thunder on Ralph the Rover's Ledge, as if they would drive down the solid rock.

Mingled with this solemn, intermittent roar of the sea was the continuous clink of picks, chisels, and hammers, and the loud clang of the two forges; that on the beacon being distinctly different from the other, owing to the wooden erection on which it stood rendering it deep and thunderous. Torches and forge fires cast a glare over all, rendering the foam pale green and the rocks deep red. Some of the active figures at work stood out black and sharp against the light, while others shone in its blaze like red-hot fiends. Above all sounded an occasional cry from the sea-gulls, as they swooped down into the magic circle of light, and then soared away shrieking into darkness.

"Hard work's not easy," observed James Dove, pausing in the midst of his labours to wipe his brow.

"True for ye; but as we've got to arn our brid be the sweat of our brows, we're in the fair way to fortin," said Ned O'Connor, blowing away energetically with the big bellows.

Ned had been reappointed to this duty since the erection of the second forge, which was in Ruby's charge. It was our hero's hammer that created such a din up in the beacon, while Dove wrought down on the rock.

"We'll have a gale to-night," said the smith; "I know that by the feelin' of the air."

"Well, I can't boast o' much knowledge o' feelin'," said O'Connor; "but I believe you're right, for the fish towld me the news this mornin'."

This remark of Ned had reference to a well-ascertained fact, that, when a storm was coming, the fish invariably left the neighbourhood of the rock; doubtless in order to seek the security of depths which are not affected by winds or waves.

While Dove and his comrade commented on this subject, two of the other men had retired to the south-eastern end of the rock to take a look at the weather. These were Peter Logan, the foreman, whose position required him to have a care for the safety of the men as well as for the progress of the work, and our friend Bremner, who had just descended from the cooking-room, where he had been superintending the preparation of supper.

"It will be a stiff breeze, I fear, to-night," said Logan.

"D'ye think so I" said Bremner; "it seems to me so calm that I would think a storm a'most impossible. But the fish never tell lies."

"True. You got no fish to-day, I believe?" said Logan.

"Not a nibble," replied the other.

As he spoke, he was obliged to rise from a rock on which he had seated himself, because of a large wave, which, breaking on the outer reefs, sent the foam a little closer to his toes than was agreeable.

"That was a big one, but yonder is a bigger," cried Logan.

The wave to which he referred was indeed a majestic wall of water. It came on with such an awful appearance of power, that some of the men who perceived it could not repress a cry of astonishment.

In another moment it fell, and, bursting over the rocks with a terrific roar, extinguished the forge fire, and compelled the men to take refuge in the beacon.

Jamie Dove saved his bellows with difficulty. The other men, catching up their things as they best might, crowded up the ladder in a more or less draggled condition.

The beacon house was gained by means of one of the main beams, which had been converted into a stair, by the simple process of nailing small battens thereon, about a foot apart from each other. The men could only go up one at a time, but as they were active and accustomed to the work, were all speedily within their place of refuge. Soon afterwards the sea covered the rock, and the place where they had been at work was a mass of seething foam.

Still there was no wind; but dark clouds had begun to rise on the seaward horizon.

The sudden change in the appearance of the rock after the last torches were extinguished was very striking. For a few seconds there seemed to be no light at all. The darkness of a coal mine appeared to have settled down on the scene. But this soon passed away, as the men's eyes became accustomed to the change, and then the dark loom of the advancing billows, the pale light of the flashing foam, and occasional gleams of phosphorescence, and glimpses of black rocks in the midst of all, took the place of the warm, busy scene which the spot had presented a few minutes before.

"Supper, boys!" shouted Bremner.

Peter Bremner, we may remark in passing, was a particularly useful member of society. Besides being small and corpulent, he was a capital cook. He had acted during his busy life both as a groom and a house-servant; he had been a soldier, a sutler, a writer's clerk, and an apothecary—in which latter profession he had acquired the art of writing and suggesting recipes, and a taste for making collections in natural history. He was very partial to the use of the lancet, and quite a terrible adept at tooth-drawing. In short, Peter was the *factotum* of the beacon house, where, in addition to his other offices, he filled those of barber and steward to the admiration of all.

But Bremner came out in quite a new and valuable light after he went to reside in the beacon—namely, as a storyteller. During the long periods of inaction that ensued, when the men were imprisoned there by storms, he lightened many an hour that would have otherwise hung heavily on their hands, and he cheered the more timid among them by speaking lightly of the danger of their position.

On the signal for supper being given, there was a general rush down the ladders into the kitchen, where as comfortable a meal as one could wish for was smoking in pot and pan and platter.

As there were twenty-three to partake, it was impossible, of course, for all to sit down to table. They were obliged to stow themselves away on such articles of furniture as came most readily to hand, and eat as they best could. Hungry men find no difficulty in doing this. For some time the conversation was restricted to a word or two. Soon, however, as appetite began to be appeased, tongues began to loosen. The silence was first broken by a groan.

"Ochone!" exclaimed O'Connor, as well as a mouthful of pork and potatoes would allow him; "was it *you* that groaned like a dyin' pig?"

The question was put to Forsyth, who was holding his head between his hands, and swaying his body to and fro in agony.

"Hae ye the colic, freen'?" enquired John Watt, in a tone of sympathy.

"No—n—o," groaned Forsyth, "it's a—a—too-tooth!"

"Och! is that all?"

"Have it out, man, at once."

"Ram a red-hot skewer into it."

"No, no; let it alone, and it'll go away."

Such was the advice tendered, and much more of a similar nature, to the suffering man.

"There's nothink like 'ot water an' cold," said Joe Dumsby in the tones of an oracle. "Just fill your mouth with bilin' 'ot Water, an' dip your face in a basin o' cold, and it's sartain to cure."

"Or kill," suggested Jamie Dove.

"It's better now," said Forsyth, with a sigh of relief. "I scrunched a bit o' bone into it; that was all."

"There's nothing like the string and the red-hot poker," suggested Ruby Brand. "Tie the one end o' the string to a post and t'other end to the tooth, an' stick a red-hot poker to your nose. Away it comes at once."

"Hoot! nonsense," said Watt. "Ye might as weel tie a string to his lug an' dip him into the sea. Tak' my word for't, there's naethin' like pooin'."

"D'you mean pooh pooin'?" enquired Dumsby.

Watt's reply was interrupted by a loud gust of wind, which burst upon the beacon house at that moment and shook it violently.

Everyone started up, and all clustered round the door and windows to observe the appearance of things without. Every object was shrouded in thick darkness, but a flash of lightning revealed the approach of the storm which had been predicted, and which had already commenced to blow.

All tendency to jest instantly vanished, and for a time some of the men stood watching the scene outside, while others sat smoking their pipes by the fire in silence.

"What think ye of things?" enquired one of the men, as Ruby came up from the mortar-gallery, to which he had descended at the first gust of the storm.

"I don't know what to think," said he gravely. "It's clear enough that we shall have a stiffish gale. I think little of that with a tight craft below me and plenty of sea-room; but I don't know what to think of a *beacon* in a gale."

As he spoke another furious burst of wind shook the place, and a flash of vivid lightning was speedily followed by a crash of thunder, that caused some hearts there to beat faster and harder than usual.

"Pooh!" cried Bremner, as he proceeded coolly to wash up his dishes, "that's nothing, boys. Has not this old timber house weathered all the gales o' last winter, and d'ye think it's goin' to come down before a summer breeze? Why, there's a lighthouse in France, called the Tour de Cordouan, which rises light out o' the sea, an' I'm told it had some fearful gales to try its metal when it was buildin'. So don't go an' git narvous."

"Who's gittin' narvous?" exclaimed George Forsyth, at whom Bremner had looked when he made the last remark.

"Sure ye misjudge him," cried O'Connor. "It's only another twist o' the toothick. But it's all very well in you to spake lightly o' gales in that fashion. Wasn't the Eddystone Lighthouse cleared away one stormy night, with the engineer and all the men, an' was niver more heard on?"

"That's true," said Ruby. "Come, Bremner, I have heard you say that you had read all about that business. Let's hear the story; it will help to while away the time, for there's no chance of anyone gettin' to sleep with such a row outside."

"I wish it may be no worse than a row outside," said Forsyth in a doleful tone, as he shook his head and looked round on the party anxiously.

280

"Wot! another fit o' the toothick?" enquired O'Connor ironically.

"Don't try to put us in the dismals," said Jamie Dove, knocking the ashes out of his pipe, and refilling that solace of his leisure hours. "Let us hear about the Eddystone, Bremner; it'll cheer up our spirits a bit."

"Will it though?" said Bremner, with a look that John Watt described as "awesome", "Well, we shall see."

"You must know, boys—"

"'Ere, light your pipe, my 'earty," said Dumsby.

"Hold yer tongue, an' don't interrupt him," cried one of the men, flattening Dumsby's cap over his eyes.

"And don't drop yer *h*aitches," observed another, "'cause if ye do they'll fall into the sea an' be drownded, an' then ye'll have none left to put into their wrong places when ye wants 'em."

"Come, Bremner, go on."

"Well, then, boys," began Bremner, "you must know that it is more than a hundred years since the Eddystone Lighthouse was begun—in the year 1696, if I remember rightly—that would be just a hundred and thirteen years to this date. Up to that time these rocks were as

281

great a terror to sailors as the Bell Rock is now, or, rather, as it was last year, for now that this here comfortable beacon has been put up, it's no longer a terror to nobody—"

"Except Geordie Forsyth," interposed O'Connor.

"Silence," cried the men.

"Well," resumed Bremner, "as you all know, the Eddystone Rocks lie in the British Channel, fourteen miles from Plymouth and ten from the Ram Head, an' open to a most tremendious sea from the Bay o' Biscay and the Atlantic, as I knows well, for I've passed the place in a gale, close enough a'most to throw a biscuit on the rocks.

"They are named the Eddystone Rocks because of the whirls and eddies that the tides make among them; but for the matter of that, the Bell Rock might be so named on the same ground. Howsever, it's six o' one an' half a dozen o' t'other. Only there's this difference, that the highest point o' the Eddystone is barely covered at high water, while here the rock is twelve or fifteen feet below water at high tide.

"Well, it was settled by the Trinity Board in 1696, that a lighthouse should be put up, and a Mr Winstanley was engaged to do it. He was an uncommon clever an' ingenious man. He used to exhibit wonderful waterworks in

London; and in his house, down in Essex, he used to astonish his friends, and frighten them sometimes, with his queer contrivances. He had invented an easy chair which laid hold of anyone that sat down in it, and held him prisoner until Mr Winstanley set him free. He made a slipper also, and laid it on his bedroom floor, and when anyone put his foot into it he touched a spring that caused a ghost to rise from the hearth. He made a summer house, too, at the foot of his garden, on the edge of a canal, and if anyone entered into it and sat down, he very soon found himself adrift on the canal.

"Such a man was thought to be the best for such a difficult work as the building of a lighthouse on the Eddystone, so he was asked to undertake it, and agreed, and began it well. He finished it, too, in four years, his chief difficulty being the distance of the rock from land, and the danger of goin' backwards and forwards. The light was first shown on the 14th November, 1698. Before this the engineer had resolved to pass a night in the building, which he did with a party of men; but he was compelled to pass more than a night, for it came on to blow furiously, and they were kept prisoners for eleven days, drenched with spray all the time, and hard up for provisions.

"It was said the sprays rose a hundred feet above the lantern of this first Eddystone Lighthouse. Well, it stood till the year 1703, when repairs became necessary, and Mr Winstanley went down to Plymouth to superintend. It had been prophesied that this lighthouse would certainly be carried away. But dismal prophecies are always made about unusual things. If men were to mind prophecies there would be precious little done in this world. Howsever, the prophecies unfortunately came true. Winstanley's friends advised him not to go to stay in it, but he was so confident of the strength of his work that he said he only wished to have the chance o' bein' there in the greatest storm that ever blew, that he might see what effect it would have on the buildin'. Poor man! he had his wish. On the night of the 26th November a terrible storm arose, the worst that had been for many years, and swept the lighthouse entirely away. Not a vestige of it or the people on it was ever seen afterwards. Only a few bits of the iron fastenings were left fixed in the rocks."

"That was terrible," said Forsyth, whose uneasiness was evidently increasing with the rising storm.

"Ay, but the worst of it was," continued Bremner, "that, owing to the absence of the light, a large East Indiaman went on the rocks immediately after, and became a total wreck. This, however, set the Trinity House on putting up another, which was begun in 1706, and the light shown in 1708. This tower was ninety-two feet high, built partly of wood and partly of stone. It was a strong building, and stood for forty-nine years. Mayhap it would have been standin' to this day but for an accident, which you shall hear of before I have done. While this lighthouse was building, a French privateer carried off all the workmen prisoners to France, but they were set at liberty by the King, because their work was of such great use to all nations.

"The lighthouse, when finished, was put in charge of two keepers, with instructions to hoist a flag when anything was wanted from the shore. One of these men became suddenly ill, and died. Of course his comrade hoisted the signal, but the weather was so bad that it was found impossible to send a boat off for four weeks. The poor keeper was so afraid that people might suppose he had murdered his companion that he kept the corpse beside him all that time. What his feelin's could have been I don't know, but they must have been awful; for, besides the horror of such a position in such a lonesome place, the body decayed to an extent—"

"That'll do, lad; don't be too partickler," said Jamie Dove.

The others gave a sigh of relief at the interruption, and Bremner continued—

"There were always *three* keepers in the Eddystone after that. Well, it was in the year 1755, on the 2nd December, that one o' the keepers went to snuff the candles, for they only burned candles in the lighthouses at that time, and before that time great open grates with coal fires were the most common; but there were not many lights either of one kind or another in those days. On gettin' up to the lantern he found it was on fire. All the efforts they made failed to put it out, and it was soon burned down. Boats put off to them, but they only succeeded in saving the keepers; and of them, one went mad on reaching the shore, and ran off, and never was heard of again; and another, an old man, died from the effects of melted lead which had run down his throat from the roof of the burning lighthouse. They did not believe him when he said he had swallowed lead, but after he died it was found to be a fact.

"The tower became red-hot, and burned for five days before it was utterly destroyed. This was the end o' the second Eddystone. Its builder was a Mr John Rudyerd, a silk mercer of London.

"The third Eddystone, which has now stood for half a century as firm as the rock itself, and which bids fair to stand till the end of time, was begun in 1756 and completed in 1759. It was lighted by means of twenty-four candles. Of Mr Smeaton, the engineer who built it, those who knew him best said that 'he had never undertaken anything without completing it to the satisfaction of his employers.'

"D'ye know, lads," continued Bremner in a half-musing tone, "I've sometimes been led to couple this character of Smeaton with the text that he put round the top of the first room of the lighthouse—'Except the Lord build the house, they labour in vain that build it;' and also the words, 'Praise God,' which he cut in Latin on the last stone, the lintel of the lantern door. I think these words had somethin' to do with the success of the last Eddystone Lighthouse."

"I agree with you," said Robert Selkirk, with a nod of hearty approval; "and, moreover, I think the Bell Rock Lighthouse stands a good chance of equal success, for whether he means to carve texts on the stones or not I don't know, but I feel assured that *our* engineer is animated by the same spirit."

When Bremner's account of the Eddystone came to a close, most of the men had finished their third or fourth pipes, yet no one proposed going to rest.

The storm without raged so furiously that they felt a strong disinclination to separate. At last, however, Peter Logan rose, and said he would turn in for a little. Two or three of the others also rose, and were about to ascend to their barrack, when a heavy sea struck the building, causing it to quiver to its foundation.

Chapter Twenty Three

The Storm

"'Tis a fearful night," said Logan, pausing with his foot on the first step of the ladder. "Perhaps we had better sit up."

"What's the use?" said O'Connor, who was by nature reckless. "Av the beacon howlds on, we may as well slape as not; an' if it don't howld on, why, we'll be none the worse o' slapin' anyhow."

"*I* mean to sit up," said Forsyth, whose alarm was aggravated by another fit of violent toothache.

"So do I," exclaimed several of the men, as another wave dashed against the beacon, and a quantity of spray came pouring down from the rooms above.

This latter incident put an end to further conversation. While some sprang up the ladder to see where the leak had occurred, Ruby opened the door, which was on the lee-side of the building, and descended to the mortar-gallery to look after his tools, which lay there.

Here he was exposed to the full violence of the gale, for, as we have said, this first floor of the beacon was not protected by sides. There was sufficient light to enable him to see all round for a considerable distance. The sight was not calculated to comfort him.

The wind was whistling with what may be termed a vicious sound among the beams, to one of which Ruby was obliged to cling to prevent his being carried away. The sea was bursting, leaping, and curling wildly over the rocks, which were now quite covered, and as he looked down through the chinks in the boards of the floor, he could see the foam whirling round the beams of his trembling abode, and leaping up as if to seize him. As the tide rose higher and higher, the waves roared straight through below the floor, their curling backs rising terribly near to where he stood, and the sprays drenching him and the whole edifice completely.

As he gazed into the dark distance, where the turmoil of waters seemed to glimmer with ghostly light against a sky of the deepest black, he missed the light of the *Smeaton*, which, up to that time, had been moored as near to the lee of the rock as was consistent with safety. He fancied she must have gone down, and it was not till next day that the people on the beacon knew that she had parted her cables, and had been obliged to make for the Firth of Forth for shelter from the storm.

While he stood looking anxiously in the direction of the tender, a wave came so near to the platform that he almost involuntarily leaped up the ladder for safety. It broke before reaching the beacon, and the spray dashed right over it, carrying away several of the smith's tools.

"Ho, boys! lend a hand here, some of you," shouted Ruby, as he leaped down on the mortar-gallery again.

Jamie Dove, Bremner, O'Connor, and several others were at his side in a moment, and, in the midst of tremendous sprays, they toiled to secure the movable articles that lay there. These were passed up to the sheltered parts of the house; but not without great danger to all who stood on the exposed gallery below.

Presently two of the planks were torn up by a sea, and several bags of coal, a barrel of small-beer, and a few casks containing lime and sand, were all swept away. The men would certainly have shared the fate of these, had they not clung to the beams until the sea had passed.

As nothing remained after that which could be removed to the room above, they left the mortar-gallery to its fate, and returned to the kitchen, where they were met by the anxious glances and questions of their comrades.

The fire, meanwhile, could scarcely be got to burn, and the whole place was full of smoke, besides being wet with the sprays that burst over the roof, and found out all the crevices that had not been sufficiently stopped up. Attending to these leaks occupied most of the men at intervals during the night. Ruby and his friend the smith spent much of the time in the doorway, contemplating the gradual destruction of their workshop.

For some time the gale remained steady, and the anxiety of the men began to subside a little, as they became accustomed to the ugly twisting of the great beams, and found that no evil consequences followed.

In the midst of this confusion, poor Forsyth's anxiety of mind became as nothing compared with the agony of his toothache!

Bremner had already made several attempts to persuade the miserable man to have it drawn, but without success.

"I could do it quite easy," said he, "only let me get a hold of it, an' before you could wink I'd have it out."

"Well, you may try," cried Forsyth in desperation, with a face of ashy paleness.

It was an awful situation truly. In danger of his life; suffering the agonies of toothache, and with the prospect of torments unbearable from an inexpert hand; for Forsyth did not believe in Bremner's boasted powers.

"What'll you do it with?" he enquired meekly.

"Jamie Dove's small pincers. Here they are," said Bremner, moving about actively in his preparations, as if he enjoyed such work uncommonly.

By this time the men had assembled round the pair, and almost forgot the storm in the interest of the moment.

"Hold him, two of you," said Bremner, when his victim was seated submissively on a cask.

"You don't need to hold me," said Forsyth, in a gentle tone.

"Don't we!" said Bremner. "Here, Dove, Ned, grip his arms, and some of you stand by to catch his legs; but you needn't touch them unless he kicks. Ruby, you're a strong fellow; hold his head."

The men obeyed. At that moment Forsyth would have parted with his dearest hopes in life to have escaped, and the toothache, strange to say, left him entirely; but he was a plucky fellow at bottom; having agreed to have it done, he would not draw back.

Bremner introduced the pincers slowly, being anxious to get a good hold of the tooth. Forsyth uttered a groan in anticipation! Alarmed lest he should struggle too soon, Bremner made a sudden grasp and caught the tooth. A wrench followed; a yell was the result, and the pincers slipped!

This was fortunate, for he had caught the wrong tooth.

"Now be aisy, boy," said Ned O'Connor, whose sympathies were easily roused.

"Once more," said Bremner, as the unhappy man opened his mouth. "Be still, and it will be all the sooner over."

Again Bremner inserted the instrument, and fortunately caught the right tooth. He gave a terrible tug, that produced its corresponding howl; but the tooth held on. Again! again! again! and the beacon house resounded with the deadly yells of the unhappy man, who struggled violently, despite the strength of those who held him.

"Och! poor sowl!" ejaculated O'Connor.

Bremner threw all his strength into a final wrench, which tore away the pincers and left the tooth as firm as ever!

Forsyth leaped up and dashed his comrades right and left.

"That'll do," he roared, and darted up the ladder into the apartment above, through which he ascended to the barrack-room, and flung himself on his bed. At the same time a wave burst on the beacon with such force that every man there, except Forsyth, thought it would be carried away. The wave not only sprang up against the house, but the spray, scarcely less solid than the wave, went quite over it, and sent down showers of water on the men below.

Little cared Forsyth for that. He lay almost stunned on his couch, quite regardless of the storm. To his surprise, however, the toothache did not return. Nay, to make a long story short, it never again returned to that tooth till the end of his days!

The storm now blew its fiercest, and the men sat in silence in the kitchen listening to the turmoil, and to the thundering blows given by the sea to their wooden house. Suddenly the beacon received a shock so awful, and so thoroughly different from any that it had previously received, that the men sprang to their feet in consternation.

Ruby and the smith were looking out at the doorway at the time, and both instinctively grasped the woodwork near them, expecting every instant that the whole structure would be carried away; but it stood fast. They speculated a good deal on the force of the blow they had received, but no one hit on the true cause; and it was not until some days later that they discovered that a huge rock of fully a ton weight had been washed against the beams that night.

While they were gazing at the wild storm, a wave broke up the mortar-gallery altogether, and sent its remaining contents into the sea. All disappeared in a moment; nothing was left save the powerful beams to which the platform had been nailed.

There was a small boat attached to the beacon. It hung from two davits, on a level with the kitchen, about thirty feet above the rock. This had got filled by the sprays, and the weight of water proving too much for the tackling, it gave way at the bow shortly after the destruction of the mortar-gallery, and the boat hung suspended by the stern-tackle. Here it swung for a few minutes, and then was carried away by a sea. The same sea sent an eddy of foam round towards the door and drenched the kitchen, so that the door had to be shut, and as the fire had gone out, the men had to sit and await their fate by the light of a little oil-lamp.

They sat in silence, for the noise was now so great that it was difficult to hear voices, unless when they were raised to a high pitch.

Thus passed that terrible night; and the looks of the men, the solemn glances, the closed eyes, the silently moving lips, showed that their thoughts were busy reviewing bygone days and deeds; perchance in making good resolutions for the future—"if spared!"

Morning brought a change. The rush of the sea was indeed still tremendous, but the force of the gale was broken and the danger was past.

Chapter Twenty Four

A Chapter of Accidents

Time rolled on, and the lighthouse at length began to grow.

It did not rise slowly, as does an ordinary building. The courses of masonry having been formed and fitted on shore during the winter, had only to be removed from the workyard at Arbroath to the rock, where they were laid, mortared, wedged, and trenailed, as fast as they could be landed.

Thus, foot by foot it grew, and soon began to tower above its foundation.

From the foundation upwards for thirty feet it was built solid. From this point rose the spiral staircase leading to the rooms above. We cannot afford space to trace its erection step by step, neither is it desirable that we should do so. But it is proper to mention, that there were, as might be supposed, leading points in the process—eras, as it were, in the building operations.

The first of these, of course, was the laying of the foundation stone, which was done ceremoniously, with all the honours. The next point was the occasion when the tower showed itself for the first time above water at full tide. This was a great event. It was proof positive that the sea had been conquered; for many a time before that event happened had the sea done its best to level the whole erection with the rock.

Three cheers announced and celebrated the fact, and a "glass" all round stamped it on the memories of the men.

Another noteworthy point was the connexion—the marriage, if the simile may be allowed—of the tower and the beacon. This occurred when the former rose to a few feet above high-water mark, and was effected by means of a rope-bridge, which was dignified by the sailors with the name of "Jacob's ladder."

Heretofore the beacon and lighthouse had stood in close relation to each other. They were thenceforward united by a stronger tie; and it is worthy of record that their attachment lasted until the destruction of the beacon after the work was done. Jacob's ladder was fastened a little below the doorway of the beacon. Its other end rested on, and rose with, the wall of the tower. At first it sloped downward from beacon to tower; gradually it became horizontal; then it sloped upward. When this happened it was removed, and replaced by a regular wooden bridge, which extended from the doorway of the one structure to that of the other.

Along this way the men could pass to and fro at all tides, and during any time of the day or night.

This was a matter of great importance, as the men were no longer so dependent on tides as they had been, and could often work as long as their strength held out.

Although the work was regular, and, as some might imagine, rather monotonous, there were not wanting accidents and incidents to enliven the routine of daily duty. The landing of the boats in rough weather with stones, etcetera, was a never-failing source of anxiety, alarm, and occasionally amusement. Strangers sometimes visited the rock, too, but these visits were few and far between.

Accidents were much less frequent, however, than might have been expected in a work of the kind. It was quite an event, something to talk about for days afterwards, when poor John Bonnyman, one of the masons, lost a finger. The balance crane was the cause of this accident. We may remark, in passing, that this balance crane was a very peculiar and clever contrivance, which deserves a little notice.

It may not have occurred to readers who are unacquainted with mechanics that the raising of ponderous stones to a great height is not an easy matter. As long as the lighthouse was low, cranes were easily raised on the rock, but when it became too high for the cranes to reach their heads up to the top of the tower, what was to be done? Block-tackles could not be fastened to the skies! Scaffolding in such a situation would not have survived a moderate gale.

In these circumstances Mr Stevenson constructed a *balance* crane, which was fixed in the centre of the tower, and so arranged that it could be raised along with the rising works. This crane resembled a cross in form. At one arm was hung a movable weight, which could be run out to its extremity, or fixed at any part of it. The other arm was the one by means of which the stones were hoisted. When a stone had to be raised, its weight was ascertained, and the movable weight was so fixed as *exactly* to counterbalance it. By this simple contrivance all the cumbrous and troublesome machinery of long guys and bracing-chains extending from the crane to the rock below were avoided.

Well, Bonnyman was attending to the working of the crane, and directing the lowering of a stone into its place, when he inadvertently laid his left hand on a part of the machinery where it was brought into contact with the chain, which passed over his forefinger, and cut it so nearly off that it was left hanging by a mere shred of skin. The poor man was at once sent off in a fast rowing boat to Arbroath, where the finger was removed and properly dressed. (See note 1.)

A much more serious accident occurred at another time, however, which resulted in the death of one of the seamen belonging to the *Smeaton*.

It happened thus. The *Smeaton* had been sent from Arbroath with a cargo of stones one morning, and reached the rock about half-past six o'clock a.m. The mate and one of the men, James Scott, a youth of eighteen years of age, got into the sloop's boat to make fast the hawser to the floating buoy of her moorings.

The tides at the time were very strong, and the mooring-chain when sweeping the ground had caught hold of a rock or piece of wreck, by which the chain was so shortened, that when the tide flowed the buoy got almost under water, and little more than the ring appeared at the surface. When the mate and Scott were in the act of making the hawser fast to the ring, the chain got suddenly disentangled at the bottom, and the large buoy, measuring about seven feet in length by three in diameter in the middle, vaulted upwards with such force that it upset the boat, which instantly filled with water. The mate with great difficulty succeeded in getting hold of the gunwale, but Scott seemed to have been stunned by the buoy, for he lay motionless for a few minutes on the water, apparently unable to make any exertion to save himself, for he did not attempt to lay hold of the oars or thwarts which floated near him.

A boat was at once sent to the rescue, and the mate was picked up, but Scott sank before it reached the spot.

This poor lad was a great favourite in the service, and for a time his melancholy end cast a gloom over the little community at the Bell Rock. The circumstances of the case were also peculiarly distressing in reference to the boy's mother, for her husband had been for three years past confined in a French prison, and her son had been the chief support of the family. In order in some measure to make up to the poor woman for the loss of the monthly aliment regularly allowed her by her lost son, it was suggested that a younger brother of the deceased might be taken into the service. This appeared to be a rather delicate proposition, but it was left to the landing-master to arrange according to circumstances. Such was the resignation, and at the same time the spirit of the poor woman, that she readily accepted the proposal, and in a few days the younger Scott was actually afloat in the place of his brother. On this distressing case being represented to the Board, the Commissioners granted an annuity of 5 pounds to the lad's mother.

The painter who represents only the sunny side of nature portrays a one-sided, and therefore a false view of things, for, as everyone knows, nature is not all sunshine. So, if an author makes his pen-and-ink pictures represent only the amusing and picturesque view of things, he does injustice to his subject.

We have no pleasure, good reader, in saddening you by accounts of "fatal accidents", but we have sought to convey to you a correct impression of things, and scenes, and incidents at the building of the Bell Rock Lighthouse, as they actually were, and looked, and occurred. Although there was much, *very* much, of risk, exposure, danger, and trial connected with the erection of that building, there was, in the good providence of God, *very* little of severe accident or death. Yet that little must be told,—at least touched upon,—else will our picture remain incomplete as well as untrue.

Now, do not imagine, with a shudder, that these remarks are the prelude to something that will harrow up your feelings. Not so. They are merely the apology, if apology be needed, for the introduction of another "accident."

Well, then. One morning the artificers landed on the rock at a quarter-past six, and as all hands were required for a piece of special work that day, they breakfasted on the beacon, instead of returning to the tender, and spent the day on the rock.

The special work referred to was the raising of the crane from the eighth to the ninth course— an operation which required all the strength that could be mustered for working the guy-tackles. This, be it remarked, was before the

303

balance crane, already described, had been set up; and as the top of the crane stood at the time about thirty-five feet above the rock, it became much more unmanageable than heretofore.

At the proper hour all hands were called, and detailed to their several posts on the tower, and about the rock. In order to give additional purchase or power in tightening the tackle, one of the blocks of stone was suspended at the end of the movable beam of the crane, which, by adding greatly to the weight, tended to slacken the guys or supporting-ropes in the direction to which the beam with the stone was pointed, and thereby enabled the men more easily to brace them one after another.

While the beam was thus loaded, and in the act of swinging round from one guy to another, a great strain was suddenly brought upon the opposite tackle, with the end of which the men had very improperly neglected to take a turn round some stationary object, which would have given them the complete command of the tackle.

Owing to this simple omission, the crane, with the large stone at the end of the beam, got a preponderancy to one side, and, the tackle alluded to having rent, it fell upon the building with a terrible crash.

The men fled right and left to get out of its way; but one of them, Michael Wishart, a mason, stumbled over an uncut trenail and rolled on his back, and the ponderous crane fell upon him. Fortunately it fell so that his body lay between the great shaft and the movable beam, and thus he escaped with his life, but his feet were entangled with the wheel-work, and severely injured.

Wishart was a robust and spirited young fellow, and bore his sufferings with wonderful firmness while he was being removed. He was laid upon one of the narrow frame-beds of the beacon, and despatched in a boat to the tender. On seeing the boat approach with the poor man stretched on a bed covered with blankets, and his face overspread with that deadly pallor which is the usual consequence of excessive bleeding, the seamen's looks betrayed the presence of those well-known but indescribable sensations which one experiences when brought suddenly into contact with something horrible. Relief was at once experienced, however, when Wishart's voice was heard feebly accosting those who first stepped into the boat.

He was immediately sent on shore, where the best surgical advice was obtained, and he began to recover steadily, though slowly. Meanwhile, having been one of the principal masons, Robert Selkirk was appointed to his vacant post.

And now let us wind up this chapter of accidents with an account of the manner in which a party of strangers, to use a slang but expressive phrase, came to grief during a visit to the Bell Rock.

One morning, a trim little vessel was seen by the workmen making for the rock at low tide. From its build and size, Ruby at once judged it to be a pleasure yacht. Perchance some delicate shades in the seamanship, displayed in managing the little vessel, had influenced the sailor in forming his opinion. Be this as it may, the vessel brought up under the lee of the rock and cast anchor.

It turned out to be a party of gentlemen from Leith, who had run down the firth to see the works. The weather was fine, and the sea calm, but these yachters had yet to learn that fine weather and a calm sea do not necessarily imply easy or safe landing at the Bell Rock! They did not know that the *swell* which had succeeded a recent gale was heavier than it appeared to be at a distance; and, worst of all, they did not know, or they did not care to remember, that "there is a time for all things," and that the time for landing at the Bell Rock is limited.

Seeing that the place was covered with workmen, the strangers lowered their little boat and rowed towards them.

"They're mad," said Logan, who, with a group of the men, watched the motions of their would-be visitors.

"No," observed Joe Dumsby; "they are brave, but hignorant."

"*Faix*, they won't be ignorant long!" cried Ned O'Connor, as the little boat approached the rock, propelled by two active young rowers in Guernsey shirts, white trousers, and straw hats. "You're stout, lads, both of ye, an' purty good hands at the oar, *for gintlemen*; but av ye wos as strong as Samson it would puzzle ye to stem these breakers, so ye better go back."

The yachters did not hear the advice, and they would not have taken it if they had heard it. They rowed straight up towards the landing-place, and, so far, showed themselves expert selectors of the right channel; but they soon came within the influence of the seas, which burst on the rock and sent up jets of spray to leeward.

These jets had seemed very pretty and harmless when viewed from the deck of the yacht, but they were found on a nearer approach to be quite able, and, we might almost add, not unwilling, to toss up the boat like a ball, and throw it and its occupants head over heels into the air.

But the rowers, like most men of their class, were not easily cowed. They watched their

307

opportunity—allowed the waves to meet and rush on, and then pulled into the midst of the foam, in the hope of crossing to the shelter of the rock before the approach of the next wave.

Heedless of a warning cry from Ned O'Connor, whose anxiety began to make him very uneasy, the amateur sailors strained every nerve to pull through, while their companion who sat at the helm in the stern of the boat seemed to urge them on to redoubled exertions. Of course their efforts were in vain. The next billow caught the boat on its foaming crest, and raised it high in the air. For one moment the wave rose between the boat and the men on the rock, and hid her from view, causing Ned to exclaim, with a genuine groan, "Arrah! they's gone!"

But they were not; the boat's head had been carefully kept to the sea, and, although she had been swept back a considerable way, and nearly half-filled with water, she was still afloat.

The chief engineer now hailed the gentlemen, and advised them to return and remain on board their vessel until the state of the tide would permit him to send a proper boat for them.

In the meantime, however, a large boat from the floating light, pretty deeply laden with lime, cement, and sand, approached, when the strangers, with a view to avoid giving trouble, took their passage in her to the rock. The accession of three passengers to a boat, already in a lumbered state, put her completely out of trim, and, as it unluckily happened, the man who steered her on this occasion was not in the habit of attending the rock, and was not sufficiently aware of the run of the sea at the entrance of the eastern creek.

Instead, therefore, of keeping close to the small rock called *Johnny Gray*, he gave it, as Ruby expressed it, "a wide berth." A heavy sea struck the boat, drove her to leeward, and, the oars getting entangled among the rocks and seaweed, she became unmanageable. The next sea threw her on a ledge, and, instantly leaving her, she canted seaward upon her gunwale, throwing her crew and part of her cargo into the water.

All this was the work of a few seconds. The men had scarce time to realise their danger ere they found themselves down under the water; and when they rose gasping to the surface, it was to behold the next wave towering over them, ready to fall on their heads. When it fell it scattered crew, cargo, and boat in all directions.

Some clung to the gunwale of the boat, others to the seaweed, and some to the thwarts and oars which floated about, and which quickly carried them out of the creek to a considerable distance from the spot where the accident happened.

The instant the boat was overturned, Ruby darted towards one of the rock boats which lay near to the spot where the party of workmen who manned it had landed that morning. Wilson, the landing-master, was at his side in a moment.

"Shove off, lad, and jump in!" cried Wilson.

There was no need to shout for the crew of the boat. The men were already springing into her as she floated off. In a few minutes all the men in the water were rescued, with the exception of one of the strangers, named Strachan.

This gentleman had been swept out to a small insulated rock, where he clung to the seaweed with great resolution, although each returning sea laid him completely under water, and hid him for a second or two from the spectators on the rock. In this situation he remained for ten or twelve minutes; and those who know anything of the force of large waves will understand how severely his strength and courage must have been tried during that time.

When the boat reached the rock the most difficult part was still to perform, as it required the greatest nicety of management to guide her in a rolling sea, so as to prevent her from being carried forcibly against the man whom they sought to save.

"Take the steering-oar, Ruby; you are the best hand at this," said Wilson.

Ruby seized the oar, and, notwithstanding the breach of the seas and the narrowness of the passage, steered the boat close to the rock at the proper moment.

"Starboard, noo, stiddy!" shouted John Watt, who leant suddenly over the bow of the boat and seized poor Strachan by the hair. In another moment he was pulled inboard with the aid of Selkirk's stout arms, and the boat was backed out of danger.

"Now, a cheer, boys!" cried Ruby.

The men did not require urging to this. It burst from them with tremendous energy, and was echoed back by their comrades on the rock, in the midst of whose wild hurrah, Ned O'Connor's voice was distinctly heard to swell from a cheer into a yell of triumph!

The little rock on which this incident occurred was called *Strachan's Ledge*, and it is known by that name at the present day.

Note 1. It is right to state that this man afterwards obtained a light-keeper's situation from the Board of Commissioners of Northern Lights, who seem to have taken a kindly interest in all their servants, especially those of them who had suffered in the service.

Chapter Twenty Five

The Bell Rock in a Fog—Narrow Escape of the Smeaton

Change of scene is necessary to the healthful working of the human mind; at least, so it is said. Acting upon the assumption that the saying is true, we will do our best in this chapter for the human minds that condescend to peruse these pages, by leaping over a space of time, and by changing at least the character of the scene, if not the locality.

We present the Bell Rock under a new aspect, that of a dense fog and a dead calm.

This is by no means an unusual aspect of things at the Bell Rock, but as we have hitherto dwelt chiefly on storms it may be regarded as new to the reader.

It was a June morning. There had been few breezes and no storms for some weeks past, so that the usual swell of the ocean had gone down, and there were actually no breakers on the rock at low water, and no ruffling of the surface at all at high tide. The tide had, about two hours before, overflowed the rock and driven the men into the beacon house, where, having breakfasted, they were at the time enjoying themselves with pipes and small talk.

The lighthouse had grown considerably by this time. Its unfinished top was more than eighty feet above the foundation; but the fog was so dense that only the lower part of the column could be seen from the beacon, the summit being lost, as it were, in the clouds.

Nevertheless that summit, high though it was, did not yet project beyond the reach of the sea. A proof of this had been given in a very striking manner, some weeks before the period about which we now write, to our friend George Forsyth.

George was a studious man, and fond of reading the Bible critically. He was proof against laughter and ridicule, and was wont sometimes to urge the men into discussions. One of his favourite arguments was somewhat as follows—

"Boys," he was wont to say, "you laugh at me for readin' the Bible carefully. You would not laugh at a schoolboy for reading his books carefully, would you? Yet the learnin' of the way of salvation is of far more consequence to me than book learnin' is to a schoolboy. An astronomer is never laughed at for readin' his books o' geometry an' suchlike day an' night— even to the injury of his health—but what is an astronomer's business to *him* compared with the concerns of my soul to *me*? Ministers tell me there are certain things I must know and believe if I would be saved—such as the death and resurrection of our Saviour Jesus Christ; and they also point out that the Bible speaks of certain Christians, who did well in refusin' to receive the Gospel at the hands of the apostles, without first enquirin' into these things, to see if they were true. Now, lads, *if* these things that so many millions believe in, and that *you* all profess to believe in, are lies, then you may well laugh at me for enquirin' into them; but if they be true, why, I think the devils themselves must be laughing at *you* for *not* enquirin' into them!"

Of course, Forsyth found among such a number of intelligent men, some who could argue with him, as well as some who could laugh at him. He also found one or two who sympathised openly, while there were a few who agreed in their hearts, although they did not speak.

Well, it was this tendency to study on the part of Forsyth that led him to cross the wooden bridge between the beacon and the lighthouse during his leisure hours, and sit reading at the top of the spiral stair, near one of the windows of the lowest room.

Forsyth was sitting at his usual window one afternoon at the end of a storm. It was a comfortless place, for neither sashes nor glass had at that time been put in, and the wind howled up and down the shaft dreadfully. The man was robust, however, and did not mind that.

The height of the building was at that time fully eighty feet. While he was reading there a tremendous breaker struck the lighthouse with such force that it trembled distinctly. Forsyth started up, for he had never felt this before, and fancied the structure was about to fall. For a moment or two he remained paralysed, for he heard the most terrible and inexplicable sounds going on overhead. In fact, the wave that shook the building had sent a huge volume of spray right over the top, part of which fell into the lighthouse, and what poor Forsyth heard was about a ton of water coming down through storey after storey, carrying lime, mortar, buckets, trowels, and a host of other things, violently along with it.

To plunge down the spiral stair, almost headforemost, was the work of a few seconds. Forsyth accompanied the descent with a yell of terror, which reached the ears of his comrades in the beacon, and brought them to the door, just in time to see their comrade's long legs carry him across the bridge in two bounds. Almost at the same instant the water and rubbish burst out of the doorway of the lighthouse, and flooded the bridge.

But let us return from this digression, or rather, this series of digressions, to the point where we branched off: the aspect of the beacon in the fog, and the calm of that still morning in June.

Some of the men inside were playing draughts, others were finishing their breakfast; one was playing "Auld Lang Syne", with many extempore flourishes and trills, on a flute, which was very much out of tune. A few were smoking, of course (where exists the band of Britons who can get on without that!) and several were sitting astride on the cross-beams below, bobbing—not exactly for whales, but for any monster of the deep that chose to turn up.

The men fishing, and the beacon itself, loomed large and mysterious in the half-luminous fog. Perhaps this was the reason that the sea-gulls flew so near them, and gave forth an occasional and very melancholy cry, as if of complaint at the changed appearance of things.

"There's naethin' to be got the day," said John Watt, rather peevishly, as he pulled up his line and found the bait gone.

Baits are *always* found gone when lines are pulled up! This would seem to be an angling law of nature. At all events, it would seem to have been a very aggravating law of nature on the present occasion, for John Watt frowned and growled to himself as he put on another bait.

"There's a bite!" exclaimed Joe Dumsby, with a look of doubt, at the same time feeling his line.

"Poo'd in then," said Watt ironically.

"No, 'e's hoff," observed Joe.

"Hm! he never was on," muttered Watt.

"What are you two growling at?" said Ruby, who sat on one of the beams at the other side.

"At our luck, Ruby," said Joe. "Ha! was that a nibble?" ("Naethin' o' the kind," from Watt.) "It was! as I live it's large; an 'addock, I think."

"A naddock!" sneered Watt; "mair like a bit o' tangle than—eh! losh me! it *is* a fish—"

"Well done, Joe!" cried Bremner, from the doorway above, as a large rock-cod was drawn to the surface of the water.

"Stay, it's too large to pull up with the line. I'll run down and gaff it," cried Ruby, fastening his own line to the beam, and descending to the water by the usual ladder, on one of the main beams. "Now, draw him this way—gently, not too roughly—take time. Ah! that was a miss—he's off; no! Again; now then—"

Another moment, and a goodly cod of about ten pounds weight was wriggling on the iron hook which Ruby handed up to Dumsby, who mounted with his prize in triumph to the kitchen.

From that moment the fish began to "take."

While the men were thus busily engaged, a boat was rowing about in the fog, vainly endeavouring to find the rock.

It was the boat of two fast friends, Jock Swankie and Davy Spink.

These worthies were in a rather exhausted condition, having been rowing almost incessantly from daybreak.

"I tell 'ee what it is," said Swankie; "I'll be hanged if I poo another stroke."

He threw his oar into the boat, and looked sulky.

"It's my belief," said his companion, "that we ought to be near aboot Denmark be this time."

"Denmark or Rooshia, it's a' ane to me," rejoined Swankie; "I'll hae a smoke."

So saying, he pulled out his pipe and tobacco-box, and began to cut the tobacco. Davy did the same.

Suddenly both men paused, for they heard a sound. Each looked enquiringly at the other, and then both gazed into the thick fog.

"Is that a ship?" said Davy Spink.

They seized their oars hastily.

"The beacon, as I'm a leevin' sinner!" exclaimed Swankie.

If Spink had not backed his oar at that moment, there is some probability that Swankie would have been a dead, instead of a living, sinner in a few minutes, for they had almost run upon the north-east end of the Bell Rock, and distinctly heard the sound of voices on the beacon. A shout settled the question at once, for it was replied to by a loud holloa from Ruby.

In a short time the boat was close to the beacon, and the water was so very calm that day, that they were able to venture to hand the packet of letters with which they had come off into the beacon, even although the tide was full.

"Letters," said Swankie, as he reached out his hand with the packet.

"Hurrah!" cried the men, who were all assembled on the mortar-gallery, looking down at the fishermen, excepting Ruby, Watt, and Dumsby, who were still on the cross-beams below.

"Mind the boat; keep her aff," said Swankie, stretching out his hand with the packet to the utmost, while Dumsby descended the ladder and held out *his* hand to receive it.

"Take care," cried the men in chorus, for news from shore was always a very exciting episode in their career, and the idea of the packet being lost filled them with sudden alarm.

The shout and the anxiety together caused the very result that was dreaded. The packet fell into the sea and sank, amid a volley of yells.

It went down slowly. Before it had descended a fathom, Ruby's head cleft the water, and in a moment he returned to the surface with the packet in his hand amid a wild cheer of joy; but this was turned into a cry of alarm, as Ruby was carried away by the tide, despite his utmost efforts to regain the beacon.

The boat was at once pushed off but so strong was the current there, that Ruby was carried past the rock, and a hundred yards away to sea, before the boat overtook him.

The moment he was pulled into her he shook himself, and then tore off the outer covering of the packet in order to save the letters from being wetted. He had the great satisfaction of finding them almost uninjured. He had the greater satisfaction, thereafter, of feeling that he had done a deed which induced every man in the beacon that night to thank him half a dozen times over; and he had the greatest possible satisfaction in finding that among the rest he had saved two letters addressed to himself, one from Minnie Gray, and the other from his uncle.

The scene in the beacon when the contents of the packet were delivered was interesting. Those who had letters devoured them, and in many cases read them (unwittingly) half-aloud. Those who had none read the newspapers, and those who had neither papers nor letters listened.

Ruby's letter ran as follows (we say his *letter*, because the other letter was regarded, comparatively, as nothing):—

"**Arbroath**, etcetera.

"**Darling Ruby**,—I have just time to tell you that we have made a discovery which will surprise you. Let me detail it to you circumstantially. Uncle Ogilvy and I were walking on the pier a few days ago, when we overheard a conversation between two sailors, who did not see that we were approaching. We would not have stopped to listen, but the words we heard arrested our attention, so— O what a pity! there, Big Swankie has come for our letters. Is it not strange that *he* should be the man to take them off? I meant to have given you *such* an account of it, especially a description of the case. They won't wait. Come ashore as soon as you can, dearest Ruby."

The letter broke off here abruptly. It was evident that the writer had been obliged to close it abruptly, for she had forgotten to sign her name.

"'A description of the case;' *what* case?" muttered Ruby in vexation. "O Minnie, Minnie, in your anxiety to go into details you have omitted to give me the barest outline. Well, well, darling, I'll just take the will for the deed, but I *wish* you had—"

Here Ruby ceased to mutter, for Captain Ogilvy's letter suddenly occurred to his mind. Opening it hastily, he read as follows:—

"**Dear Neffy**,—I never was much of a hand at spellin', an' I'm not rightly sure o' that word, howsever, it reads all square, so ittle do. If I had been the inventer o' writin' I'd have had signs for a lot o' words. Just think how much better it would ha' bin to have put a regular D like that instead o' writin' s-q-u-a-r-e. Then *round* would have bin far better O, like that. An' crooked thus," (draws a squiggly line); "see how significant an' suggestive, if I may say so; no humbug—all fair an' above-board, as the pirate said, when he ran up the black flag to the peak.

"But avast speckillatin' (shiver my timbers! but that last was a pen-splitter), that's not what I sat down to write about. My object in takin' up the pen, neffy, is two-fold,

323

"'Double, double, toil an' trouble,'

"as Macbeath said,—if it wasn't Hamlet.

"We want you to come home for a day or two, if you can git leave, lad, about this strange affair. Minnie said she was goin' to give you a full, true, and partikler account of it, so it's of no use my goin' over the same course. There's that blackguard Swankie come for the letters. Ha! it makes me chuckle. No time for more—"

This letter also concluded abruptly, and without a signature.

"There's a pretty kettle o' fish!" exclaimed Ruby aloud.

"So 'tis, lad; so 'tis," said Bremner, who at that moment had placed a superb pot of codlings on the fire; "though why ye should say it so positively when nobody's denyin' it, is more nor I can tell."

Ruby laughed, and retired to the mortar-gallery to work at the forge and ponder. He always found that he pondered best while employed in hammering, especially if his feelings were ruffled.

Seizing a mass of metal, he laid it on the anvil, and gave it five or six heavy blows to straighten it a little, before thrusting it into the fire.

Strange to say, these few blows of the hammer were the means, in all probability, of saving the sloop *Smeaton* from being wrecked on the Bell Rock!

That vessel had been away with Mr Stevenson at Leith, and was returning, when she was overtaken by the calm and the fog. At the moment that Ruby began to hammer, the *Smeaton* was within a stone's cast of the beacon, running gently before a light air which had sprung up.

No one on board had the least idea that the tide had swept them so near the rock, and the ringing of the anvil was the first warning they got of their danger.

The lookout on board instantly sang out, "Starboard har–r–r–d–! beacon ahead!" and Ruby looked up in surprise, just as the *Smeaton* emerged like a phantom-ship out of the fog. Her sails fluttered as she came up to the wind, and the crew were seen hurrying to and fro in much alarm.

Mr Stevenson himself stood on the quarterdeck of the little vessel, and waved his hand to assure those on the beacon that they had sheered off in time, and were safe.

This incident tended to strengthen the engineer in his opinion that the two large bells which were being cast for the lighthouse, to be rung by the machinery of the revolving light, would be of great utility in foggy weather.

While the *Smeaton* was turning away, as if with a graceful bow to the men on the rock, Ruby shouted:

"There are letters here for you, sir."

The mate of the vessel called out at once, "Send them off in the shore-boat; we'll lay-to."

No time was to be lost, for if the *Smeaton* should get involved in the fog it might be very difficult to find her; so Ruby at once ran for the letters, and, hailing the shore-boat which lay quite close at hand, jumped into it and pushed off.

They boarded the *Smeaton* without difficulty and delivered the letters.

Instead of returning to the beacon, however, Ruby was ordered to hold himself in readiness to go to Arbroath in the shore-boat with a letter from Mr Stevenson to the superintendent of the workyard.

"You can go up and see your friends in the town, if you choose," said the engineer, "but be sure to return by tomorrow's forenoon tide. We cannot dispense with your services longer than a few hours, my lad, so I shall expect you to make no unnecessary delay."

"You may depend upon me, sir," said Ruby, touching his cap, as he turned away and leaped into the boat.

A light breeze was now blowing, so that the sails could be used. In less than a quarter of an hour sloop and beacon were lost in the fog, and Ruby steered for the harbour of Arbroath, overjoyed at this unexpected and happy turn of events, which gave him an opportunity of solving the mystery of the letters, and of once more seeing the sweet face of Minnie Gray.

But an incident occurred which delayed these desirable ends, and utterly changed the current of Ruby's fortunes for a time.

Chapter Twenty Six

A Sudden and Tremendous Change in Ruby's Fortunes

What a variety of appropriate aphorisms there are to express the great truths of human experience! "There is many a slip 'twixt the cup and the lip" is one of them. Undoubtedly there is. So is there "many a miss of a sweet little kiss." "The course of true love," also, "never did run smooth." Certainly not. Why should it? If it did we should doubt whether the love were true. Our own private belief is that the course of true love is always uncommonly rough, but collective human wisdom has seen fit to put the idea in the negative form. So let it stand.

Ruby had occasion to reflect on these things that day, but the reflection afforded him no comfort whatever.

The cause of his inconsolable state of mind is easily explained.

The boat had proceeded about halfway to Arbroath when they heard the sound of oars, and in a few seconds a ship's gig rowed out of the fog towards them. Instead of passing them the gig was steered straight for the boat, and Ruby saw that it was full of men-of-war's men.

He sprang up at once and seized an oar.

"Out oars!" he cried. "Boys, if ever you pulled hard in your lives, do so now. It's the press-gang!"

Before those few words were uttered the two men had seized the oars, for they knew well what the press-gang meant, and all three pulled with such vigour that the boat shot over the smooth sea with double speed. But they had no chance in a heavy fishing boat against the picked crew of the light gig. If the wind had been a little stronger they might have escaped, but the wind had decreased, and the small boat overhauled them yard by yard.

Seeing that they had no chance, Ruby said, between his set teeth:

"Will ye fight, boys?"

"*I* will," cried Davy Spink sternly, for Davy had a wife and little daughter on shore, who depended entirely on his exertions for their livelihood, so he had a strong objection to go and fight in the wars of his country.

"What's the use?" muttered Big Swankie, with a savage scowl. He, too, had a strong disinclination to serve in the Royal Navy, being a lazy man, and not overburdened with courage. "They've got eight men of a crew, wi' pistols an' cutlashes."

"Well, it's all up with us," cried Ruby, in a tone of sulky anger, as he tossed his oar overboard, and, folding his arms on his breast, sat sternly eyeing the gig as it approached.

Suddenly a beam of hope shot into his heart. A few words will explain the cause thereof.

About the time the works at the Bell Rock were in progress, the war with France and the Northern Powers was at its height, and the demand for men was so great that orders were issued for the establishment of an impress service at Dundee, Arbroath, and Aberdeen. It became therefore necessary to have some protection for the men engaged in the works. As the impress officers were extremely rigid in the execution of their duty, it was resolved to have the seamen carefully identified, and, therefore, besides being described in the usual manner in the protection-bills granted by the Admiralty, each man had a ticket given to him descriptive of his person, to which was attached a silver medal emblematical of the lighthouse service.

That very week Ruby had received one of the protection-medals and tickets of the Bell Rock, a circumstance which he had forgotten at the moment. It was now in his pocket, and might perhaps save him.

When the boat ranged up alongside, Ruby recognised in the officer at the helm the youth who had already given him so much annoyance. The officer also recognised Ruby, and, with a glance of surprise and pleasure, exclaimed:

"What! have I bagged you at last, my slippery young lion?"

Ruby smiled as he replied, "Not *quite* yet, my persevering young jackall." (He was sorely tempted to transpose the word into jackass, but he wisely restrained himself.) "I'm not so easily caught as you think."

"Eh! how? what mean you?" exclaimed the officer, with an expression of surprise, for he knew that Ruby was now in his power. "I have you safe, my lad, unless you have provided yourself with a pair of wings. Of course, I shall leave one of you to take your boat into harbour, but you may be sure that I'll not devolve that pleasant duty upon *you*."

"I have not provided myself with wings exactly," returned Ruby, pulling out his medal and ticket; "but here is something that will do quite as well."

The officer's countenance fell, for he knew at once what it was. He inspected it, however, closely.

"Let me see," said he, reading the description on the ticket, which ran thus: —

"Bell Rock Workyard, Arbroath,

"20th June, 1810.

"Ruby Brand, seaman and blacksmith, in the service of the Honourable the Commissioners of the Northern Lighthouses, aged 25 years, 5 feet 10 inches high, very powerfully made, fair complexion, straight nose, dark-blue eyes, and curling auburn hair."

This description was signed by the engineer of the works; and on the obverse was written, *"The bearer, Ruby Brand, is serving as a blacksmith in the erection of the Bell Rock Lighthouse."*

"This is all very well, my fine fellow," said the officer, "but I have been deceived more than once with these medals and tickets. How am I to know that you have not stolen it from someone?"

"By seeing whether the description agrees," replied Ruby.

"Of course, I know that as well as you, and I don't find the description quite perfect. I would say that your hair is light-brown, now, not auburn, and your nose is a little Roman, if anything; and there's no mention of whiskers, or that delicate moustache. Why, look here," he added, turning abruptly to Big Swankie, "this might be the description of your comrade as well as, if not better than, yours. What's your name?"

"Swankie, sir," said that individual ruefully, yet with a gleam of hope that the advantages of the Bell Rock medal might possibly, in some unaccountable way, accrue to himself, for he was sharp enough to see that the officer would be only too glad to find any excuse for securing Ruby.

"Well, Swankie, stand up, and let's have a look at you," said the officer, glancing from the paper to the person of the fisherman, and commenting thereon. "Here we have 'very powerfully made'—no mistake about that—strong as Samson; 'fair complexion'—that's it exactly; 'auburn hair'—so it is. Auburn is a very undecided colour; there's a great deal of red in it, and no one can deny that Swankie has a good deal of red in *his* hair."

There was indeed no denying this, for it was altogether red, of an intense carroty hue.

"You see, friend," continued the officer, turning to Ruby, "that the description suits Swankie very well."

"True, as far as you have gone," said Ruby, with a quiet smile; "but Swankie is six feet two in his stockings, and his nose is turned up, and his hair don't curl, and his eyes are light-green, and his complexion is sallow, if I may not say yellow—"

"Fair, lad; fair," said the officer, laughing in spite of himself. "Ah! Ruby Brand, you are jealous of him! Well, I see that I'm fated not to capture you, so I'll bid you good day. Meanwhile your companions will be so good as to step into my gig."

The two men rose to obey. Big Swankie stepped over the gunwale, with the fling of a sulky, reckless man, who curses his fate and submits to it. Davy Spink had a very crestfallen, subdued look. He was about to follow, when a thought seemed to strike him. He turned hastily round, and Ruby was surprised to see that his eyes were suffused with tears, and that his features worked with the convulsive twitching of one who struggles powerfully to restrain his feelings.

"Ruby Brand," said he, in a deep husky voice, which trembled at first, but became strong as he went on; "Ruby Brand, I deserve nae good at your hands, yet I'll ask a favour o' ye. Ye've seen the wife and the bairn, the wee ane wi' the fair curly pow. Ye ken the auld hoose. It'll be mony a lang day afore I see them again, if iver I come back ava. There's naebody left to care for them. They'll be starvin' soon, lad. Wull ye—wull ye look-doon?"

Poor Davy Spink stopped here, and covered his face with his big sunburnt hands.

A sudden gush of sympathy filled Ruby's heart. He started forward, and drawing from his pocket the letter with which he was charged, thrust it into Spink's hand, and said hurriedly—

"Don't fail to deliver it the first thing you do on landing. And hark'ee, Spink, go to Mrs Brand's cottage, and tell them there *why* I went away. Be sure you see them *all*, and explain *why it was*. Tell Minnie Gray that I will be *certain* to return, if God spares me."

Without waiting for a reply he sprang into the gig, and gave the other boat a shove, that sent it several yards off.

"Give way, lads," cried the officer, who was delighted at this unexpected change in affairs, though he had only heard enough of the conversation to confuse him as to the cause of it.

"Stop! stop!" shouted Spink, tossing up his arms.

"I'd rather not," returned the officer.

Davy seized the oars, and, turning his boat in the direction of the gig, endeavoured to overtake it. As well might the turkey-buzzard attempt to catch the swallow. He was left far behind, and when last seen faintly through the fog, he was standing up in the stern of the boat wringing his hands.

Ruby had seated himself in the bow of the gig, with his face turned steadily towards the sea, so that no one could see it. This position he maintained in silence until the boat ranged up to what appeared like the side of a great mountain, looming through the mist.

Then he turned round, and, whatever might have been the struggle within his breast, all traces of it had left his countenance, which presented its wonted appearance of good-humoured frankness.

We need scarcely say that the mountain turned out to be a British man-of-war. Ruby was quickly introduced to his future messmates, and warmly received by them. Then he was left to his own free will during the remainder of that day, for the commander of the vessel was a kind man, and did not like to add to the grief of the impressed men by setting them to work at once.

Thus did our hero enter the Royal Navy; and many a long and weary day and month passed by before he again set foot in his native town.

Chapter Twenty Seven

Other Things Besides Murder "Will Out"

Meanwhile Davy Spink, with his heart full, returned slowly to the shore.

He was long of reaching it, the boat being very heavy for one man to pull. On landing he hurried up to his poor little cottage, which was in a very low part of the town, and in a rather out-of-the-way corner of that part.

"Janet," said he, flinging himself into a rickety old armchair that stood by the fireplace, "the press-gang has catched us at last, and they've took Big Swankie away, and, worse than that—"

"Oh!" cried Janet, unable to wait for more, "that's the best news I've heard for mony a day. Ye're sure they have him safe?"

"Ay, sure enough," said Spink dryly; "but ye needna be sae glad aboot it, for. Swankie was aye good to *you*."

"Ay, Davy," cried Janet, putting her arm round her husband's neck, and kissing him, "but he wasna good to *you*. He led ye into evil ways mony a time when ye would rather hae keepit oot o' them. Na, na, Davy, ye needna shake yer heed; I ken'd fine."

"Weel, weel, hae'd yer ain way, lass, but Swankie's awa' to the wars, and so's Ruby Brand, for they've gotten him as weel."

"Ruby Brand!" exclaimed the woman.

"Ay, Ruby Brand; and this is the way they did it."

Here Spink detailed to his helpmate, who sat with folded hands and staring eyes opposite to her husband, all that had happened. When he had concluded, they discussed the subject together. Presently the little girl came bouncing into the room, with rosy cheeks, sparkling eyes, a dirty face, and fair ringlets very much dishevelled, and with a pitcher of hot soup in her hands.

Davy caught her up, and kissing her, said abruptly, "Maggie, Big Swankie's awa' to the wars."

The child looked enquiringly in her father's face, and he had to repeat his words twice before she quite realised the import of them.

"Are ye jokin', daddy?"

"No, Maggie; it's true. The press-gang got him and took him awa', an' I doot we'll never see him again."

The little girl's expression changed while he spoke, then her lip trembled, and she burst into tears.

"See there, Janet," said Spink, pointing to Maggie, and looking earnestly at his wife.

"Weel-a-weel," replied Janet, somewhat softened, yet with much firmness, "I'll no deny that the man was fond o' the bairn, and it liked him weel enough; but, my certes! he wad hae made a bad man o' you if he could. But I'm real sorry for Ruby Brand; and what'll the puir lassie Gray do? Ye'll hae to gang up an' gie them the message."

"So I will; but that's like somethin' to eat, I think?"

Spink pointed to the soup.

"Ay, it's a' we've got, so let's fa' to; and haste ye, lad. It's a sair heart she'll hae this night—wae's me!"

While Spink and his wife were thus employed, Widow Brand, Minnie Gray, and Captain Ogilvy were seated at tea, round the little table in the snug kitchen of the widow's cottage.

It might have been observed that there were two teapots on the table, a large one and a small, and that the captain helped himself out of the small one, and did not take either milk or sugar. But the captain's teapot did not necessarily imply tea. In fact, since the death of the captain's mother, that small teapot had been accustomed to strong drink only. It never tasted tea.

"I wonder if Ruby will get leave of absence," said the captain, throwing himself back in his armchair, in order to be able to admire, with greater ease, the smoke, as it curled towards the ceiling from his mouth and pipe.

"I do hope so," said Mrs Brand, looking up from her knitting, with a little sigh. Mrs Brand usually followed up all her remarks with a little sigh. Sometimes the sigh was *very* little. It depended a good deal on the nature of her remark whether the sigh was of the little, less, or least description; but it never failed, in one or other degree, to close her every observation.

"I *think* he will," said Minnie, as she poured a second cup of tea for the widow.

"Ay, that's right, lass," observed the captain; "there's nothin' like hope—

"'The pleasures of hope told a flatterin' tale Regardin' the fleet when Lord Nelson set sail.'

"Fill me out another cup of tea, Hebe."

It was a pleasant little fiction with the captain to call his beverage "tea". Minnie filled out a small cupful of the contents of the little teapot, which did, indeed, resemble tea, but which smelt marvellously like hot rum and water.

"Enough, enough. Come on, Macduff! Ah! Minnie, this is prime Jamaica; it's got such a— but I forgot; you don't understand nothin' about nectar of this sort."

The captain smoked in silence for a few minutes, and then said, with a sudden chuckle—

"Wasn't it odd, sister, that we should have found it all out in such an easy sort o' way? If criminals would always tell on themselves as plainly as Big Swankie did, there would be no use for lawyers."

"Swankie would not have spoken so freely," said Minnie, with a laugh, "if he had known that we were listening."

"That's true, girl," said the captain, with sudden gravity; "and I don't feel quite easy in my mind about that same eavesdropping. It's a dirty thing to do—especially for an old sailor, who likes everything to be fair and above-board; but then, you see, the natur' o' the words we couldn't help hearin' justified us in waitin' to hear more. Yes, it was quite right, as it turned out. A little more tea, Minnie. Thank'ee, lass. Now go, get the case, and let us look over it again."

The girl rose, and, going to a drawer, quickly returned with a small red leather case in her hand. It was the identical jewel-case that Swankie had found on the dead body at the Bell Rock!

"Ah! that's it; now, let us see; let us see." He laid aside his pipe, and for some time felt all his pockets, and looked round the room, as if in search of something.

"What are you looking for, uncle?"

"The specs, lass; these specs'll be the death o' me."

Minnie laughed. "They're on your brow, uncle!"

"So they are! Well, well—"

The captain smiled deprecatingly, and, drawing his chair close to the table, began to examine the box.

Its contents were a strange mixture, and it was evident that the case had not been made to hold them.

There was a lady's gold watch, of very small size, and beautifully formed; a set of ornaments, consisting of necklace, bracelets, ring, and ear-rings of turquoise and pearls set in gold, of the most delicate and exquisite chasing; also, an antique diamond cross of great beauty, besides a number of rings and bracelets of considerable value.

As the captain took these out one by one, and commented on them, he made use of Minnie's pretty hand and arm to try the effect of each, and truly the ornaments could not have found a more appropriate resting-place among the fairest ladies of the land.

Minnie submitted to be made use of in this way with a pleased and amused expression; for, while she greatly admired the costly gems, she could not help smiling at the awkwardness of the captain in putting them on.

"Read the paper again," said Minnie, after the contents of the box had been examined.

The captain took up a small parcel covered with oiled cloth, which contained a letter. Opening it, he began to read, but was interrupted by Mrs Brand, who had paid little attention to the jewels.

"Read it out loud, brother," said she, "I don't hear you well. Read it out; I love to hear of my darling's gallant deeds."

The captain cleared his throat, raised his voice, and read slowly:—

"'Lisbon, 10th March, 1808.

"'Dear Captain Brand,—I am about to quit this place for the East in a few days, and shall probably never see you again. Pray accept the accompanying case of jewels as a small token of the love and esteem in which you are held by a heart-broken father. I feel assured that if it had been in the power of man to have saved my drowning child your gallant efforts would have been successful. It was ordained otherwise; and I now pray that I may be enabled to say "God's will be done." But I cannot bear the sight of these ornaments. I have no relatives—none at least who deserve them half so well as yourself. Do not pain me by refusing them. They may be of use to you if you are ever in want of money, being worth, I believe, between three and four hundred pounds. Of course, you cannot misunderstand my motive in mentioning this. No amount of money could in any measure represent the gratitude I owe to the man who risked his life to save my child. May God bless you, sir.'"

The letter ended thus, without signature; and the captain ceased to read aloud. But there was an addition to the letter written in pencil, in the hand of the late Captain Brand, which neither he nor Minnie had yet found courage to read to the poor widow. It ran thus:—

"Our doom is sealed. My schooner is on the Bell Rock. It is blowing a gale from the North East, and she is going to pieces fast. We are all standing under the lee of a ledge of rock—six

344

of us. In half an hour the tide will be roaring over the spot. God in Christ help us! It is an awful end. If this letter and box is ever found, I ask the finder to send it, with my blessing, to Mrs Brand, my beloved wife, in Arbroath."

The writing was tremulous, and the paper bore the marks of having been soiled with seaweed. It was unsigned. The writer had evidently been obliged to close it hastily.

After reading this in silence the captain refolded the letter.

"No wonder, Minnie, that Swankie did not dare to offer such things for sale. He would certainly have been found out. Wasn't it lucky that we heard him tell Spink the spot under his floor where he had hidden them?"

At that moment there came a low knock to the door. Minnie opened it, and admitted Davy Spink, who stood in the middle of the room twitching his cap nervously, and glancing uneasily from one to another of the party.

"Hallo, Spink!" cried the captain, pushing his spectacles up on his forehead, and gazing at the fisherman in surprise, "you don't seem to be quite easy in your mind. Hope your fortunes have not sprung a leak!"

"Weel, Captain Ogilvy, they just have; gone to the bottom, I might a'most say. I've come to tell ye—that—the fact is, that the press-gang have catched us at last, and ta'en awa' my mate, Jock Swankie, better kenn'd as Big Swankie."

"Hem—well, my lad, in so far as that does damage to you, I'm sorry for it; but as regards society at large, I rather think that Swankie havin' tripped his anchor is a decided advantage. If you lose by this in one way, you gain much in another; for your mate's companionship did ye no good. Birds of a feather should flock together. You're better apart, for I believe you to be an honest man, Spink."

Davy looked at the captain in unfeigned astonishment.

"Weel, ye're the first man that iver said that, an' I thank 'ee, sir, but you're wrang, though I wush ye was right. But that's no' what I cam' to tell ye."

Here the fisherman's indecision of manner returned.

"Come, make a clean breast of it, lad. There are none here but friends."

"Weel, sir, Ruby Brand—"

He paused, and Minnie turned deadly pale, for she jumped at once to the right conclusion. The widow, on the other hand, listened for more with deep anxiety, but did not guess the truth.

"The fact is, Ruby's catched too, an' he's awa' to the wars, and he sent me to—ech, sirs! the auld wuman's fentit."

Poor Widow Brand had indeed fallen back in her chair in a state bordering on insensibility. Minnie was able to restrain her feelings so as to attend to her. She and the captain raised her gently, and led her into her own room, from whence the captain returned, and shut the door behind him.

"Now, Spink," said he, "tell me all about it, an' be partic'lar."

Davy at once complied, and related all that the reader already knows, in a deep, serious tone of voice, for he felt that in the captain he had a sympathetic listener.

When he had concluded, Captain Ogilvy heaved a sigh so deep that it might have been almost considered a groan, then he sat down on his armchair, and, pointing to the chair from which the widow had recently risen, said, "Sit down, lad."

As he advanced to comply, Spink's eyes for the first time fell on the case of jewels. He started, paused, and looked with a troubled air at the captain.

"Ha!" exclaimed the latter with a grin; "you seem to know these things; old acquaintances, eh?"

"It wasna' me that stole them," said Spink hastily.

"I did not say that anyone stole them."

"Weel, I mean that—that—"

He stopped abruptly, for he felt that in whatever way he might attempt to clear himself, he would unavoidably criminate, by implication, his absent mate.

"I know what you mean, my lad; sit down."

Spink sat down on the edge of the chair, and looked at the other uneasily.

"Have a cup of tea?" said the captain abruptly, seizing the small pot and pouring out a cupful.

"Thank 'ee—I—I niver tak' tea."

"Take it to-night, then. It will do you good."

Spink put the cup to his lips, and a look of deep surprise overspread his rugged countenance as he sipped the contents. The captain nodded. Spink's look of surprise changed into a confidential smile; he also nodded, winked, and drained the cup to the bottom.

"Yes," resumed the captain; "you mean that you did not take the case of jewels from old Brand's pocket on that day when you found his body on the Bell Rock, though you were present, and saw your comrade pocket the booty. You see I know all about it, Davy, an' your only fault lay in concealing the matter, and in keepin' company with that scoundrel."

The gaze of surprise with which Spink listened to the first part of this speech changed to a look of sadness towards the end of it.

"Captain Ogilvy," said he, in a tone of solemnity that was a strong contrast to his usual easy, careless manner of speaking, "you ca'd me an honest man, an' ye think I'm clear o' guilt in this matter, but ye're mista'en. Hoo ye cam' to find oot a' this I canna divine, but I can tell ye somethin' mair than ye ken. D'ye see that bag?"

He pulled a small leather purse out of his coat pocket, and laid it with a little bang on the table.

The captain nodded.

"Weel, sir, that was *my* share o' the plunder, thretty goolden sovereigns. We tossed which o' us was to hae them, an' the siller fell to me. But I've niver spent a boddle o't. Mony a time have I been tempit, an' mony a time wad I hae gi'en in to the temptation, but for a certain lass ca'd Janet, that's been an angel, it's my belief,

349

sent doon frae heeven to keep me frae gawin to the deevil a'thegither. But be that as it may, I've brought the siller to them that owns it by right, an' so my conscience is clear o't at lang last."

The sigh of relief with which Davy Spink pushed the bag of gold towards his companion, showed that the poor man's mind was in truth released from a heavy load that had crushed it for years.

The captain, who had lit his pipe, stared at the fisherman through the smoke for some time in silence; then he began to untie the purse, and said slowly, "Spink, I said you were an honest man, an' I see no cause to alter my opinion."

He counted out the thirty gold pieces, put them back into the bag, and the bag into his pocket. Then he continued, "Spink, if this gold was mine I would—but no matter, it's not mine, it belongs to Widow Brand, to whom I shall deliver it up. Meantime, I'll bid you good night. All these things require reflection. Call back here to-morrow, my fine fellow, and I'll have something to say to you. Another cup of tea?"

"Weel, I'll no objec'."

Davy Spink rose, swallowed the beverage, and left the cottage. The captain returned, and stood for some time irresolute with his hand on the handle of the door of his sister's room. As he listened, he heard a sob, and the tones of Minnie's voice as if in prayer. Changing his mind, he walked softly across the kitchen into his own room, where, having trimmed the candle, refilled and lit his pipe, he sat down at the table, and, resting his arms thereon, began to meditate.

Chapter Twenty Eight

The Lighthouse Completed—Ruby's Escape from Trouble by a Desperate Venture

There came a time at last when the great work of building the Bell Rock Lighthouse drew to a close. Four years after its commencement it was completed, and on the night of the 1st of February, 1811, its bright beams were shed for the first time far and wide over the sea.

It must not be supposed, however, that this lighthouse required four years to build it. On the contrary, the seasons in which work could be done were very short. During the whole of the first season of 1807, the aggregate time of low-water work, caught by snatches of an hour or two at a tide, did not amount to fourteen days of ten hours! while in 1808 it fell short of four weeks.

A great event is worthy of very special notice. We should fail in our duty to our readers if we were to make only passing reference to this important event in the history of our country.

That 1st of February, 1811, was the birthday of a new era, for the influence of the Bell Rock Light on the shipping interests of the kingdom (not merely of Scotland, by any means), was far greater than people generally suppose.

Here is a *fact* that may well be weighed with attention; that might be not inappropriately inscribed in diamond letters over the lintel of the lighthouse door. Up to the period of the building of the lighthouse, the known history of the Bell Rock was a black record of wreck, ruin, and death. Its unknown history, in remote ages, who shall conceive, much less tell? *Up* to that period, seamen dreaded the rock and shunned it—ay, so earnestly as to meet destruction too often in their anxious efforts to avoid it. *From* that period the Bell Rock has been a friendly point, a guiding star—hailed as such by storm-tossed mariners—marked as such on the charts of all nations. *From* that date not a single night for more than half a century has passed, without its wakeful eye beaming on the waters, or its fog-bells sounding on the air; and, best of all, *not a single wreck has occurred on that rock from that period down to the present day*!

Say not, good reader, that much the same may be said of all lighthouses. In the first place, the history of many lighthouses is by no means so happy as that of this one. In the second place, all lighthouses are not of equal importance. Few stand on an equal footing with the Bell Rock, either in regard to its national importance or its actual pedestal. In the last place, it is our subject of consideration at present, and we object to odious comparisons while we sing its praises!

Whatever may be said of the other lights that guard our shores, special gratitude is due to the Bell Rock—to those who projected it—to the engineer who planned and built it—to God, who inspired the will to dare, and bestowed the skill to accomplish, a work so difficult, so noble, so prolific of good to man!

The nature of our story requires that we should occasionally annihilate time and space.

Let us then leap over both, and return to our hero, Ruby Brand.

His period of service in the Navy was comparatively brief, much more so than either he or his friends anticipated. Nevertheless, he spent a considerable time in his new profession, and, having been sent to foreign stations, he saw a good deal of what is called "service", in which he distinguished himself, as might have been expected, for coolness and courage.

But we must omit all mention of his warlike deeds, and resume the record of his history at that point which bears more immediately on the subject of our tale.

It was a wild, stormy night in November. Ruby's ship had captured a French privateer in the German Ocean, and, a prize crew having been put aboard, she was sent away to the nearest port, which happened to be the harbour of Leith, in the Firth of Forth. Ruby had not been appointed one of the prize crew; but he resolved not to miss the chance of again seeing his native town, if it should only be a distant view through a telescope. Being a favourite with his commander, his plea was received favourably, and he was sent on board the Frenchman.

Those who know what it is to meet with an unexpected piece of great good fortune, can imagine the delight with which Ruby stood at the helm on the night in question, and steered for *home*! He was known by all on board to be the man who understood best the navigation of the Forth, so that implicit trust was placed in him by the young officer who had charge of the prize.

The man-of-war happened to be short-handed at the time the privateer was captured, owing to her boats having been sent in chase of a suspicious craft during a calm. Some of the French crew were therefore left on board to assist in navigating the vessel.

This was unfortunate, for the officer sent in charge turned out to be a careless man, and treated the Frenchmen with contempt. He did not keep strict watch over them, and the result was, that, shortly after the storm began, they took the English crew by surprise, and overpowered them.

Ruby was the first to fall. As he stood at the wheel, indulging in pleasant dreams, a Frenchman stole up behind him, and felled him with a handspike. When he recovered he found that he was firmly bound, along with his comrades, and that the vessel was lying-to. One of the Frenchmen came forward at that moment, and addressed the prisoners in broken English.

"Now, me boys," said he, "you was see we have konker you again. You behold the sea?" pointing over the side; "well, that bees your bed to-night if you no behave. Now, I wants to know, who is best man of you as onderstand die cost? Speak de trut', else you die."

The English lieutenant at once turned to Ruby.

"Well, cast him loose; de rest of you go b'low—good day, ver' moch indeed."

Here the Frenchman made a low bow to the English, who were led below, with the exception of Ruby.

"Now, my goot mans, you onderstand dis cost?"

"Yes. I know it well."

"It is dangereoux?"

"It is—very; but not so much so as it used to be before the Bell Rock Light was shown."

"Have you see dat light?"

"No; never. It was first lighted when I was at sea; but I have seen a description of it in the newspapers, and should know it well."

"Ver goot; you will try to come to dat light an' den you will steer out from dis place to de open sea. Afterwards we will show you to France. If you try mischief—voilà!"

The Frenchman pointed to two of his comrades who stood, one on each side of the wheel, with pistols in their hands, ready to keep Ruby in order.

"Now, cut him free. Go, sare; do your dooty."

Ruby stepped to the wheel at once, and, glancing at the compass, directed the vessel's head in the direction of the Bell Rock.

The gale was rapidly increasing, and the management of the helm required his undivided attention; nevertheless his mind was busy with anxious thoughts and plans of escape. He thought with horror of a French prison, for there were old shipmates of his who had been captured years before, and who were pining in exile still. The bare idea of being separated indefinitely, perhaps for ever, from Minnie, was so terrible, that for a moment he meditated an attack, single-handed, on the crew; but the muzzle of a pistol on each side of him induced him to pause and reflect!

Reflection, however, only brought him again to the verge of despair. Then he thought of running up to Leith, and so take the Frenchmen prisoners; but this idea was at once discarded, for it was impossible to pass up to Leith Roads without seeing the Bell Rock light, and the Frenchmen kept a sharp lookout. Then he resolved to run the vessel ashore and wreck her, but the thought of his comrades down below induced him to give that plan up.

Under the influence of these thoughts he became inattentive, and steered rather wildly once or twice.

"Stiddy. Ha! you tink of how you escape?"

"Yes, I do," said Ruby, doggedly.

"Good, and have you see how?"

"No," replied Ruby, "I tell you candidly that I can see no way of escape."

"Ver good, sare; mind your helm."

At that moment a bright star of the first magnitude rose on the horizon, right ahead of them.

"Ha! dat is a star," said the Frenchman, after a few moments' observation of it.

"Stars don't go out," replied Ruby, as the light in question disappeared.

"It is de light'ouse den?"

"I don't know," said Ruby, "but we shall soon see."

Just then a thought flashed into Ruby's mind. His heart beat quick, his eye dilated, and his lip was tightly compressed as it came and went. Almost at the same moment another star rose right ahead of them. It was of a deep red colour; and Ruby's heart beat high again, for he was now certain that it was the revolving light of the Bell Rock, which shows a white and red light alternately every two minutes.

"*Voilà*! that must be him now," exclaimed the Frenchman, pointing to the light, and looking enquiringly at Ruby.

"I have told you," said the latter, "that I never saw the light before. I believe it to be the Bell Rock Light; but it would be as well to run close and see. I think I could tell the very stones of the tower, even in a dark night. Anyhow, I know the rock itself too well to mistake it."

"Be there plenty watter?"

"Ay; on the east side, close to the rock, there is enough water to float the biggest ship in your navy."

"Good; we shall go close."

There was a slight lull in the gale at this time, and the clouds broke a little, allowing occasional glimpses of moonlight to break through and tinge the foaming crests of the waves. At last the light, that had at first looked like a bright star, soon increased, and appeared like a glorious sun in the stormy sky. For a few seconds it shone intensely white and strong, then it slowly died away and disappeared; but almost before one could have time to wonder what had become of it, it returned in the form of a brilliant red sun, which also shone for a few seconds, steadily, and then, like the former, slowly died out. Thus, alternating, the red and white suns went round.

In a few minutes the tall and graceful column itself became visible, looking pale and spectral against the black sky. At the same time the roar of the surf broke familiarly on Ruby's ears. He steered close past the north end of the rock, so close that he could see the rocks, and knew that it was low water. A gleam of moonlight broke out at the time, as if to encourage him.

"Now," said Ruby, "you had better go about, for if we carry on at this rate, in the course we are going, in about an hour you will either be a dead man on the rocks of Forfar, or enjoying yourself in a Scotch prison!"

"Ha! ha!" laughed the Frenchman, who immediately gave the order to put the vessel about; "good, ver good; bot I was not wish to see the Scottish prison, though I am told the mountains be ver superb."

While he was speaking, the little vessel lay over on her new course, and Ruby steered again past the north side of the rock. He shaved it so close that the Frenchman shouted, "*Prenez garde*," and put a pistol to Ruby's ear.

"Do you think I wish to die?" asked Ruby, with a quiet smile. "Now, captain, I want to point out the course, so as to make you sure of it. Bid one of your men take the wheel, and step up on the bulwarks with me, and I will show you."

This was such a natural remark in the circumstances, and moreover so naturally expressed, that the Frenchman at once agreed. He ordered a seaman to take the wheel, and then stepped with Ruby upon the bulwarks at the stern of the vessel.

"Now, you see the position of the lighthouse," said Ruby, "well, you must keep your course due east after passing it. If you steer to the nor'ard o' that, you'll run on the Scotch coast; if you bear away to the south'ard of it, you'll run a chance, in this state o' the tide, of getting wrecked among the Farne Islands; so keep her head *due east*."

Ruby said this very impressively; so much so, that the Frenchman looked at him in surprise.

"Why you so particulare?" he enquired, with a look of suspicion.

"Because I am going to leave you," said Ruby, pointing to the Bell Rock, which at that moment was not much more than a hundred yards to leeward. Indeed, it was scarcely so much, for the outlying rock at the northern end named *Johnny Gray*, lay close under their lee as the vessel passed. Just then a great wave burst upon it, and, roaring in wild foam over the ledges, poured into the channels and pools on the other side. For one instant Ruby's courage wavered, as he gazed at the flood of boiling foam.

"What you say?" exclaimed the Frenchman, laying his hand on the collar of Ruby's jacket.

The young sailor started, struck the Frenchman a backhanded blow on the chest, which hurled him violently against the man at the wheel, and, bending down, sprang with a wild shout into the sea.

So close had he steered to the rock, in order to lessen the danger of his reckless venture, that the privateer just weathered it. There was not, of course, the smallest chance of recapturing Ruby. No ordinary boat could have lived in the sea that was running at the time, even in open water, much less among the breakers of the

Bell Rock. Indeed, the crew felt certain that the English sailor had allowed despair to overcome his judgment, and that he must infallibly be dashed to pieces on the rocks, so they did not check their onward course, being too glad to escape from the immediate neighbourhood of such a dangerous spot.

Meanwhile Ruby buffeted the billows manfully. He was fully alive to the extreme danger of the attempt, but he knew exactly what he meant to do. He trusted to his intimate knowledge of every ledge and channel and current, and had calculated his motions to a nicety.

He knew that at the particular state of the tide at the time, and with the wind blowing as it then did, there was a slight eddy at the point of *Cunningham's Ledge*. His life, he felt, depended on his gaining that eddy. If he should miss it, he would be dashed against *Johnny Gray's* rock, or be carried beyond it and cast upon *Strachan's Ledge* or *Scoreby's Point*, and no man, however powerful he might be, could have survived the shock of being launched on any of these rocks. On the other hand, if, in order to avoid these dangers, he should swim too much to windward, there was danger of his being carried on the crest of a billow and hurled upon the weather-side of *Cunningham's Ledge*, instead of getting into the eddy under its lee.

All this Ruby had seen and calculated when he passed the north end of the rock the first time, and he had fixed the exact spot where he should take the plunge on repassing it. He acted so promptly that a few minutes sufficed to carry him towards the eddy, the tide being in his favour. But when he was about to swim into it, a wave burst completely over the ledge, and, pouring down on his head, thrust him back. He was almost stunned by the shock, but retained sufficient presence of mind to struggle on. For a few seconds he managed to bear up against wind and tide, for he put forth his giant strength with the energy of a desperate man, but gradually he was carried away from the rock, and for the first time his heart sank within him.

Just then one of those rushes or swirls of water, which are common among rocks in such a position, swept him again forward, right into the eddy which he had struggled in vain to reach, and thrust him violently against the rock. This back current was the precursor of a tremendous billow, which came towering on like a black moving wall. Ruby saw it, and, twining his arm amongst the seaweed, held his breath.

The billow fell! Only those who have seen the Bell Rock in a storm can properly estimate the roar that followed. None but Ruby himself could tell what it was to feel that world of water rushing overhead. Had it fallen directly upon him, it would have torn him from his grasp and killed him, but its full force had been previously spent on *Cunningham's Ledge*. In another moment it passed, and Ruby, quitting his hold, struck out wildly through the foam. A few strokes carried him through *Sinclair's* and *Wilson's* tracks into the little pool formerly mentioned as *Port Stevenson*.

(The author has himself bathed in Port Stevenson, so that the reader may rely on the fidelity of this description of it and the surrounding ledges.)

Here he was in comparative safety. True, the sprays burst over the ledge called *The Last Hope* in heavy masses, but these could do him no serious harm, and it would take a quarter of an hour at least for the tide to sweep into the pool. Ruby therefore swam quietly to *Trinity Ledge*, where he landed, and, stepping over it, sat down to rest, with a thankful heart, on *Smith's Ledge*, the old familiar spot where he and Jamie Dove had wrought so often and so hard at the forge in former days.

He was now under the shadow of the Bell Rock Lighthouse, which towered high above his head; and the impression of immovable solidity which its cold, grey, stately column conveyed to his mind, contrasted powerfully with the howling wind and the raging sea around. It seemed to him, as he sat there within three yards of its granite base, like the impersonation of repose in the midst of turmoil; of peace surrounded by war; of calm and solid self-possession in the midst of fretful and raging instability.

No one was there to welcome Ruby. The lightkeepers, high up in the apartments in their wild home, knew nothing and heard nothing of all that had passed so near them. The darkness of the night and the roaring of the storm was all they saw or heard of the world without, as they sat in their watch tower reading or trimming their lamps.

But Ruby was not sorry for this; he felt glad to be alone with God, to thank Him for his recent deliverance.

Exhausting though the struggle had been, its duration was short, so that he soon recovered his wonted strength. Then, rising, he got upon the iron railway, or "rails", as the men used to call it, and a few steps brought him to the foot of the metal ladder conducting to the entrance-door.

Climbing up, he stood at last in a place of safety, and disappeared within the doorway of the lighthouse.

Chapter Twenty Nine

The Wreck

Meantime the French privateer sped onward to her doom.

The force with which the French commander fell when Ruby cast him off, had stunned him so severely that it was a considerable time before he recovered. The rest of the crew were therefore in absolute ignorance of how to steer.

In this dilemma they lay-to for a short time, after getting away to a sufficient distance from the dangerous rock, and consulted what was to be done. Some advised one course, and some another, but it was finally suggested that one of the English prisoners should be brought up and commanded to steer out to sea.

This advice was acted on, and the sailor who was brought up chanced to be one who had a partial knowledge of the surrounding coasts. One of the Frenchmen who could speak a few words of English, did his best to convey his wishes to the sailor, and wound up by producing a pistol, which he cocked significantly.

"All right," said the sailor, "I knows the coast, and can run ye straight out to sea. That's the Bell Rock Light on the weather-bow, I s'pose."

"Oui, dat is de Bell Roke."

"Wery good; our course is due nor'west."

So saying, the man took the wheel and laid the ship's course accordingly.

Now, he knew quite well that this course would carry the vessel towards the harbour of Arbroath, into which he resolved to run at all hazards, trusting to the harbour-lights to guide him when he should draw near. He knew that he ran the strongest possible risk of getting himself shot when the Frenchmen should find out his faithlessness, but he hoped to prevail on them to believe the harbour-lights were only another lighthouse, which they should have to pass on their way out to sea, and then it would be too late to put the vessel about and attempt to escape.

But all his calculations were useless, as it turned out, for in half an hour the men at the bow shouted that there were breakers ahead, and before the helm could be put down, they struck with such force that the topmasts went overboard at once, and the sails, bursting their sheets and tackling, were blown to ribbons.

Just then a gleam of moonlight struggled through the wrack of clouds, and revealed the dark cliffs of the Forfar coast, towering high above them. The vessel had struck on the rocks at the entrance to one of those rugged bays with which that coast is everywhere indented.

At the first glance, the steersman knew that the doom of all on board was fixed, for the bay was one of those which are surrounded by almost perpendicular cliffs; and although, during calm weather, there was a small space between the cliffs and the sea, which might be termed a beach, yet during a storm the waves lashed with terrific fury against the rocks, so that no human being might land there.

It chanced at the time that Captain Ogilvy, who took great delight in visiting the cliffs in stormy weather, had gone out there for a midnight walk with a young friend, and when the privateer struck, he was standing on the top of the cliffs.

He knew at once that the fate of the unfortunate people on board was almost certain, but, with his wonted energy, he did his best to prevent the catastrophe.

"Run, lad, and fetch men, and ropes, and ladders. Alarm the whole town, and use your legs well. Lives depend on your speed," said the captain, in great excitement.

The lad required no second bidding. He turned and fled like a greyhound.

The lieges of Arbroath were not slow to answer the summons. There were neither lifeboats nor mortar-apparatus in those days, but there were the same willing hearts and stout arms then as now, and in a marvellously short space of time, hundreds of the able-bodied men of the town, gentle and semple, were assembled on these wild cliffs, with torches, rope, etcetera; in short, with all the appliances for saving life that the philanthropy of the times had invented or discovered.

But, alas! these appliances were of no avail. The vessel went to pieces on the outer point of rocks, and part of the wreck, with the crew clinging to it, drifted into the bay.

The horrified people on the cliffs looked down into that dreadful abyss of churning water and foam, into which no one could descend. Ropes were thrown again and again, but without avail. Either it was too dark to see, or the wrecked men were paralysed. An occasional shriek was heard above the roar of the tempest, as, one after another, the exhausted men fell into the water, or were wrenched from their hold of the piece of wreck.

At last one man succeeded in catching hold of a rope, and was carefully hauled up to the top of the cliff.

It was found that this was one of the English sailors. He had taken the precaution to tie the rope under his arms, poor fellow, having no strength left to hold on to it; but he was so badly bruised as to be in a dying state when laid on the grass.

"Keep back and give him air," said Captain Ogilvy, who had taken a prominent part in the futile efforts to save the crew, and who now knelt at the sailor's side, and moistened his lips with a little brandy.

The poor man gave a confused and rambling account of the circumstances of the wreck, but it was sufficiently intelligible to make the captain acquainted with the leading particulars.

"Were there many of your comrades aboard?" he enquired. The dying man looked up with a vacant expression. It was evident that he did not quite understand the question, but he began again to mutter in a partly incoherent manner.

"They're all gone," said he, "every man of 'em but me! All tied together in the hold. They cast us loose, though, after she struck. All gone! all gone!"

After a moment he seemed to try to recollect something.

"No," said he, "we weren't all together. They took Ruby on deck, and I never saw *him* again. I wonder what they did—"

Here he paused.

"Who, did you say?" enquired the captain with deep anxiety.

"Ruby—Ruby Brand," replied the man.

"What became of him, said you?"

"Don't know."

"Was *he* drowned?"

"Don't know," repeated the man.

The captain could get no other answer from him, so he was compelled to rest content, for the poor man appeared to be sinking.

A sort of couch had been prepared for him, on which he was carried into the town, but before he reached it he was dead. Nothing more could be done that night, but next day, when the tide was out, men were lowered down the precipitous sides of the fatal bay, and the bodies of the unfortunate seamen were sent up to the top of the cliffs by means of ropes. These ropes cut deep grooves in the turf, as the bodies were hauled up one by one and laid upon the grass, after which they were conveyed to the town, and decently interred.

The spot where this melancholy wreck occurred is now pointed out to the visitor as "The Seamen's Grave", and the young folk of the town have, from the time of the wreck, annually recut the grooves in the turf, above referred to, in commemoration of the event, so that these grooves may be seen there at the present day.

It may easily be imagined that poor Captain Ogilvy returned to Arbroath that night with dark forebodings in his breast.

He could not, however, imagine how Ruby came to be among the men on board of the French prize; and tried to comfort himself with the thought that the dying sailor had perhaps been a comrade of Ruby's at some time or other, and was, in his wandering state of mind, mixing him up with the recent wreck.

As, however, he could come to no certain conclusion on this point, he resolved not to tell what he had heard either to his sister or Minnie, but to confine his anxieties, at least for the present, to his own breast.

Chapter Thirty

Old Friends in New Circumstances

Let us now return to Ruby Brand; and in order that the reader may perfectly understand the proceedings of that bold youth, let us take a glance at the Bell Rock Lighthouse in its completed condition.

We have already said that the lower part, from the foundation to the height of thirty feet, was built of solid masonry, and that at the top of this solid part stood the entrance-door of the building—facing towards the south.

The position of the door was fixed after the solid part had been exposed to a winter's storms. The effect on the building was such that the most sheltered or lee-side was clearly indicated; the weather-side being thickly covered with limpets, barnacles, and short green seaweed, while the lee-side was comparatively free from such incrustations.

The walls at the entrance-door are nearly seven feet thick, and the short passage that pierces them leads to the foot of a spiral staircase, which conducts to the lowest apartment in the tower, where the walls decrease in thickness to three feet. This room is the provision store. Here are kept water-tanks and provisions of all kinds, including fresh vegetables which, with fresh water, are supplied once a fortnight to the rock all the year round. The provision store is the smallest apartment, for, as the walls of the tower decrease in thickness as they rise, the several apartments necessarily increase as they ascend.

The second floor is reached by a wooden staircase or ladder, leading up through a "manhole" in the ceiling. Here is the lightroom store, which contains large tanks of polished metal for the oil consumed by the lights. A whole year's stock of oil, or about 1100 gallons, is stored in these tanks. Here also is a small carpenter's bench and tool-box, besides an endless variety of odds and ends,—such as paint-pots, brushes, flags, waste for cleaning the reflectors, etcetera, etcetera.

Another stair, similar to the first, leads to the third floor, which is the kitchen of the building. It stands about sixty-six feet above the foundation. We shall have occasion to describe it and the rooms above presently. Meanwhile, let it suffice to say, that the fourth floor contains the men's sleeping-berths, of which there are six, although three men is the usual complement on the rock. The fifth floor is the library, and above that is the lantern; the whole building, from base to summit, being 115 feet high.

At the time when Ruby entered the door of the Bell Rock Lighthouse, as already described, there were three keepers in the building, one of whom was on his watch in the lantern, while the other two were in the kitchen.

These men were all old friends. The man in the lantern was George Forsyth, who had been appointed one of the light-keepers in consideration of his good services and steadiness. He was seated reading at a small desk. Close above him was the blazing series of lights, which revolved slowly and steadily by means of machinery, moved by a heavy weight. A small bell was struck slowly but regularly by the same machinery, in token that all was going on well. If that bell had ceased to sound, Forsyth would at once have leaped up to ascertain what was wrong with the lights. So long as it continued to ring he knew that all was well, and that he might continue his studies peacefully—not quietly, however, for, besides the rush of wind against the thick plate-glass of the lantern, there was the never-ceasing roar of the ventilator, in which the heated air from within and the cold air from without met and kept up a terrific war. Keepers get used to that sound, however, and do not mind it.

Each keeper's duty was to watch for three successive hours in the lantern.

Not less familiar were the faces of the occupants of the kitchen. To this apartment Ruby ascended without anyone hearing him approach, for one of the windows was open, and the roar of the storm effectually drowned his light footfall. On reaching the floor immediately below the kitchen he heard the tones of a violin, and when his head emerged through the manhole of the kitchen floor, he paused and listened with deep interest, for the air was familiar.

Peeping round the corner of the oaken partition that separated the manhole from the apartment, he beheld a sight which filled his heart with gladness, for there, seated on a camp-stool, with his back leaning against the dresser, his face lighted up by the blaze of a splendid fire, which burned in a most comfortable-looking kitchen range, and his hands drawing forth most pathetic music from a violin, sat his old friend Joe Dumsby, while opposite to him on a similar camp-stool, with his arm resting on a small table, and a familiar black pipe in his mouth, sat that worthy son of Vulcan, Jamie Dove.

The little apartment glowed with ruddy light, and to Ruby, who had just escaped from a scene of such drear and dismal aspect, it appeared, what it really was, a place of the most luxurious comfort.

Dove was keeping time to the music with little puffs of smoke, and Joe was in the middle of a prolonged shake, when Ruby passed through the doorway and stood before them.

Dove's eyes opened to their widest, and his jaw dropt, so did his pipe, and the music ceased abruptly, while the face of both men grew pale.

"I'm not a ghost, boys," said Ruby, with a laugh, which afforded immense relief to his old comrades. "Come, have ye not a welcome for an old messmate who swims off to visit you on such a night as this?"

Dove was the first to recover. He gasped, and, holding out both arms, exclaimed, "Ruby Brand!"

"And no mistake!" cried Ruby, advancing and grasping his friend warmly by the hands.

For at least half a minute the two men shook each other's hands lustily and in silence. Then they burst into a loud laugh, while Joe, suddenly recovering, went crashing into a Scotch reel with energy so great that time and tune were both sacrificed. As if by mutual impulse, Ruby and Dove began to dance! But this was merely a spurt of feeling, more than half-involuntary. In the middle of a bar Joe flung down the fiddle, and, springing up, seized Ruby round the neck and hugged him, an act which made him aware of the fact that he was dripping wet.

"Did ye *swim* hoff to the rock?" he enquired, stepping back, and gazing at his friend with a look of surprise, mingled with awe.

"Indeed I did."

"But how? why? what mystery are ye rolled up in?" exclaimed the smith.

"Sit down, sit down, and quiet yourselves," said Ruby, drawing a stool near to the fire, and seating himself. "I'll explain, if you'll only hold your tongues, and not look so scared like."

"No, Ruby; no, lad, you must change yer clothes first," said the smith, in a tone of authority; "why, the fire makes you steam like a washin' biler. Come along with me, an' I'll rig you out."

"Ay, go hup with 'im, Ruby. Bless me, this is the most amazin' hincident as ever 'appened to me. Never saw nothink like it."

As Dove and Ruby ascended to the room above, Joe went about the kitchen talking to himself, poking the fire violently, overturning the camp-stools, knocking about the crockery on the dresser, and otherwise conducting himself like a lunatic.

Of course Ruby told Dove parts of his story by fits and starts as he was changing his garments; of course he had to be taken up to the lightroom and go through the same scene there with Forsyth that had occurred in the kitchen; and, of course, it was not until all the men, himself included, had quite exhausted themselves, that he was able to sit down at the kitchen fire and give a full and connected account of himself, and of his recent doings.

After he had concluded his narrative, which was interrupted by frequent question and comment, and after he had refreshed himself with a cup of tea, he rose and said—

"Now, boys, it's not fair to be spending all the night with you here, while my old comrade Forsyth sits up yonder all alone. I'll go up and see him for a little."

"We'll go hup with 'ee, lad," said Dumsby.

"No ye won't," replied Ruby; "I want him all to myself for a while; fair play and no favour, you know, used to be our watchword on the rock in old times. Besides, his watch will be out in a little, so ye can come up and fetch him down."

"Well, go along with you," said the smith. "Hallo! that must have been a big 'un."

This last remark had reference to a distinct tremor in the building, caused by the falling of a great wave upon it.

"Does it often get raps like that?" enquired Ruby, with a look of surprise.

"Not often," said Dove, "once or twice durin' a gale, mayhap, when a bigger one than usual chances to fall on us at the right angle. But the lighthouse shakes worst just the gales begin to take off and when the swell rolls in heavy from the east'ard."

"Ay, that's the time," quoth Joe. "W'y, I've 'eard all the cups and saucers on the dresser rattle with the blows o' them heavy seas, but the gale is gittin' to be too strong to-night to shake us much."

"Too strong!" exclaimed Ruby.

"Ay. You see w'en it blows very hard, the breakers have not time to come down on us with a 'eavy tellin' blow, they goes tumblin' and swashin' round us and over us, hammerin' away wildly everyhow, or nohow, or anyhow, just like a hexcited man fightin' in a hurry. The after-swell, *that's* wot does it. *That's* wot comes on slow, and big, and easy but powerful, like a great prize-fighter as knows what he can do, and means to do it."

"A most uncomfortable sort of residence," said Ruby, as he turned to quit the room.

"Not a bit, when ye git used to it," said the smith. "At first we was rather skeered, but we don't mind now. Come, Joe, give us 'Rule, Britannia'—'pity she don't rule the waves straighter,' as somebody writes somewhere."

So saying, Dove resumed his pipe, and Dumsby his fiddle, while Ruby proceeded to the staircase that led to the rooms above.

Just as he was about to ascend, a furious gust of wind swept past, accompanied by a wild roar of the sea; at the same moment a mass of spray dashed against the small window at his side. He knew that this window was at least sixty feet above the rock, and he was suddenly filled with a strong desire to have a nearer view of the waves that had force to mount so high. Instead, therefore, of ascending to the lantern, he descended to the doorway, which was open, for, as the storm blew from the eastward, the door was on the lee-side.

There were two doors—one of metal, with thick plate-glass panels at the inner end of the passage; the other, at the outer end of it, was made of thick solid wood bound with metal, and hung so as to open outwards. When the two leaves of this heavy door were shut they were flush with the tower, so that nothing was presented for the waves to act upon. But this door was never closed except in cases of storm from the southward.

The scene which presented itself to our hero when he stood in the entrance passage was such as neither pen nor pencil can adequately depict. The tide was full, or nearly so, and had the night been calm the water would have stood about twelve or fourteen feet on the sides of the tower, leaving a space of about the same height between its surface and the spot at the top of the copper ladder where Ruby stood; but such was the wild commotion of the sea that this space was at one moment reduced to a few feet, as the waves sprang up towards the doorway, or nearly doubled, as they sank hissing down to the very rock.

Acres of white, leaping, seething foam covered the spot where the terrible Bell Rock lay. Never for a moment did that boiling cauldron get time to show one spot of dark-coloured water. Billow after billow came careering on from the open sea in quick succession, breaking with indescribable force and fury just a few yards to windward of the foundations of the lighthouse, where the outer ledges of the rock, although at the time deep down in the water, were sufficiently near the surface to break their first full force, and save the tower from destruction, though not from many a tremendous blow and overwhelming deluge of water.

When the waves hit the rock they were so near that the lighthouse appeared to receive the shock. Rushing round it on either side, the cleft billows met again to leeward, just opposite the door, where they burst upwards in a magnificent cloud of spray to a height of full thirty feet. At one time, while Ruby held on by the man-ropes at the door and looked over the edge, he could see a dark abyss with the foam shimmering pale far below; another instant, and the solid building perceptibly trembled, as a green sea hit it fair on the weather-side. A continuous roar and hiss followed as the billow swept round, filled up the dark abyss, and sent the white water gleaming up almost into the doorway. At the same moment the sprays flew by on either side of the column, so high that a few drops were thrown on the lantern. To Ruby's eye these sprays appeared to be clouds driving across the sky, so high were they above his head. A feeling of awe crept over him as his mind gradually began to realise the world of water which, as it were, overwhelmed him—water and foam roaring and flying everywhere—the heavy seas thundering on the column at his back—the sprays from behind arching almost over the lighthouse, and meeting those that burst up in front, while an eddy of wind sent a cloud swirling in at the doorway, and drenched him to the skin! It was an exhibition of the might of God in the storm such as he had never seen before, and a brief sudden exclamation of thanksgiving burst from the youth's lips, as he thought of how hopeless his case would have been had the French vessel passed the lighthouse an hour later than it did.

The contrast between the scene outside and that inside the Bell Rock Lighthouse at that time was indeed striking. Outside there was madly raging conflict; inside there were peace, comfort, security: Ruby, with his arms folded, standing calmly in the doorway; Jamie Dove and Joe Dumsby smoking and fiddling in the snug kitchen; George Forsyth reading (the *Pilgrim's Progress* mayhap, or *Robinson Crusoe*, for both works were in the Bell Rock library) by the bright blaze of the crimson and white lamps, high up in the crystal lantern.

If a magician had divided the tower in two from top to bottom while some ship was staggering past before the gale, he would have presented to the amazed mariners the most astonishing picture of "war without and peace within" that the world ever saw!

Chapter Thirty One

Midnight Chat in a Lantern

"I'll have to borrow another shirt and pair of trousers from you, Dove," said Ruby with a laugh, as he returned to the kitchen.

"What! been having another swim?" exclaimed the smith.

"Not exactly, but you see I'm fond o' water. Come along, lad."

In a few minutes the clothes were changed, and Ruby was seated beside Forsyth, asking him earnestly about his friends on shore.

"Ah! Ruby," said Forsyth, "I thought it would have killed your old mother when she was told of your bein' caught by them sea-sharks, and taken off to the wars. You must know I came to see a good deal of your friends, through—through—hoot! what's the name? the fair-haired lass that lives with—"

"Minnie?" suggested Ruby, who could not but wonder that any man living should forget *her* name for a moment.

"Ay, Minnie it is. She used to come to see my wife about some work they wanted her to do, and I was now and again sent up with a message to the cottage, and Captain Ogilvy always invited me in to take a glass out of his old teapot. Your mother used to ask me ever so many questions about you, an' what you used to say and do on the rock when this lighthouse was buildin'. She looked so sad and pale, poor thing; I really thought it would be all up with her, an' I believe it would, but for Minnie. It was quite wonderful the way that girl cheered your mother up, by readin' bits o' the Bible to her, an' tellin' her that God would certainly send you back again. She looked and spoke always so brightly too."

"Did she do that?" exclaimed Ruby, with emotion.

Forsyth looked for a moment earnestly at his friend.

"I mean," continued Ruby, in some confusion, "did she look bright when she spoke of my bein' away?"

"No lad, it was when she spoke of you comin' back; but I could see that her good spirits was partly put on to keep up the old woman."

For a moment or two the friends remained silent.

Suddenly Forsyth laid his hand on the other's shoulder, and said impressively: "Ruby Brand, it's my belief that that girl is rather fond of you."

Ruby looked up with a bright smile, and said, "D'you think so? Well, d'ye know, I believe she is."

"Upon my word, youngster," exclaimed the other, with a look of evident disgust, "your conceit is considerable. I had thought to be somewhat confidential with you in regard to this idea of mine, but you seem to swallow it so easy, and to look upon it as so natural a thing, that—that— Do you suppose you've nothin' to do but ask the girl to marry you and she'll say 'Yes' at once?"

"I do," said Ruby quietly; "nay, I am sure of it."

Forsyth's eyes opened very wide indeed at this. "Young man," said he, "the sea must have washed all the modesty you once had out of you—"

"I hope not," interrupted the other, "but the fact is that I put the question you have supposed to Minnie long ago, and she *did* say 'Yes' to it then, so it's not likely she's goin' to draw back now."

"Whew! that alters the case," cried Forsyth, seizing his friend's hand, and wringing it heartily.

"Hallo! you two seem to be on good terms, anyhow," observed Jamie Dove, whose head appeared at that moment through the hole in the floor by which the lantern communicated with the room below. "I came to see if anything had gone wrong, for your time of watch is up."

"So it is," exclaimed Forsyth, rising and crossing to the other side of the apartment, where he applied his lips to a small tube in the wall.

"What are you doing?" enquired Ruby.

"Whistling up Joe," said Forsyth. "This pipe runs down to the sleepin' berths, where there's a whistle close to Joe's ear. He must be asleep. I'll try again."

He blew down the tube a second time and listened for a reply, which came up a moment or two after in a sharp whistle through a similar tube reversed; that is, with the mouthpiece below and the whistle above.

Soon after, Joe Dumsby made his appearance at the trap-door, looking very sleepy.

"I feels as 'eavy as a lump o' lead," said he. "Wot an 'orrible thing it is to be woke out o' a comf'r'able sleep."

Just as he spoke the lighthouse received a blow so tremendous that all the men started and looked at each other for a moment in surprise.

"I say, is it warranted to stand *anything*?" enquired Ruby seriously.

"I hope it is," replied the smith, "else it'll be a blue lookout for *us*. But we don't often get such a rap as that. D'ye mind the first we ever felt o' that sort, Forsyth? It happened last month. I was on watch at the time, Forsyth was smokin' his pipe in the kitchen, and Dumsby was in bed, when a sea struck us with such force that I thought we was done for. In a moment Forsyth and Joe came tumblin' up the ladder—Joe in his shirt. 'It must have been a ship sailed right against us,' says Forsyth, and with that we all jumped on the rail that runs round the lantern there and looked out, but no ship could be seen, though it was a moonlight night. You see there's plenty o' water at high tide to let a ship of two hundred tons, drawin' twelve feet, run slap into us, and we've sometimes feared this in foggy weather; but it was just a blow of the sea. We've had two or three like it since, and are gettin' used to it now."

"Well, we can't get used to do without sleep," said Forsyth, stepping down through the trap-door, "so I'll bid ye all good night."

"'Old on! Tell Ruby about Junk before ye go," cried Dumsby. "Ah! well, I'll tell 'im myself. You must know, Ruby, that we've got what they calls an hoccasional light-keeper ashore, who larns the work out 'ere in case any of us

390

reg'lar keepers are took ill, so as 'e can supply our place on short notice. Well, 'e was out 'ere larnin' the dooties one tremendous stormy night, an' the poor fellow was in a mortial fright for fear the lantern would be blowed right hoff the top o' the stone column, and 'imself along with it. You see, the door that covers the manhole there is usually shut when we're on watch, but Junk (we called 'im Junk 'cause 'e wos so like a lump o' fat pork), 'e kep the door open all the time an' sat close beside it, so as to be ready for a dive. Well, it was my turn to watch, so I went up, an' just as I puts my fut on the first step o' the lantern-ladder there comes a sea like wot we had a minit ago; the wind at the same time roared in the wentilators like a thousand fiends, and the spray dashed agin the glass. Junk gave a yell, and dived. He thought it wos all over with 'im, and wos in sich a funk that he came down 'ead foremost, and would sartinly 'ave broke 'is neck if 'e 'adn't come slap into my buzzum! I tell 'e it was no joke, for 'e wos fourteen stone if 'e wos an ounce, an'—"

"Come along, Ruby," said Dove, interrupting; "the sooner we dive too the better, for there's no end to that story when Dumsby get off in full swing. Good night!"

"Good night, lads, an' better manners t'ye!" said Joe, as he sat down beside the little desk where the lightkeepers were wont during the lonely watch-hours of the night to read, or write, or meditate.

Chapter Thirty Two

Everyday Life on the Bell Rock, and Old Memories Recalled

The sun shone brightly over the sea next morning; so brightly and powerfully that it seemed to break up and disperse by force the great storm-clouds which hung about the sky, like the fragments of an army of black bullies who had done their worst and been baffled.

The storm was over; at least, the wind had moderated down to a fresh, invigorating breeze. The white crests of the billows were few and far between, and the wild turmoil of waters had given place to a grand procession of giant waves, that thundered on the Bell Rock Lighthouse, at once with more dignity and more force than the raging seas of the previous night.

It was the sun that awoke Ruby, by shining in at one of the small windows of the library, in which he slept. Of course it did not shine in his face, because of the relative positions of the library and the sun, the first being just below the lantern, and the second just above the horizon, so that the rays struck upwards, and shone with dazzling brilliancy on the dome-shaped ceiling. This was the second time of wakening for Ruby that night, since he lay down to rest. The first wakening was occasioned by the winding up of the machinery which kept the lights in motion, and the chain of which, with a ponderous weight attached to it, passed through a wooden pilaster close to his ear, causing such a sudden and hideous din that the sleeper, not having been warned of it, sprang like a Jack-in-the-box out of bed into the middle of the room, where he first stared vacantly around him like an unusually surprised owl, and then, guessing the cause of the noise, smiled pitifully, as though to say, "Poor fellow, you're easily frightened," and tumbled back into bed, where he fell asleep again instantly.

On the second time of wakening Ruby rose to a sitting posture, yawned, looked about him, yawned again, wondered what o'clock it was, and then listened.

No sound could be heard save the intermittent roar of the magnificent breakers that beat on the Bell Rock. His couch was too low to permit of his seeing anything but sky out of his windows, three of which, about two feet square, lighted the room. He therefore jumped up, and, while pulling on his garments, looked towards the east, where the sun greeted and almost blinded him. Turning to the north window, a bright smile lit up his countenance, and "A blessing rest on you" escaped audibly from his lips, as he kissed his hand towards the cliffs of Forfarshire, which were seen like a faint blue line on the far-off horizon, with the town of Arbroath just rising above the morning mists.

He gazed out at this north window, and thought over all the scenes that had passed between him and Minnie from the time they first met, down to the day when they last parted. One of the sweetest of the mental pictures that he painted that morning with unwonted facility, was that of Minnie sitting at his mother's feet, comforting her with the words of the Bible.

At length he turned with a sigh to resume his toilette. Looking out at the southern window, he observed that the rocks were beginning to be uncovered, and that the "rails", or iron pathway that led to the foot of the entrance-door ladder, were high enough out of the water to be walked upon. He therefore hastened to descend.

We know not what appearance the library presented at the time when Ruby Brand slept in it; but we can tell, from personal experience, that, at the present day, it is a most comfortable and elegant apartment. The other rooms of the lighthouse, although thoroughly substantial in their furniture and fittings, are quite plain and devoid of ornament, but the library, or "stranger's room", as it is sometimes called, being the guest-chamber, is fitted up in a style worthy of a lady's boudoir, with a Turkey carpet, handsome chairs, and an elaborately carved oak table, supported appropriately by a centre stem of three twining dolphins. The dome of the ceiling is painted to represent stucco panelling, and the partition which cuts off the small segment of this circular room that is devoted to passage and staircase, is of panelled oak. The thickness of this partition is just sufficient to contain the bookcase; also a cleverly contrived bedstead, which can be folded up during the day out of sight. There is also a small cupboard of oak, which serves the double purpose of affording shelf accommodation and concealing the iron smoke-pipe which rises from the kitchen, and, passing through the several storeys, projects a few feet above the lantern. The centre window is ornamented with marble sides and top, and above it stands a marble bust of Robert Stevenson, the engineer of the building, with a marble slab below bearing testimony to the skill and energy with which he had planned and executed the work.

If not precisely what we have described it to be at the present time, the library must have been somewhat similar on that morning when our hero issued from it and descended to the rock.

The first stair landed him at the entrance to the sleeping-berths. He looked into one, and observed Forsyth's head and arms lying in the bed, in that peculiarly negligent style that betokens deep and sweet repose. Dumsby's rest was equally sound in the next berth. This fact did not require proof by ocular demonstration; his nose announced it sonorously over the whole building.

Passing to the kitchen, immediately below, Ruby found his old messmate, Jamie Dove, busy in the preparation of breakfast.

"Ha! Ruby, good mornin'; you keep up your early habits, I see. Can't shake yer paw, lad, 'cause I'm up to the elbows in grease, not to speak o' sutt an' ashes."

"When did you learn to cook, Jamie?" said Ruby, laughing.

"When I came here. You see we've all got to take it turn and turn about, and it's wonderful how soon a feller gets used to it. I'm rather fond of it, d'ye know? We haven't overmuch to work on in the way o' variety, to be sure, but what we have there's lots of it, an' it gives us occasion to exercise our wits to invent somethin' new. It's wonderful what can be done with fresh beef, cabbage, carrots, potatoes, flour, tea, bread, mustard, sugar, pepper, an' the like, if ye've got a talent that way."

"You've got it all off by heart, I see," said Ruby.

"True, boy, but it's not so easy to get it all off yer stomach sometimes. What with confinement and want of exercise we was troubled with indigestion at first, but we're used to it now, and I have acquired quite a fancy for cooking. No doubt you'll hear Forsyth and Joe say that I've half-pisoned them four or five times, but that's all envy; besides, a feller can't learn a trade without doin' a little damage to somebody or something at first. Did you ever taste blackbird pie?"

"No," replied Ruby, "never."

"Then you shall taste one to-day, for we caught fifty birds last week."

"Caught fifty birds?"

"Ay, but I'll tell ye about it some other time. Be off just now, and get as much exercise out o' the rock as ye can before breakfast."

The smith resumed his work as he said this, and Ruby descended.

He found the sea still roaring over the rock, but the rails were so far uncovered that he could venture on them, yet he had to keep a sharp lookout, for, whenever a larger breaker than usual struck the rock, the gush of foaming water that flew over it was so great that a spurt or two would sometimes break up between the iron bars, and any one of these spurts would have sufficed to give him a thorough wetting.

In a short time, however, the sea went back and left the rails free. Soon after that Ruby was joined by Forsyth and Dumsby, who had come down for their morning promenade.

They had to walk in single file while taking exercise, as the tramway was not wide enough for two, and the rock, even when fully uncovered, did not afford sufficient level space for comfortable walking, although at low water (as the reader already knows) it afforded fully a hundred yards of scrambling ground, if not more.

They had not walked more than a few minutes when they were joined by Jamie Dove, who announced breakfast, and proceeded to take two or three turns by way of cooling himself. Thereafter the party returned to the kitchen, where they sat down to as good a meal as any reasonable man could desire.

There was cold boiled beef—the remains of yesterday's dinner—and a bit of broiled cod, a native of the Bell Rock, caught from the doorway at high water the day before. There was tea also, and toast—buttered toast, hot out of the oven.

Dove was peculiarly good at what may be styled toast-cooking. Indeed, all the lightkeepers were equally good. The bread was cut an inch thick, and butter was laid on as plasterers spread plaster with a trowel. There was no scraping off a bit here to put it on there; no digging out pieces from little caverns in the bread with the point of the knife; no repetition of the work to spread it thinner, and, above all, no omitting of corners and edges;— no, the smallest conceivable fly could not have found the minutest atom of dry footing on a Bell Rock slice of toast, from its centre to its circumference. Dove had a liberal heart, and he laid on the butter with a liberal hand. Fair play and no favour was his motto, quarter-inch thick was his gauge, railway speed his practice. The consequence was that the toast floated, as it were, down the throats of the men, and compensated to some extent for the want of milk in the tea.

"Now, boys, sit in," cried Dove, seizing the teapot.

"We have not much variety," observed Dumsby to Ruby, in an apologetic tone.

"Variety!" exclaimed Forsyth, "what d'ye call that?" pointing to the fish.

"Well, that *is* a hextra morsel, I admit," returned Joe; "but we don't get that every day; 'owsever, wot there is is good, an' there's plenty of it, so let's fall to."

Forsyth said grace, and then they all "fell to", with appetites peculiar to that isolated and breezy spot, where the wind blows so fresh from the open sea that the nostrils inhale culinary odours, and the palates seize culinary products, with unusual relish.

There was something singularly unfeminine in the manner in which the duties of the table were performed by these stalwart guardians of the Rock. We are accustomed to see such duties performed by the tender hands of woman, or, it may be, by the expert fingers of trained landsmen; but in places where woman may not or can not act with propriety,—as on shipboard, or in sea-girt towers,—men go through such feminine work in a way that does credit to their versatility,—also to the strength of culinary materials and implements.

The way in which Jamie Dove and his comrades knocked about the pans, teapots, cups and saucers, etcetera, without smashing them, would have astonished, as well as gratified, the hearts of the fraternity of tinsmiths and earthenware manufacturers.

We have said that everything in the lighthouse was substantial and very strong. All the woodwork was oak, the floors and walls of solid stone,—hence, when Dove, who had no nerves or physical feelings, proceeded with his cooking, the noise he caused was tremendous. A man used to woman's gentle ways would, on seeing him poke the fire, have expected that the poker would certainly penetrate not only the coals, but the back of the grate also, and perchance make its appearance at the outside of the building itself, through stones, joggles, dovetails, trenails, pozzolano mortar, and all the strong materials that have withstood the fury of winds and waves for the last half-century!

Dove treated the other furniture in like manner; not that he treated it ill,—we would not have the reader imagine this for a moment. He was not reckless of the household goods. He was merely indifferent as to the row he made in using them.

But it was when the cooking was over, and the table had to be spread, that the thing culminated. Under the impulse of lightheartedness, caused by the feeling that his labours for the time were nearly ended, and that his reward was about to be reaped, he went about with irresistible energy, like the proverbial bull in a china shop, without reaching that creature's destructive point. It was then that a beaming smile overspread his countenance, and he raged about the kitchen with Vulcan-like joviality. He pulled out the table from the wall to the centre of the apartment, with a swing that produced a prolonged crash. Up went its two leaves with two minor crashes. Down went the four plates and the cups and saucers, with such violence and rapidity that they all seemed to be dancing on the board together. The beef all but went over the side of its dish by reason of the shock of its sudden stoppage on touching the table, and the pile of toast was only saved from scatteration by the strength of the material, so to speak, with which its successive layers were cemented.

When the knives, forks, and spoons came to be laid down, the storm seemed to lull, because these were comparatively light implements, so that this period—which in shore-going life is usually found to be the exasperating one—was actually a season of relief. But it was always followed by a terrible squall of scraping wooden legs and clanking human feet when the camp-stools were set, and the men came in and sat down to the meal.

The pouring out of the tea, however, was the point that would have called forth the admiration of the world—had the world seen it. What a contrast between the miserable, sickly, slow-dribbling silver and other teapots of the land, and this great teapot of the sea! The Bell Rock teapot had no sham, no humbug about it. It was a big, bold-looking one, of true Britannia metal, with vast internal capacity and a gaping mouth.

Dove seized it in his strong hand as he would have grasped his biggest fore-hammer. Before you could wink, a sluice seemed to burst open; a torrent of rich brown tea spouted at your cup, and it was full—the saucer too, perhaps—in a moment.

But why dwell on these luxurious scenes? Reader, you can never know them from experience unless you go to visit the Bell Rock; we will therefore cease to tantalise you.

During breakfast it was discussed whether or not the signal-ball should be hoisted.

The signal-ball was fixed to a short staff on the summit of the lighthouse, and the rule was that it should be hoisted at a fixed hour every morning *when all was well*, and kept up until an answering signal should be made from a signal-tower in Arbroath where the keepers' families dwelt, and where each keeper in succession spent a fortnight with his family, after a spell of six weeks on the rock. It was the duty of the keeper on shore to watch for the hoisting of the ball (the "All's well" signal) each morning on the lighthouse, and to reply to it with a similar ball on the signal-tower.

If, on any occasion, the hour for signalling should pass without the ball on the lighthouse being shown, then it was understood that something was wrong, and the attending boat of the establishment was sent off at once to ascertain the cause, and afford relief if necessary. The keeping down of the ball was, however, an event of rare occurrence, so that when it did take place the poor wives of the men on the rock were usually thrown into a state of much perturbation and anxiety, each naturally supposing that her husband must be seriously ill, or have met with a bad accident.

It was therefore natural that there should be some hesitation about keeping down the ball merely for the purpose of getting a boat off to send Ruby ashore.

"You see," said Forsyth, "the day after to-morrow the 'relief boat' is due, and it may be as well just to wait for that, Ruby, and then you can go ashore with your friend Jamie Dove, for it's his turn this time."

"Ay, lad, just make up your mind to stay another day," said the smith; "as they don't know you're here they can't be wearyin' for you, and I'll take ye an' introduce you to my little wife, that I fell in with on the cliffs of Arbroath not long after ye was kidnapped. Besides, Ruby, it'll do ye good to feed like a fighting cock out here another day. Have another cup o' tea?"

"An' a junk o' beef?" said Forsyth.

"An' a slice o' toast?" said Dumsby.

Ruby accepted all these offers, and soon afterwards the four friends descended to the rock, to take as much exercise as they could on its limited surface, during the brief period of low water that still remained to them.

It may easily be imagined that this ramble was an interesting one, and was prolonged until the tide drove them into their tower of refuge. Every rock, every hollow, called up endless reminiscences of the busy building seasons. Ruby went over it all step by step with somewhat of the feelings that influence a man when he revisits the scene of his childhood.

There was the spot where the forge had stood.

"D'ye mind it, lad?" said Dove. "There are the holes where the hearth was fixed, and there's the rock where you vaulted over the bellows when ye took that splendid dive after the fair-haired lassie into the pool yonder."

"Mind it? Ay, I should think so!"

Then there were the holes where the great beams of the beacon had been fixed, and the iron bats, most of which latter were still left in the rock, and some of which may be seen there at the present day. There was also the pool into which poor Selkirk had tumbled with the vegetables on the day of the first dinner on the rock, and that other pool into which Forsyth had plunged after the mermaids; and, not least interesting among the spots of note, there was the ledge, now named the "Last Hope", on which Mr Stevenson and his men had stood on the day when the boat had been carried away, and they had expected, but were mercifully preserved from, a terrible tragedy.

After they had talked much on all these things, and long before they were tired of it, the sea drove them to the rails; gradually, as it rose higher, it drove them into the lighthouse, and then each man went to his work—Jamie Dove to his kitchen, in order to clean up and prepare dinner, and the other two to the lantern, to scour and polish the reflectors, refill and trim the lamps, and, generally, to put everything in order for the coming night.

Ruby divided his time between the kitchen and lantern, lending a hand in each, but, we fear, interrupting the work more than he advanced it.

That day it fell calm, and the sun shone brightly.

"We'll have fog to-night," observed Dumsby to Brand, pausing in the operation of polishing a reflector, in which his fat face was mirrored with the most indescribable and dreadful distortions.

"D'ye think so?"

"I'm sure of it."

"You're right," remarked Forsyth, looking from his elevated position to the seaward horizon, "I can see it coming now."

"I say, what smell is that?" exclaimed Ruby, sniffing.

"Somethink burnin'," said Dumsby, also sniffing.

"Why, what can it be?" murmured Forsyth, looking round and likewise sniffing. "Hallo! Joe, look out; you're on fire!"

Joe started, clapped his hand behind him, and grasped his inexpressibles, which were smouldering warmly. Ruby assisted, and the fire was soon put out, amidst much laughter.

"'Ang them reflectors!" said Joe, seating himself, and breathing hard after his alarm and exertions; "it's the third time they've set me ablaze."

"The reflectors, Joe?" said Ruby.

"Ay, don't ye see? They've nat'rally got a focus, an' w'en I 'appen to be standin' on a sunny day in front of 'em, contemplatin' the face o' natur', as it wor, through the lantern panes, if I gits into the focus by haccident, d'ye see, it just acts like a burnin'-glass."

Ruby could scarcely believe this, but after testing the truth of the statement by actual experiment he could no longer doubt it.

Presently a light breeze sprang up, rolling the fog before it, and then dying away, leaving the lighthouse enshrouded.

During fog there is more danger to shipping than at any other time. In the daytime, in ordinary weather, rocks and lighthouses can be seen. At night, lights can be seen, but during fog nothing can be seen until danger may be too near to be avoided. The two great fog-bells of the lighthouse were therefore set a-going, and they rang out their slow deep-toned peal all that day and all that night, as the bell of the Abbot of Aberbrothoc is said to have done in days of yore.

That night Ruby was astonished, and then he was stunned! First, as to his astonishment. While he was seated by the kitchen fire chatting with his friend the smith, sometime between nine o'clock and midnight, Dumsby summoned him to the lantern to "help in catching to-morrow's dinner!"

Dove laughed at the summons, and they all went up.

The first thing that caught Ruby's eye at one of the window panes was the round visage of an owl, staring in with its two large eyes as if it had gone mad with amazement, and holding on to the iron frame with its claws. Presently its claws lost hold, and it fell off into outer darkness.

"What think ye o' that for a beauty?" said Forsyth.

Ruby's eyes, being set free from the fascination of the owl's stare, now made him aware of the fact that hundreds of birds of all kinds—crows, magpies, sparrows, tomtits, owls, larks, mavises, blackbirds, etcetera, etcetera—were fluttering round the lantern outside, apparently bent on ascertaining the nature of the wonderful light within.

"Ah! poor things," said Forsyth, in answer to Ruby's look of wonder, "they often visit us in foggy weather. I suppose they get out to sea in the fog and can't find their way back to land, and then some of them chance to cross our light and take refuge on it."

"Now I'll go out and get to-morrow's dinner," said Dumsby. He went out accordingly, and, walking round the balcony that encircled the base of the lantern, was seen to put his hand up and quietly take down and wring the necks of such birds as he deemed suitable for his purpose. It seemed a cruel act to Ruby, but when he came to think of it he felt that, as they were to be stewed at any rate, the more quickly they were killed the better!

He observed that the birds kept fluttering about, alighting for a few moments and flying off again, all the time that Dumsby was at work, yet Dumsby never failed to seize his prey.

Presently the man came in with a small basket full of *game*. "Now, Ruby," said he, "I'll bet a sixpence that you don't catch a bird within five minutes."

"I don't bet such large sums usually, but I'll try," said Ruby, going out.

He tried and failed. Just as the five minutes were expiring, however, the owl happened to alight before his nose, so he "nabbed" it, and carried it in triumphantly.

"*That* ain't a bird," said Dumsby.

"It's not a fish," retorted Ruby; "but how is it that you caught them so easily, and I found it so difficult?"

"Because, lad, you must do it at the right time. You watch w'en the focus of a revolvin' light is comin' full in a bird's face. The moment it does so 'e's dazzled, and you grab 'im. If you grab too soon or too late, 'e's away. That's 'ow it is, and they're capital heatin', as you'll *find*."

Thus much for Ruby's astonishment. Now for his being stunned.

Late that night the fog cleared away, and the bells were stopped. After a long chat with his friends, Ruby mounted to the library and went to bed. Later still the fog returned, and the bells were again set a-going. Both of them being within a few feet of Ruby's head, they awakened him with a bang that caused him to feel as if the room in which he lay were a bell and his own head the tongue thereof.

At first the sound was solemnising, then it was saddening. After a time it became exasperating, and then maddening. He tried to sleep, but he only tossed. He tried to meditate, but he only wandered—not "in dreams", however. He tried to laugh, but the laugh degenerated into a growl. Then he sighed, and the sigh ended in a groan. Finally, he got up and walked up and down the floor till his legs were cold, when he turned into bed again, very tired, and fell asleep, but not to rest—to dream.

He dreamt that he was at the forge again, and that he and Dove were trying to smash their anvils with the sledge-hammers—bang and bang about. But the anvil would not break. At last he grew desperate, hit the horn off, and then, with another terrific blow, smashed the whole affair to atoms!

This startled him a little, and he awoke sufficiently to become aware of the fog-bells.

Again he dreamed. Minnie was his theme now, but, strange to say, he felt little or no tenderness towards her. She was beset by a hundred ruffians in pea-jackets and sou'westers. Something stirred him to madness. He rushed at the foe, and began to hit out at them right and left. The hitting was slow, but sure—regular as clock-work. First the right, then the left, and at each blow a seaman's nose was driven into his head, and a seaman's body lay flat on the ground. At length they were all floored but one—the last and the biggest. Ruby threw all his remaining strength into one crashing blow, drove his fist right through his antagonist's body, and awoke with a start to find his knuckles bleeding.

"Hang these bells!" he exclaimed, starting up and gazing round him in despair. Then he fell back on his pillow in despair, and went to sleep in despair.

Once more he dreamed. He was going to church now, dressed in a suit of the finest broadcloth, with Minnie on his arm, clothed in pure white, emblematic, it struck him, of her pure gentle spirit. Friends were with him, all gaily attired, and very happy, but unaccountably silent. Perhaps it was the noise of the wedding-bells that rendered their voices inaudible. He was struck by the solemnity as well as the pertinacity of these wedding-bells as he entered the church. He was puzzled too, being a Presbyterian, why he was to be married in church, but being a man of liberal mind, he made no objection to it.

They all assembled in front of the pulpit, into which the clergyman, a very reverend but determined man, mounted with a prayer book in his hand. Ruby was puzzled again. He had not supposed that the pulpit was the proper

413

place, but modestly attributed this to his ignorance.

"Stop those bells!" said the clergyman, with stern solemnity; but they went on.

"Stop them, I say!" he roared in a voice of thunder.

The sexton, pulling the ropes in the middle of the church, paid no attention.

Exasperated beyond endurance, the clergyman hurled the prayer book at the sexton's head, and felled him! Still the bells went on of their own accord.

"Stop! sto–o–o–op! I say," he yelled fiercely, and, hitting the pulpit with his fist, he split it from top to bottom.

Minnie cried "Shame!" at this, and from that moment the bells ceased.

Whether it was that the fog-bells ceased at that time, or that Minnie's voice charmed Ruby's thoughts away, we cannot tell, but certain it is that the severely tried youth became entirely oblivious of everything. The marriage-party vanished with the bells; Minnie, alas, faded away also; finally, the roar of the sea round the Bell Rock, the rock itself, its lighthouse and its inmates, and all connected with it, faded from the sleeper's mind, and: —

"Like the baseless fabric of a vision
Left not a wrack behind."

Chapter Thirty Three

Conclusion

Facts are facts; there is no denying that. They cannot be controverted; nothing can overturn them, or modify them, or set them aside. There they stand in naked simplicity; mildly contemptuous alike of sophists and theorists.

Immortal facts! Bacon founded on you; Newton found you out; Dugald Stewart and all his fraternity reasoned on you, and followed in your wake. What *would* this world be without facts? Rest assured, reader, that those who ignore facts and prefer fancies are fools. We say it respectfully. We have no intention of being personal, whoever you may be.

On the morning after Ruby was cast on the Bell Rock, our old friend Ned O'Connor (having been appointed one of the lighthouse-keepers, and having gone for his fortnight ashore in the order of his course) sat on the top of the signal-tower at Arbroath with a telescope at his eye directed towards the lighthouse, and became aware of a fact,—a fact which seemed to be contradicted by those who ought to have known better.

Ned soliloquised that morning. His soliloquy will explain the circumstances to which we refer; we therefore record it here. "What's that? Sure there's something wrong wid me eye intirely this mornin'. Howld on," (he wiped it here, and applying it again to the telescope, proceeded); "wan, tshoo, three, *four*! No mistake about it. Try agin. Wan, tshoo, three, *four*! An' yet the ball's up there as cool as a cookumber, tellin' a big lie; ye know ye are," continued Ned, apostrophising the ball, and readjusting the glass. "There ye are, as bold as brass—av ye're not copper—tellin' me that everythin's goin' on as usual, whin I can see with me two eyes (one after the other) that there's *four* men on the rock, whin there should be only *three*! Well, well," continued Ned, after a pause, and a careful examination of the Bell Rock, which being twelve miles out at sea could not be seen very distinctly in its lower parts, even through a good glass, "the day afther to-morrow'll settle the question, Misther Ball, for then the Relief goes off, and faix, if I don't guv' ye the lie direct I'm not an Irishman."

With this consolatory remark, Ned O'Connor descended to the rooms below, and told his wife, who immediately told all the other wives and the neighbours, so that ere long the whole town of Arbroath became aware that there was a mysterious stranger, a *fourth* party, on the Bell Rock!

Thus it came to pass that, when the relieving boat went off, numbers of fishermen and sailors and others watched it depart in the morning, and increased numbers of people of all sorts, among whom were many of the old hands who had wrought at the building of the lighthouse, crowded the pier to watch its return in the afternoon.

As soon as the boat left the rock, those who had "glasses" announced that there was an "extra man in her."

Speculation remained on tiptoe for nearly three hours, at the end of which time the boat drew near.

"It's a man, anyhow," observed Captain Ogilvy, who was one of those near the outer end of the pier.

"I say," observed his friend the "leftenant", who was looking through a telescope, "if—that's—not—Ruby—Brand—I'll eat my hat without sauce!"

"You don't mean—let me see," cried the captain, snatching the glass out of his friend's hand, and applying it to his eye. "I do believe!—yes! it is Ruby, or his ghost!"

By this time the boat was near enough for many of his old friends to recognise him, and Ruby, seeing that some of the faces were familiar to him, rose in the stern of the boat, took off his hat and waved it.

This was the signal for a tremendous cheer from those who knew our hero; and those who did not know him, but knew that there was something peculiar and romantic in his case, and in the manner of his arrival, began to cheer from sheer sympathy; while the little boys, who were numerous, and who love to cheer for cheering's sake alone, yelled at the full pitch of their lungs, and waved their ragged caps as joyfully as if the King of England were about to land upon their shores!

The boat soon swept into the harbour, and Ruby's friends, headed by Captain Ogilvy, pressed forward to receive and greet him. The captain embraced him, the friends surrounded him, and almost pulled him to pieces; finally, they lifted him on their shoulders, and bore him in triumphal procession to his mother's cottage.

And where was Minnie all this time? She had indeed heard the rumour that something had occurred at the Bell Rock; but, satisfied from what she heard that it would be nothing very serious, she was content to remain at home and wait for the news. To say truth, she was too much taken up with her own sorrows and anxieties to care as much for public matters as she had been wont to do.

When the uproarious procession drew near, she was sitting at Widow Brand's feet, "comforting her" in her usual way.

Before the procession turned the corner of the street leading to his mother's cottage, Ruby made a desperate effort to address the crowd, and succeeded in arresting their attention.

"Friends, friends!" he cried, "it's very good of you, very kind; but my mother is old and feeble; she might be hurt if we were to come on her in this fashion. We must go in quietly."

"True, true," said those who bore him, letting him down, "so, good day, lad; good day. A shake o' your flipper; give us your hand; glad you're back, Ruby; good luck to 'ee, boy!"

Such were the words, followed by three cheers, with which his friends parted from him, and left him alone with the captain.

"We must break it to her, nephy," said the captain, as they moved towards the cottage.

"'Still so gently o'er me stealin', Memory will bring back the feelin'.'

"It won't do to go slap into her, as a British frigate does into a French line-o'-battle ship. I'll go in an' do the breakin' business, and send out Minnie to you."

Ruby was quite satisfied with the captain's arrangement, so, when the latter went in to perform his part of this delicate business, the former remained at the door-post, expectant.

"Minnie, lass, I want to speak to my sister," said the captain, "leave us a bit—and there's somebody wants to see *you* outside."

"Me, uncle!"

"Ay, *you*; look alive now."

Minnie went out in some surprise, and had barely crossed the threshold when she found herself pinioned in a strong man's arms! A cry escaped her as she struggled, for one instant, to free herself; but a glance was sufficient to tell who it was that held her. Dropping her head on Ruby's breast, the load of sorrow fell from her heart. Ruby pressed his lips upon her forehead, and they both *rested* there.

It was one of those pre-eminently sweet resting-places which are vouchsafed to some, though not to all, of the pilgrims of earth, in their toilsome journey through the wilderness towards that eternal rest, in the blessedness of which all minor resting-places shall be forgotten, whether missed or enjoyed by the way.

Their rest, however, was not of long duration, for in a few minutes the captain rushed out, and exclaiming "she's swounded, lad," grasped Ruby by the coat and dragged him into the cottage, where he found his mother lying in a state of insensibility on the floor.

Seating himself by her side on the floor, he raised her gently, and placing her in a half-sitting, half-reclining position in his lap, laid her head tenderly on his breast. While in this position Minnie administered restoratives, and the widow, ere long opened her eyes and looked up. She did not speak at first, but, twining her arms round Ruby's neck, gazed steadfastly into his face; then, drawing him closer to her heart, she fervently exclaimed "Thank God!" and laid her head down again with a deep sigh.

She too had found a resting-place by the way on that day of her pilgrimage.

Now, reader, we feel bound to tell you in confidence that there are few things more difficult than drawing a story to a close! Our tale is done, for Ruby is married to Minnie, and the Bell Rock Lighthouse is finished, and most of those who built it are scattered beyond the possibility of reunion. Yet we are loath to shake hands with them and to bid *you* farewell.

Nevertheless, so it must be, for if we were to continue the narrative of the after-careers of our friends of the Bell Rock, the books that should be written would certainly suffice to build a new lighthouse.

But we cannot make our bow without a parting word or two.

Ruby and Minnie, as we have said, were married. They lived in the cottage with their mother, and managed to make it sufficiently large to hold them all by banishing the captain into the scullery.

Do not suppose that this was done heartlessly, and without the captain's consent. By no means. That worthy son of Neptune assisted at his own banishment. In fact, he was himself the chief cause of it, for when a consultation was held after the honeymoon, as to "what was to be done now," he waved his hand, commanded silence, and delivered himself as follows:—

"Now, shipmates all, give ear to me, an' don't ventur' to interrupt. It's nat'ral an' proper, Ruby, that you an' Minnie and your mother should wish to live together; as the old song says, 'Birds of a feather flock together,' an' the old song's right; and as the thing ought to be, an' you all want it to be, so it *shall* be. There's only one little difficulty in the way, which is, that the ship's too small to hold us, by reason of the after-cabin bein' occupied by an old seaman of the name of Ogilvy. Now, then, not bein' pigs, the question is, what's to be done? I will answer that question: the seaman of the name of Ogilvy shall change his quarters."

Observing at this point that both Ruby and his bride opened their mouths to speak, the captain held up a threatening finger, and sternly said, "Silence!" Then he proceeded—

"I speak authoritatively on this point, havin' conversed with the seaman Ogilvy, and diskivered his sentiments. That seaman intends to resign the cabin to the young couple, and to hoist his flag for the futur' in the fogs'l."

He pointed, in explanation, to the scullery; a small, dirty-looking apartment off the kitchen, which was full of pots and pans and miscellaneous articles of household, chiefly kitchen, furniture.

Ruby and Minnie laughed at this, and the widow looked perplexed, but perfectly happy and at her ease, for she knew that whatever arrangement the captain should make, it would be agreeable in the end to all parties.

"The seaman Ogilvy and I," continued the captain, "have gone over the fogs'l" (meaning the forecastle) "together, and we find that, by the use of mops, buckets, water, and swabs, the place can be made clean. By the use of paper, paint, and whitewash, it can be made respectable; and, by the use of furniture, pictures, books, and 'baccy, it can be made comfortable. Now, the question that I've got to propound this day to the judge and jury is— Why not?"

Upon mature consideration, the judge and jury could not answer "why not?" therefore the thing was fixed and carried out and the captain thereafter dwelt for years in the scullery, and the inmates of the cottage spent so much of their time in the scullery that it became, as it were, the parlour, or boudoir, or drawing-room of the place. When, in course of time, a number of small Brands came to howl and tumble about the cottage, they naturally gravitated towards the scullery, which then virtually became the nursery, with a stout old seaman, of the name of Ogilvy, usually acting the part of head nurse. His duties were onerous, by reason of the strength of constitution, lungs, and muscles of the young Brands, whose ungovernable desire to play with that dangerous element from which heat is evolved, undoubtedly qualified them for the honorary title of Fire-Brands.

With the proceeds of the jewel-case Ruby bought a little coasting vessel, with which he made frequent and successful voyages. "Absence makes the heart grow fonder," no doubt, for Minnie grew fonder of Ruby every time he went away, and every time he came back. Things prospered with our hero, and you may be sure that he did not forget his old friends of the lighthouse. On the contrary, he and his wife became frequent visitors at the signal-tower, and the families of the lighthouse-keepers felt almost as much at home in "the cottage" as they did in their own houses. And each keeper, on returning from his six weeks' spell on the rock to take his two weeks' spell at the signal-tower, invariably made it his first business, *after* kissing his wife and children, to go up to the Brands and smoke a pipe in the scullery with that eccentric old seafaring nursery-maid of the name of Ogilvy.

In time Ruby found it convenient to build a top flat on the cottage, and above this a small turret, which overlooked the opposite houses, and commanded a view of the sea. This tower the captain converted into a point of lookout, and a summer smoking-room,—and many a time and oft, in the years that followed, did he and Ruby climb up there about nightfall, to smoke the pipe of peace, with Minnie beside them, and to watch the bright flashing of the red and white light on the Bell Rock, as it shone over the waters far and wide, like a star of the first magnitude, a star of hope and safety, guiding sailors to their desired haven; perchance reminding them of that star of Bethlehem which guided the shepherds to Him who is the Light of the World and the Rock of Ages.